Praise for
These Boots Weren't Made for Walking

"Melody Carlson has crafted a brilliant, kick-up-your-heels, laugh-out-loud winner. Welcome to the Chick Lit side of the bookshelf, Sisterchick. Keep 'em coming!"

—ROBIN JONES GUNN, best-selling author of the Sisterchicks novels and the Christy Miller series

Praise for Melody Carlson

"…any story by Carlson is worth encountering."

—BOOKLIST

"Melody Carlson's style is mature and bitingly funny, and her gift for connecting our heart to the character's plight also connects us to the complicated human condition and our need for one another."

—PATRICIA HICKMAN, best-selling author of *Fallen Angels* and *Sandpebbles*

"Melody Carlson never fails to drag us out of our Christian easy chairs and right into the coals of the confusing culture in which we all find ourselves. She never fails to reveal that place of compassion within each of us. Excellent."

—LISA SAMSON, author of *The Church Ladies* and *Tiger Lillie*

"With great confidence, I can say that Melody Carlson's story will enlighten, encourage, and empower you."

—GREGORY L. JANTZ, PH.D., Founder and Executive Director of the Center for Counseling & Health Resources Inc.

a novel

Melody Carlson

These
Boots
Weren't Made for Walking

WATERBROOK
PRESS

THESE BOOTS WEREN'T MADE FOR WALKING
PUBLISHED BY WATERBROOK PRESS
12265 Oracle Boulevard, Suite 200
Colorado Springs, Colorado 80921
A division of Random House Inc.

The characters and events in this book are fictional, and any resemblance to actual persons or events is coincidental.

ISBN: 978-1-4000-7313-9

Library of Congress Cataloging-in-Publication Data
Carlson, Melody.
  These boots weren't made for walking : a novel / Melody Carlson. — 1st ed.
    p. cm.
  ISBN 978-1-4000-7313-9
  I. Title.
  PS3553.A73257T46 2007
  813'.54—dc22

                                        2007003697

Printed in the United States of America
2007—First Edition

10 9 8 7 6 5 4 3 2 1

I should've known I'd lose my job after splurging on my first pair of Valentino boots. Actually, they were my first Valentino anything. I don't even own fake Valentino. My neighbor Monica has a fake Valentino purse, but my older sister has the real thing—along with an impressive variety of other authentic Valentino items. Callie tosses the Valentino name around with ease, as if she's on personal terms with the designer himself. And I suppose I'm slightly awed by this or perhaps just envious. Whatever the reason, I splurged awhile back, and now I'm fairly certain these boots will be my last Valentino of any kind.

The truth is, I'd been eying those sleek brown beauties since late August. It figures that Martolli's of Seattle would put them in the front window while it was still ninety degrees outside. But ignoring the fact that my feet were hot and sweaty in my Anne Klein sandals, which weren't exactly cheap, I ate the bait. I immediately began to imagine how the exquisitely shaped four-inch heels would make me look taller, thinner, and more successful and might possibly even get me that promotion I'd been stealthily pursuing all summer. While other employees were sneaking in extra-long lunches, extended vacations, shortened days, and secret trysts in the copy room, I slaved. Please, do not get me going about the copy room—those two sex maniacs, unlike me, are still gainfully employed. But back in August, I honestly believed those boots would be my ticket to happiness, a better love life, and a new-and-improved position in our marketing firm, one of the biggest and best in Seattle. It just made sense.

I must admit that I freaked over the price of those delectable boots—at first anyway. But then I rationalized, which I am quite good at, telling myself, *Okay, you're thirty-one, Cassidy, and still depressingly single, but you've got a decent job in a top firm, and your credit is reasonably good, plus you did just give twenty bucks to the Make-A-Wish Foundation at Safeway last night. Seriously, don't you deserve those boots?*

Never mind that my checking account was a little on the skinny side; I knew I'd be getting paid in a couple of weeks. It wouldn't kill me to live on ramen noodles for a few days or even forgo my morning latte for a while. I mean, a girl's gotta make sacrifices sometimes. So when the saleswoman offered me that extra ten percent discount if I opened up a Martolli's account, well, it just seemed like fate. Those soft suede boots were as good as mine!

"Why not?" I told the slightly gaunt brunette as I carefully filled out the detailed application, promising myself that I'd pay off the entire balance with my next check. I'd be broke for the rest of the month. But I do try to reserve my credit card for real emergencies or necessities or when I'm running low on cash or perhaps just desperate for a girls' night out before payday. And then I always try to pay off my cards promptly. Well, mostly anyway. No one's perfect. Having a sleek, gold credit card at Martolli's—which caters to a certain clientele, is only located in truly cosmopolitan cities, and is the only designer store in Seattle that carries Valentino—well, it seemed an arrival of sorts. I felt very grown-up.

I carried my large package home with a sense of real accomplishment, as if it were my personal trophy. Like a huntress who had tracked and stalked and finally bagged her prey, I walked victoriously down the street toward my apartment. But once I got inside my small studio, I was hit by a tidal wave of guilt. How could I possibly have spent that much money on a ridiculous pair of boots? My younger sister is always reminding me that children are starving and dying in Uganda right now, and I'm sure she'd have a cow over what I just spent on footwear. It could've fed an entire village for a year, I'm sure. They're just boots, for Pete's sake, and who really cares if they're Valentino or not? So I put the oversize bag into my closet—out of sight, out of mind—and promised myself I'd return them the very next day.

The very next day came, and I didn't return the boots. I mean, what was I going to tell the saleswoman? That I'd decided they were too expensive? How humiliating would that be anyway? Oh, sure, I could lie. My friend next-door, Monica Johnson, has no problem with this sort of thing. She's the Return Queen, with very few scruples. I was with her once at Macy's, and I actually saw a salesclerk cringe when Monica stepped up to the poor woman's register. I happen to know that Monica actually wears a lot of her purchases before she returns them, snipping the price tags and everything. (Of course, she only wears them once, or so she says, and only for special events or important job interviews.) Then, like it's no big deal, she returns the items afterward. She says she's good advertising for the stores because she's so tall and thin and gorgeous and the clothes look fantastic on her. And while I can't disagree with that, her values are not the same as mine. No matter how desperate I might be over Valentino or any designer, I could never do something that low. First of all, I don't have that kind of nerve (or maybe it's verve) to pull it off. Even if I did, I would feel too guilty. Besides, I'm a very bad liar. My ears turn bright red if I don't tell the truth. Monica won't even let me shop with her if she's returning something—she swears my expression alone would tip them off.

Somehow I let nearly two weeks slip by without returning those boots. I always had a good excuse. It was too late; it was too hot; I was too tired. I'd tell myself that I would return those boots the next day right after work, but I just couldn't bring myself to actually do it. Never mind that I'd taken them out of their beautiful box a few times. I'd stroked the buttery-soft suede and fingered the cool trim that runs down the side, a detail that's meant to elongate the leg. Yes, I even inhaled the sweet smell of leather, rubbing it across my cheek, carefully avoiding drooling on the lovely boots that I kept telling myself *must* be returned.

Finally, at the end of September, one of those perfect boot days

cropped up. The weather was crisp and cool, with leaves just starting to turn. I pulled out one of my favorite cool-weather suits, a
gorgeous Ralph Lauren tweed that simply begged for those brown
Valentino boots. The skirt was just the perfect length for knee-high
boots. They were made for each other.

Oh, why not? With a sense of adventure, maybe even danger,
I pulled out the slick Martolli's bag once again. I slipped out the
large, impressive Valentino box, and slowly, almost reverently,
opened the lid. I carefully removed the amazing boots. I took my
time examining each detail, and I asked myself, *Why shouldn't I
keep them?* They were, after all, exquisite. Oh, that luxurious feel
of fine Italian leather—so smooth, softer than a baby's bottom.
Maybe that's the thing that got me, since I'm sure to be middle-
aged before I ever have a chance to hold a baby of my own. No
matter how I hint, Eric barely seems to notice that my body clock
is ticking faster than ever. Sometimes I imagine the hands on my
clock whirling around so rapidly that I could use it as a fan. Perhaps I'll need it for hot flashes someday. Anyway, I knew I deserved
these boots!

So I pulled on the first boot, giving it a firm tug to get it over
my rather high instep before I zipped it snugly around my calf.
"Maybe *these* babies will get Eric's attention," I grunted to myself
as I tugged on the second boot. Maybe this head-turning footwear
could show that slow-moving man that I'm a hot babe and worth
paying serious attention to. Or maybe I could just give him a big
kick in the—

I reeled in my imagination. I was, after all, getting dressed for work.

That's when it occurred to me that perhaps these boots might be just the number to get my boss's attention today. Really, as I strutted around my apartment, it seemed highly plausible that these incredibly cool boots might actually help my slightly arrogant, I'm-so-cool, thirty-something boss, George, see that I, Cassidy Cantrell, had something going on as well. These expensive and impressive boots were proof that I, too, was up-and-coming, hip and cool, and someone my boss should be watching a bit more closely. In fact, these boots seemed to almost shout, "Look out! This girl is going places! She is real promotion material!"

With both boots on, I checked out my image in the full-length mirror. And if I do say so myself, I did look pretty hot. Okay, I was well aware of the fact that I'd put on a few extra pounds this past year, and maybe the jacket didn't button quite as smoothly as it used to, but it looked perfectly fine open. In all fairness, the weight gain was really Eric's fault. If he'd only get serious about commitment instead of playing stupid mind games... But I didn't want to go back there just yet. I needed to keep my focus positive. I had to get my head into my new role as the successful career woman, that hardworking girl who'd paid her dues, put in her time, and was now ready and willing to step up a few more rungs on the corporate ladder. I'd seen others doing it recently. Claire Hoffman had recently been made a VP. Why shouldn't it be my turn to move up? I'd done a fantastic job on my latest project—a project that was due today. A project that I would proudly turn in while wearing these boots! I couldn't wait to see George's face!

I don't know why I didn't sense something in the air when I walked into the office that morning. Looking back, I do recall an uneasy expression on the receptionist's face, as if she knew something was going down, and in retrospect, I'm certain she did. I'm sure that she and many others had been briefed. But I suppose I was too focused on those daring boots and on making a spectacular impression as I carried my project directly to George's office. I could've sent it by Claudia, my faithful assistant (actually she was the faithful assistant to several of us), but I wanted George to see me up close and personal. I wanted him to be impressed by both my work and those amazing boots.

It made so much sense at the time. But it all seems so silly now.

"George is busy," said his executive assistant, Ginnie, when I made my grand appearance. I did observe that she didn't make eye contact with me. It should've been my first clue.

"Can you call me when he's available?" I asked, holding my precious folder tightly because I wanted to present it to him personally.

"Sure." She flipped through her Day-Timer, keeping the conversation short, guarded, limited.

"Thanks," I said, starting to walk away.

"Nice boots," she called after me.

I turned to smile, but she was glued to her Day-Timer again. "Thank you," I said in a cheerful and confident tone. *Yes,* I thought as I strutted away, *these boots are already working for me.*

But by noon it was all over. George called an emergency meeting for my entire division. He made this lame little speech about how the company had been losing money these past six months and how our division in particular had really gone downhill during the last fiscal year.

"As hard as it is to do this," he said with an expression that was probably supposed to appear sad, "we have to let a few folks go." And just like that he announced that my division had been eliminated. That was about the size of it. We were no longer needed. We were expendable, dispensable, disposable, unnecessary. Call it what you like, we were toast.

We were then instructed—make that *commanded*—to quietly pack our things, pick up our checks, "which will include a generous severance package," in Personnel, and then leave. They even had extra security guards on hand to escort us from the building via the back door to the parking garage so as not to make a scene and "upset other employees." Like we weren't upset? The whole thing reminded me of the Monopoly card that says something like "Go to jail, directly to jail. Do not pass Go. Do not collect squat."

Eventually a dozen of us stood out on the street, displaced and confused and slightly shell-shocked. A couple of the guys were angry and not too concerned about who heard them discussing our situation. That's when the security guards began to strongly urge us to "clear out before we need to call for backup." Since they were armed with what appeared to be actual handguns, as well as aerosol cans of what I'm guessing was Mace, we decided not to argue.

Instead we paraded across the street and planted ourselves in the neighborhood Starbucks to lick our wounds.

I tried not to feel like a truant schoolkid, playing hooky and glancing over my shoulder to keep an eye out for police. Actually I was hoping my boss would show up, single me out, and say that it was a mistake, that he meant to fire everyone but me.

We monopolized the coffee shop, consuming far too much caffeine as we had what I now consider a very pathetic therapy session. A few hours later this scene was relocated to Clancy's, a bar that some of my co-workers, now former co-workers, often frequented after work. But already I was getting weary of the venting, complaining, and rehashing. So I decided to forgo the bar experience. I just wanted to go home, crawl into bed, and hope that things would get better tomorrow.

Maybe it was that excessive caffeine or my generally deteriorated emotional state, but I temporarily forgot about my beautiful (and did I mention expensive?) boots. I decided to skip the bus that I often rode home from work on days when I was too lazy to walk or the weather was uncooperative. After a few blocks, the things were foremost in my mind. Those high-heeled boots were definitely *not* made for walking. By the time I limped up to my apartment, my heels were aching and burning, and I had blisters the size of quarters on the balls of my feet. I was barely through the door when I sat down right on the floor and peeled off those painful Valentinos.

Then I actually threw the despicable boots across the room,

scaring my cat, Felix, half to death when a stiletto heel narrowly missed his ear. After that I simultaneously soaked my aching feet in cold water and put away a full quart of mocha almond fudge ice cream—talk about your multitasking. Between bites I called Eric, who never answered. I hit the speed dial every five minutes on the dot and left desperate messages, begging him to call. Between calls, I searched out something else to eat.

And life got kind of blurry after that.

s usual, Eric's timing was perfect. Three days after I lost what I had suddenly decided was the perfect job in marketing, with or without the stupid promotion, my missing-in-action boyfriend finally returned my calls. I'm sure I'd left him about fifty-seven messages, ranging from "Help me; I think I'm going to jump" to "Hey, it's no big deal; I can find another job" to "I must have a baby before I turn thirty-two" to "I've had it with you, Eric; we're finished."

"We need to talk," he said after I finished dumping my whole sad story on him over the phone. I'd really hoped to do it in person. I'd imagined him gathering me in his arms, smoothing my hair, and telling me it was going to be okay. But when I heard his voice on the other end, I couldn't contain myself. I was in need of some serious catharsis.

"Yeah," I said, as in "obviously." Frustrated, I peeled open another Snickers bar and took a big bite.

"Can I come over?"

"Uh, sure." I swallowed the unchewed clump of sweet chocolate and nuts, then nervously glanced around my recently ravaged apartment. It looked like someone had set loose a dozen ill-mannered chimpanzees in it. "Uh, when were you thinking of coming?"

"Now."

"Now? As in thirty minutes?" That's what it usually took Eric to get here from his apartment—which was always impeccably neat, just as he was and just the way he liked everything to be.

"Now," he said with a slight edge to his voice, "as in 'I'm downstairs.' Right now, as in 'I'm standing on the street and ready to come up,' Cassie." He sounded seriously irritated, and I wondered just who was the one going through a difficult time right now. Who was the one in need of some handholding and compassion today?

"Oh, well, come on up then." I slammed down the phone and dashed directly to the bathroom, tripping over a yellow ducky slipper and painfully stubbing my toe on the doorframe as I went. There I stood before the mirror, staring at myself in horror as I took my pathetic inventory. No makeup; blotchy skin from too much crying; dark circles under bloodshot eyes—a combination of old mascara and sleepless nights; stringy, mousy brown hair that hadn't been washed in days. I still wore the same pink fleece bathrobe I'd put on…well, I wasn't sure how long ago. Two days maybe?

I spotted some gray sweats on the bathroom floor, right where I'd dropped them before opting for the more comfy bathrobe. The sweats weren't exactly clean, but they probably smelled better than the skanky robe, so I jerked them on. It was about then that I heard Eric knocking loudly on my door and calling my name as if he'd been there for a long time. I grabbed my lip gloss and smeared some on, hoping that it was landing somewhere near my mouth as I scrambled for the door, kicking shoes and debris out of the way as I went. Amazing how a small apartment can get so totaled with just a few days of reckless living. Kind of like my life.

"Eric," I said, trying to appear calm and controlled as I opened the door for my impeccable boyfriend. As usual, every neatly cut blond hair was in its place, and his boyish face was more smoothly shaved than my legs. Somehow this picture-perfect image gave me a sense of comfort. Perhaps the universe hadn't recently spun out of control after all. Then again, there was something in his clear blue eyes that I couldn't quite read. Hopefully it was simply pity. I could've used a truckload about then.

"Cassie?" His pale brows lifted in alarm as his eyes darted around, obviously taking in the chaos behind me.

"As you can see, I really wasn't expecting you just now."

He frowned. "Sorry to catch you at a bad time."

I stepped back and opened the door wider, kicking a *People* magazine out of the way. It always bugged him that I "willingly wasted" my mind and money "on that kind of trash." But he spared me the lecture. I grabbed a splayed newspaper off my futon, which doubles as a couch, only to reveal a dirty bra underneath. I quickly stuffed that into my sweatshirt pocket and pitched the rumpled newspaper under the coffee table as I nodded toward the now-cleared futon. Clear except for the cat hair, which Eric wouldn't appreciate either. "Want to sit down?"

"No. Let's just keep this brief, okay?"

"Okay." I tried again to read his face, although it was rather expressionless. Still, I could tell by the tone of his voice and something else—like a buzzing inside of me, an alarm—that all was not well. Somehow I knew this wasn't going to be good.

"I thought about telling you this on the phone, but I've heard that's the loser way to handle it. So I decided to come and see you in person." He cleared his throat. "The reason you haven't heard from me for the last few days is because, well, there's no easy way to put this. Cassie, I've decided we need to break up."

"We need to break up?" I echoed meekly. "You've decided?"

"Yeah. I know this must seem pretty poor timing, I mean, especially after losing your job and everything, but the truth is, it's been coming for a while."

"For a while?" I sounded like a dimwitted parrot, but it was the best I could do. I was surprised that I was still standing since I was pretty sure the floor was swaying slightly.

He nodded with a sad expression. "Didn't you feel it was ending too?"

I just shrugged. I wasn't sure what I felt—well, other than that I'd just been hit by another truck, this one even bigger than the last.

"I really do like you, Cassie. But it's just not there, you know?"

Now I really studied him. "*What's* just not there?" I demanded as the past few years flashed before my eyes: all I'd done, all I'd tried to be just to make this selfish man happy. "What are you talking about?"

"You and me," he said quietly. "It's just not there."

Anger began to bubble in me as I recalled some recent tension between us. I remembered how Eric had begun pressuring me a couple of months ago, saying that he needed more out of our relationship. Of course, he only mentioned this when we were kissing, when things were getting pretty hot and passionate. And, of course, that's when I would remind him in my most tempting and seductive voice, "Sure, Eric. You can have more, but not until our wedding night."

Well, that usually shut things down pretty quickly, which worked for me. Yes, I'm one of those old-fashioned girls, and while I don't go around saying this out loud, I happen to believe the guy's not going to buy the cow when he can get the milk for free—not that I'm particularly fond of that unflattering metaphor. But the truth was, for the most part (at least when Eric wasn't all worked up and eager), he agreed with me on this basic concept. Or so it seemed. Suddenly I was starting to wonder.

Eric shook his head sadly, reminding me of a doctor who'd just given a hopeless prognosis or pronounced a patient dead. "We're just not right for each other, Cassie."

"We've been going together for more than three years, Eric." My voice ratcheted up to an obnoxiously tight and high-pitched level. I felt that I was about to cry or explode or perhaps even throw something at him. "And you decide *now* that we're not right for each other?"

He looked down at the floor. My dingy brown carpet was littered with magazines, junk mail, dirty socks, stray shoes, and even some shattered potato chips that must've escaped me during the recent eating binge. Lovely.

"Eric," I persisted, unwilling to let this relationship slip away gracefully. My anger was growing hotter, as was my assurance that I had this man pegged. "Is this because I said no to sex?" I looked directly into his eyes, wanting to hear the truth—even if it cut like a knife. Hopefully, he'd finish me off quickly.

He looked away now. "No, Cassie, it's not about sex."

I considered this. Would he lie to me? Eric was a basically honest man, a basically good man. He and I were both fairly strong Christians and went to a pretty cool church, and he was very involved in the singles' group that we both attended. In fact, he was recently made a leader at our church, second in command to the pastor who oversees all the young-adult ministries. But our church also happens to be a Bible-believing church that doesn't condone premarital sex. Oh, they never turn people of other opinions away, but they expect their leaders to respect the "rules" if they want to remain in leadership. And while I fully realized that Eric wasn't perfect, I was a little surprised at the way he'd been pressuring me about sex the past couple of months—or so it seemed. I suppose it all hit me as a bit hypocritical.

"Then what is this really about, Eric?"

He looked away again, more quickly this time, as if he was getting really uncomfortable. Perhaps he was sorry about this, or maybe I'd hit a nerve. That's when I sensed something in his expression, something I don't think I'd ever witnessed in this guy before. It smelled like guilt.

"Is there another girl?" I demanded.

He looked back at me with surprised eyes. "Who have you been talking to?"

"There is, isn't there?"

"Oh, Cassie." He slowly shook his head, but his expression reminded me of that cartoon cat Sylvester whenever the little old lady would catch him with Tweety in his fist.

"Who is she?" I said quietly but with emphasis on each word.

He shifted his weight and looked at the floor again. "I'm sorry."

"Who is she?" I demanded more loudly.

"It doesn't matter."

"It does matter!" I yelled. "It matters to me!"

"Just let it go—"

"Let it go?" My voice was so loud that Felix made a run for it.

"Come on, Cassie." He tried that soft pleading tone on me, as if he was going to persuade me against my will, as if I would let him off easy just because he was "sensitive."

I folded my arms tightly across my chest and glared at him. "Who is she, Eric?"

He exhaled loudly. "Well, I'm sure you'll find out eventually anyway."

He proceeded to tell me that he'd been spending time with Jessica Brauer, a twenty-something chick who had started coming to our church a few weeks earlier. I was the one who had originally befriended her. I felt sorry for this pretty girl sitting all by herself in the back one day. I'd invited her to our singles' group that night. And when she came, she really opened up and told the group about how she'd been raised in a pretty messed-up home and how she'd recently become a Christian and wasn't really connected with believers. As a result, I went out of my way to call her occasionally, to invite her for coffee, and Eric and I had even taken her with us to several events this past month. Apparently Eric had spent time with her on his own as well. Who knew?

"Look, it just happened, Cassie," he said as if that explained this mess. "The truth is, I think it was a God thing."

"A *God* thing?" I tossed that one back at him as if it were a hot potato.

"God brought us together, Cassie. Jessica and I both feel this way."

"You believe God set you up with Jessica so you could cheat on me?"

"It's not like we're married, Cassie. We're not even engaged—"

"That's for sure!" I opened the door for him now, like, *Here's your hat. What's your hurry?*

"Come on, Cass," he said. "Don't end it like this—"

"How do you expect me to end it?" I snapped.

"Can't we still be friends?"

"Friends?" Okay, I'm not a violent person by nature, but I sure felt like hitting him with something big and heavy just then. Instead I gathered up what little self-control remained and said, "Look, Eric, I hope you and Jessica are wonderfully happy."

He smiled as though he thought I meant it. "That's—"

"Have a great life together!" I shoved him with both hands, then slammed the door behind him.

Three

My grandmother used to say that bad things always come in groups of three. Of course, I never took this adage too seriously. But now I'm not so sure. There's no denying that two very bad things have happened. What if there's a third one coming?

As a result, I hole up in my little apartment for the next several days, waiting for the third shoe, or perhaps a boot, to fall. And as I wait, I consume calorie-laden foods like Doritos and Pepsi and Reese's peanut-butter cups, as if economists had forecast a serious junk-food shortage. Last night I wore a ball cap and trench coat when I went out to forage for my supplies. I didn't want anyone to recognize me.

Like anyone would care.

I sit around all day eating and watching disgusting soap operas and my thighs, which literally expand before me. Sometimes when I'm feeling especially fragile, I hold Felix as though he were a baby, and I tell him my troubles. As long as I scratch him in all the right places, he's a pretty good listener. We take catnaps together, and occasionally I wake up crying. I try to convince myself that I'm crying over a soap opera I just saw, that I'm brokenhearted over poor Arial, who's having Beau's baby, but he's in love with her sister Bianca, who is sleeping with his father, who has just been diagnosed with Alzheimer's and can barely remember his wife's first name. But I know the truth. And like they say, it hurts.

Finally, exactly two weeks after my termination, and eleven days after getting dumped by Eric, I tell myself enough is enough, and I force myself to start cleaning my slovenly apartment. I even sit down to open the pile of mail. My goal is to begin restoring order to my life. *What life?* I think as I use a dull steak knife to slit open the envelope that holds my new credit-card bill. I brace myself, knowing full well that it'll be a whopper because those despicable Valentino boots will be on it. But when I actually read the total, I consider taking the steak knife directly to my throat. Something is wrong—very, very wrong!

"Four thousand five hundred eighty-five dollars?" I gasp aloud. I blink and read it again. This is crazy. I know the exact price of those boots as though it's been branded on my brain. And while I admit they were stupidly expensive, they were only a fraction of this. What on earth could this be for? So I flip to the page underneath and study the itemized list of "my purchases" and am shocked to see all sorts of things listed there—things *I* never bought. Well, it's obviously a mistake. A big, stupid mistake that must be sorted out as soon as possible.

So I get on the phone and listen to a recording and punch in all kinds of numbers, then listen to more recordings, then wait and wait until I finally get to speak to a real woman. She calmly says, "It's no mistake. If you are Cassidy Cantrell, that's your card number, and according to our records, the signature matches perfectly. Unless you—"

"Wait a minute," I interrupt. "I did receive my card in the mail shortly after I opened the account. But I set it aside and *never* even signed it! How can my signature match up?"

"Oh, dear," she says. "That was a mistake."

"What?"

"You must *always* sign a charge card. A blank card is an invitation for fraud. Anyone can sign a blank card and use it."

"But who would—"

"Do you have any more questions about your account?" she asks impatiently. "Other customers are waiting."

"I want to *close* my account," I snap at her.

"Well, according to my records, it's maxed out right now and can't be used anyway. And a payment is due on the—"

"I thought that card had a $5,000 limit," I point out.

"Yes, we actually allowed you to go a bit over your—"

"I haven't gone *over* anything," I say. "Besides my Valentino boots, I haven't bought a single thing at your overpriced store."

"According to our records, your account is at $5,147 right now. The bill you received in the mail was calculated before you made your additional purchases. Now if you'd like to arrange a payment over the phone, please press the seven—"

"I don't *want* to make a payment," I nearly shout. "Just close the account, *please,* and let me talk to someone who can explain why my card's being used by someone other than me."

"Where is your card at the moment?" she asks in an acid tone.

I fumble around my still-messy apartment, wondering the very same thing. "I don't actually know," I finally admit.

"Some people should simply avoid credit accounts altogether," she tells me in a superior voice. "Credit is not for everyone."

"Thanks for the advice," I say and hang up.

I notice the brown suede boots, still in the corner by the front door where I threw them two weeks ago. They look slightly evil now, hunkered down together with their pointed toes facing each other almost as if they're conspiring, whispering secrets about me. Maybe they know something I don't, or perhaps they're really the ones responsible for this billing madness. Maybe they've been sneaking out when my back was turned, going shopping and buying things I can't afford.

I study the bill again, going over the long list of clothes—*expensive* clothes, clothes that I do *not* have in *my* closet. I read the enviable list of designer names and wish I did have them. Suddenly I remember that Monica popped in a few weeks ago, after my boot purchase and before my catastrophes, to "borrow" some milk for her granola. That woman is always out of everything and thinks nothing of borrowing what she never plans to return. I try to be a good Christian and cut her some slack since I know her good-for-nothing, live-in boyfriend, Will, is usually broke and jobless. He just seems to lounge around her apartment, usually in his T-shirt and boxers. I can't imagine why she keeps that loser around.

I make my mind replay that day, trying to remember the details. I was actually glad to see Monica, since we hadn't talked for a while and I was worried I might've said or done something to offend her. I often stick my foot in my mouth when it comes to her and Will. As usual, she looked fantastic. Her hair was perfect, and she had on a killer outfit. I remember complimenting her on the short, fitted jacket.

"This old thing?" she said with a shrug. "It's just Calvin Klein. Nothing to get overly excited about." I invited her in and even showed her my new boots since I was still trying to decide whether to keep them. I knew she'd be suitably wowed by the Valentino label. Monica knows and respects the really good designers. And she was impressed.

"These are beautiful, Cassidy." She kicked off a high-heeled shoe and actually started to try one on, even though her feet are bigger than mine.

"They'll be too small for you," I pointed out as I politely snatched the boot away. "And suede stretches so easily." I knew I'd probably offended her. Still, she told me I needed to keep them.

"Wear them and walk proud," she said with the conviction of a fashion diva. "You only live once, Cassie." Then she laughed. "And if they get stretched out, you can always let me take them off your hands." I smiled and acted as if that were funny. Like I'd even consider letting her wear those expensive boots.

But now I remember something else that happened that day. I remember that I had set my shiny new charge card on the kitchen counter. I'd already decided that it was going directly into the bottom of my lingerie drawer, where I keep other valuable things safe and out of sight. I figured with its generous $5,000 credit limit, it would be more secure in my drawer than in my purse, where I might actually be tempted to use it. So now I open my dresser to find that the card is not there. I thoroughly ransack my granny panties and 18 Hour bras but find no card. Then I check every drawer in the dresser and even the cracks and crevices in between, but I am getting the strongest feeling that I never put it there in the first place.

I try to put together exactly what happened that day. I returned my boots safely to the box and my room. Then I searched my cupboards for a clean jar to hold the milk since I didn't want to give her the whole carton and I knew she would never return a glass or a mug. After I generously filled a mayo jar with enough milk for at least two bowls of granola, Monica complained that it was two percent instead of skim, took it anyway without even thanking me, and quickly left.

The next thing I can specifically remember is the following morning, when I dressed carefully, wearing the boots just as my fashionable neighbor had recommended. Then I went to work, got fired, and totally forgot about the stupid credit card. It's probably been gone this whole time, and I never even noticed.

Love thy neighbor, I remind myself as I go into the hallway with lethal intentions toward Monica. Really, is it possible she did this to me? It seems so unbelievable. And yet I have a gut feeling that is exactly what happened. I take a deep breath. I try to calm myself. No use flying off the handle. Even so, my hands are shaking as I loudly rap on Monica's door. I have no idea how I'm going to confront her or what I'm going to say, so I determine to simply ask the question and then wait. I know she's an experienced liar, but I figure those big blue eyes of hers will give her away. Then, knowing she's the Return Queen, I will simply demand that she return all the merchandise and clear my account, and I won't even press charges. Heck, maybe I can get her to return those stupid boots as well. She could say they were defective or something.

Will answers the door, looking worse than usual. Seriously, doesn't this man ever shower or shave? I think I'm actually grimacing at him when I realize that I'm not exactly at my best either. In fact, we probably look like we could be related. He stands there blankly gazing at me as if he can't remember who I am. Well, whatever! This has nothing to do with him anyway. I'm halfway tempted to just shove him aside and go straight for Monica. But I take a breath and control myself.

"I need to talk to Monica," I proclaim in my I-mean-business voice.

"Yeah, well, get in line," he answers in a tone that sounds half dead. He starts to close the door.

"Huh?" I stick my yellow ducky slipper in the doorway to keep him from shutting me out. "What do you mean by that?"

"I mean you're not the only one who needs to talk to her."

"Is she here?"

"Nope." He folds his arms against his chest, which makes me notice the stain on the front of his grimy white T-shirt. *Ever heard of laundry soap?*

"When will she be back?" I tap my toe, which makes the duck head appear to be bobbing. I wonder if I should just blast past him, go inside, plant myself in a chair, and wait.

"Who knows?" He shrugs and looks over his shoulder toward the TV, which is blaring some loudmouthed sports commentator.

"What do you mean exactly?"

He looks back at me now, sort of studying me as if he almost remembers who I am but doesn't really care. "Haven't you heard the news?"

"What news?" I feel like screaming now. Why is this man such a jerk? And how is it that Monica has put up with him for several years?

"Monica walked out on me."

I'm about to say, "Big surprise there, bud," but then I realize what this means for me, for my unpaid credit-card bill. I grab hold of the doorframe for support. "When did she go?" I manage to ask.

He scratches his grizzly chin, thinking. "Couple of weeks ago, give or take. I haven't been keeping too good track of the time."

Okay, I feel like I just swallowed a heavy stone. It slowly drops, then wedges itself in the pit of my stomach. But maybe I didn't understand him right. "Do you mean Monica packed her bags and took her things?" I'm thinking *my things.* "Like she totally moved out?"

He slowly nods. "Which means I gotta move out too, since she's the one who's been renting this place."

"Did she leave a forwarding address?"

He sort of groans. "She didn't even leave a note. Just took off when I was gone. Just cleared out, just like that." He snaps his fingers.

"But what about her stuff? Her furniture and things?"

"Most of what's here is mine anyway, and it's not much. She took what she wanted."

"And you're absolutely sure she's not coming back?" I feel like I can hardly breathe now, like I might pass out right here in the doorway. Maybe he'll just give me a shove with his foot and close the door.

"I really don't think so." He seems to consider this. "I mean, I haven't heard a word from her since she left. Nothing. And she'd been threatening to do something like this for a long time. She was always saying she could do better than…well, you get the picture." He takes in a sharp breath and looks away, and I'm afraid he's going to cry. I don't know what I'd do if he started crying. He may be a loser and a jerk, but for Pete's sake, he's a human being. *Have a heart, Cassie!*

"I'm sorry, Will," I say to him in a soft voice. "I actually know how you feel. My boyfriend just dumped me too."

He looks back and stares at me for a long moment as if he's

taking this information in, running it around his head, and then he frowns. "It's pretty rough, huh?"

"Yeah." For no explainable reason, I feel sorry for this pathetic loser. Normally I wouldn't even give the time of day to this guy, and yet I guess I can relate. "So are you going to be okay?"

"I guess."

"Anything I can do?" Okay, now that's probably going too far. But the words are out there. I can't exactly take them back. Besides, I remind myself, I am a Christian. I am supposed to be kind and helpful and loving.

"Yeah, well." He pats his thin midsection. "I'm kinda hungry right now. I'm outta food, and the cupboards are bare, and I'm pretty broke."

"I've got a bunch of junk food," I confess. "Nothing even a little bit healthy, but it might take the edge off."

He brightens. "Hey, junk food sounds fine."

"Come on over and get what you want. It's obvious that I don't need to keep eating it." I puff out my cheeks and make a fat face. "Seriously, I've been eating like a pig since Eric dumped me. You'd be doing me a favor if you just took it all."

So Will comes over, and we commiserate as I fill a grocery bag with all my leftover chips and soda and ice cream and candy. It actually feels good to see these things go, but as I hold out the bag full of carbs and fats, I feel guilty too.

"It's not exactly health food," I say. "Not like Monica used to get for you guys." I remember how Monica gave me a bad time for only having two-percent milk to loan her. "You really need to go nonfat," she said as she was leaving. "Or if you really care about your health, you'd try to go with soy." I wonder if she had my credit card in her back pocket right then.

He nods. "Yeah, well, I'm sick of tofu and black beans. I have some opinions about food, and I think it's time I ate what I want."

"Knock yourself out with this," I say as I hand him the bag. "Just don't blame me if you feel sick later."

"Thanks." Now he looks more carefully at me. "Are you going to be okay?" he asks. "Anything I can do for you?"

I glance over at the bill that's sitting by the telephone. I know the guy is broke and can't help me in this regard, but I am curious as to how much he might know. "Yeah," I say, "you can tell me something." Then I explain my credit-card dilemma and my suspicions about his ex.

He sort of laughs. "Yep, that sounds like Monica."

"Seriously?"

"Oh, yeah. She did something like that to me when we first hooked up. It really knocked me sideways, but then she invited me to move in with her, and I thought that might make up for it. But she'd pull that kind of crud again and again. I guess it eventually became my big excuse for giving up on everything. Like what's the use? She maxed out my Visa card and ruined my credit to the point that I'll probably just go bankrupt. To be honest, I probably just stuck it out with her because she was always saying how she was going to land some great modeling job and make lots of money and pay me back." He laughs bitterly. "Like that's going to happen now."

"Wow."

"So are you going to press charges?"

I consider this. "Well, I can't be absolutely positive that it was Monica, but it's a pretty big crime. I guess I'd have to consider it."

He nods. "I can understand. I've considered it, but I doubt I ever will."

"Hey, did you notice her going on some big buying spree shortly before she left?" I ask. "I mean, maybe there's evidence she left behind, like receipts or bags or something in your apartment."

"You can look around if you want," he tells me. "The place is a mess right now, but I haven't thrown anything away since she left."

So I follow him back and carefully look around his apartment, which is just about as messy as mine, but I don't find one single piece of evidence. If Monica did this, which I feel pretty sure she did, that girl is good.

"Thanks, Will," I tell him, "but there's nothing incriminating here."

"Not surprising." He's slumped in his recliner now, a spoon already stuck into a quart of ice cream.

"Do you like Chinese food?" I ask suddenly.

He looks up, then nods.

"I'm going to order some takeout for dinner tonight," I tell him. "Come on over if you want some."

"Hey, thanks!"

Okay, I wonder if I'm going totally nuts as I halfheartedly continue to straighten my apartment. I mean, what is up with inviting Will over for Chinese? It's not bad enough that my life is in shreds, that I've lost my boyfriend and my job, that in all likelihood my neighbor has just committed felony fraud against me, but I go and invite Monica's loser boyfriend over for dinner. Seriously, what is wrong with this picture?

Four

I replace the litter in Felix's really rank-smelling cat box, which I'm sure he appreciates, and he puts it to immediate use. Then I take out the two-week-old garbage, and my nose thanks me again. But when I get back inside, it's like I really don't care that Will is coming over. Why did I bother? What's the point? It's not like that deadbeat is going to notice or care that someone went out of her way for him. And what difference would it make if he did? It's not like I care. Why waste the energy? I throw a pile of dirty clothes in the corner of the bathroom, slam the door shut, and suddenly crave a Snickers bar, which I'm fresh out of.

I walk around my tiny apartment and decide that I really don't care about anything. I don't care about my lost job. I don't care about my lost boyfriend or my ruined life. I don't even care about that crazy credit-card bill anymore. I don't think I'd care if it was for $20,000. Oh, part of me knows that I should do something about it. Maybe even call the police. But I *really* don't care. In fact, I'm starting to feel that it's probably my fault anyway. Like the woman on the phone said, I should've signed the card and put it in a safe place. I was irresponsible. Why shouldn't I have to pay?

In fact, the more I think about everything that's happened to me recently, the more I realize it's probably all my fault. I am so stupid. So incredibly stupid. If I'd been savvier, I would've sensed a change in the workplace. I would've tried harder. Crud, I would've saved the department and saved my job. I could've been Supergirl to the rescue! But instead, I became deadwood. And if I hadn't been so oblivious about my relationship with Eric, I would've gotten the signals that things were going sideways with us. I would've noticed Eric's growing interest in Jessica—the way those two would talk together, the eye contact, the body language. I would've realized that I needed to do something fast—maybe even something drastic—to keep him. I just wasn't paying attention.

But the more I think about this, the more I remember how well Jessica and Eric seemed to get along, how easily they talked and joked together. I can't help but think Jessica took advantage of me. What I assumed was a friendship was actually a cheap ruse for getting closer to Eric. Jessica used me to make a move on my man. Suddenly I see that "poor, lost lamb" as a cold, calculating, conniving boyfriend stealer. (Not unlike that despicable Bianca on the soap.)

I want to give Jessica a piece of my mind. Without really thinking this through, I grab the phone and call her, and there she is on the other end, and I am speechless. I want to hang up, but she obviously has caller ID, because she knows it's me.

"Come on, I know you're there, Cassie," she says in a gentle voice. "And I really want to talk to you. I've almost called you myself several times, but Eric said not to."

That unleashes my tongue. "Eric said not to?" I mutter. "Why not?"

"He just felt like it wouldn't help anything."

"It might help me," I point out. "I mean, consider how I feel, Jessica. I trusted you. I actually thought we were friends, and it turns out you were just—"

"We were friends, Cassie. I hope we still are. And by the way, we missed you at the singles' group and at—"

"Like I'm going to show my face around there," I practically spit at her. "I'm sure I must be the big joke by now."

"That's not fair," she says. "Those are your friends, Cassie, your good Christian friends."

"Yeah, right." I don't point out that one of them, Belinda Myers, already called to express her sympathy. What she really wanted was all the dirty details. Come to think of it, that's what I want too.

"I feel so badly," says Jessica. "And Eric does too. We never meant for it to happen. It just did."

"Yeah," I say with growing interest. "I guess I am kind of curious about that. Eric said pretty much the same thing, but honestly, Jessie, how does something like *that* just happen?"

"In all fairness, I blame myself," she says. "You know that my background isn't as squeaky clean as some people's." I'm sure she must mean me.

"And?"

"Well, things got carried away, Cassie. It's like we were only kissing, you know, and the next thing, well, you know…"

"Right," I say, thinking maybe I do know.

"Well, then we were done, and Eric told me that it was his first time." She sort of laughs. "Of course, I was certain he was kidding, but then he said no, it really was his first time. Goodness, I had no idea he was a virgin, Cassie."

It's all I can do not to hang up. Or throw up. I just stand there with my jaw hanging clear down to my ducky slippers.

"I'm sure he explained the whole thing to you already," she continues. "But I just wanted you to know how sorry I am. If I had known, you know, ahead of time…well, I probably would've been more careful. And now, of course, we *have* to get married."

"Well, of course," I snap at her.

"I mean, not as in *have to,* have to." She kind of laughs again. "I mean, I'm certainly not pregnant."

"Certainly not." I clear my throat. "Well, it's been great talking with you, Jessie. I feel *so much* better now."

"Really?" She actually buys into this, and I think maybe Eric is getting just what he deserves.

"Give Eric my regards." Then I hang up. But I am immediately stabbed with a pain that doubles me over. I grab myself around the middle. It feels like someone just jabbed me with a stomach punch, or maybe I'm developing an ulcer from all the crud I've been eating. But I physically ache inside. I try to process all that Jessie just said. They had sex! Eric gave up his precious virginity for her. Maybe I'm an idiot, but I had no idea it had gone that far. *No idea!*

I'm not sure how long I cry, but the more I cry, the worse I feel. I cannot believe this has happened. I can't believe Eric did that to me. I think I'd actually harbored the secret hope that Eric would wake up one day soon and realize that he was wrong, that he still loves me. Now I know that's not going to happen. No way!

I've never been a suicidal person. In fact, most consider me to be a perennial optimist. But I seriously wonder how difficult it would be just to check out right now. I ponder whether Eric would feel guilty. Of course, that would make me extremely happy. And it would be satisfying if Jessica felt partly to blame, assuming the girl has a conscience. On second thought, I think that Eric might simply note my premature departure as a close call for himself, like he somehow missed a bullet by not marrying me, the mentally unstable one.

Even so, and perhaps for drama's sake, I actually go to my medicine cabinet and examine the contents therein. Is it possible to kill yourself with an overdose of Correctol? Or would it just be terribly messy in the end? Then I hear a knocking at the door, and for a moment I actually think it might be Eric, coming to apologize, to tell me that it's all just a horrible misunderstanding, that Jessica made the whole thing up.

But when I open the door, I see my neighbor standing there. His pathetic expression reminds me of a mutt I found on the street when I was little. I took the smelly dog home and gave it a bath, but when Mom found out, she made me take it to the pound the next day. I still remember the look on the dog's face when I had to leave him there.

"I'm sorry," I tell Will as I wipe my nose on the sleeve of my sweatshirt. "I just had some more bad news, and I just, just…" Then I can't help it. I burst into tears again.

To my surprise, Will gently puts his arms around me, pulls me toward him, and lets me cry on his shoulder. I'm even more surprised to see that he's cleaned up some. His shirt actually smells pretty good, and when I finally step away from him, apologizing again, I notice that he's even shaved.

"We can make it another night," he says sheepishly as we both take another step back.

"No," I insist. "I want Chinese—more than ever right now." So I dig out the dog-eared menu for Ling's, and we both decide what we want, then I phone in the order. "It'll take about thirty minutes," I say. "And I think I could probably use a shower."

He nods. "Why don't you just knock on my door when it gets here?"

"Sure," I tell him, still thinking about how surreal my life has become in such a short time.

So I take a shower and actually put on real clothes. Okay, nothing great. Just jeans, which feel tighter than ever today, and an old sweater. Even so, it's better than I've done since being laid off. I pull my still-wet hair back in a ponytail, and then I even brush my teeth. But that's it. No makeup, no jewelry, no perfume. This is not a date. I'm not even sure what it is. A sympathy supper, perhaps.

Will arrives shortly after the Chinese food. "I saw the delivery van downstairs," he admits, then hands me a bottle of red wine.

"What's this?" I ask stupidly.

"Thought we could use it," he says.

I study the label, as though I should know what Shiraz is, and then mention that I don't have a corkscrew.

"Be right back," he says, disappearing out the still-open door.

I decide to take the food out, arranging it haphazardly on the breakfast bar. I don't bother to get out real plates. No point in making this seem like something it's not.

Will returns with an opened bottle and two wine glasses, which he fills, handing one to me. "Here's to better days," he says as he holds up his glass.

"Yeah," I say without enthusiasm.

"And to new beginnings," he adds.

"Sure." I stop myself from adding "whatever."

Then we both sit there and quietly eat our Chinese food, and I have to admit that it tastes pretty good. By the time we're finished, I'm amazed that I was actually considering suicide about an hour ago. I'm not sure if it's the wine or the nutrition of real food, but our conversation begins to flow more freely, and Will tells me that he used to dream of running a restaurant.

"No way," I say to him. "I never would've guessed that."

He nods. "I'm actually a good cook. I was in a culinary school when I met Monica, and, well, you know how that went."

"So you never finished?"

He shakes his head. "But I know enough to get cooking jobs. And sometimes I do. But never at any really good restaurants. Just dives mostly. I get sick of the grease and the hours and the bad management. And then I think, why bother? I mean, I'm so deep in debt, thanks to Monica, that I probably won't ever get ahead. I still have tuition bills, credit-card bills… What's the point of trying?"

I consider this. "You're the point," I say.

"Huh?"

"You're worth it, Will."

He kind of blinks at me, then nods. "Yeah, I am."

"You need to get a good job at a good restaurant, and you need to stick with it," I say with unexpected conviction. "You need to succeed for yourself. Just put the past and Monica behind you, and go for it. I mean, how old are you anyway?"

"Twenty-nine."

"That's two years younger than I am," I point out, "and I'm not ready to give up. I mean, sure, maybe life has given us lemons, Will, but we need to—"

"Make lemonade," he finishes for me.

"That's right."

We go on like this for a while, and I actually start to believe it myself. I mean, why can't people have fresh starts? Why can't we reinvent ourselves? Isn't that what life should be all about? But by the time the wine is gone, reality begins to slip in.

"It all sounds good," says Will. "But, man, I'm broke. I have to be outta the apartment by Monday. How can I get a job if I'm homeless?"

I just shake my head. "I don't know."

He brightens. "Hey, maybe you need a roommate?"

"No way," I tell him. "No offense. But that just wouldn't work for me."

He nods. "Yeah, I figured."

"Sorry."

"It's okay." Then he thanks me for dinner and says he should go. I don't try to stop him. But I do feel sort of bad once he leaves. I mean, it's like I had him all hopeful and excited and for what? *For what?*

His earlier despondency wraps itself around me as I go to bed. Really, why should we even try? What good does it do? Where does all your hard work and sincere effort land you? What's the point?

For the first time since my life started caving in, I cry out to God. I tell him how desperate I feel, how I want to give up. I beg him to do something—anything—to help me out here. *I can't do this on my own,* I admit. *I need your help!* And then I cry myself to sleep.

I wake up to the jangling sound of the phone ringing. I groggily make my way over to it, pick it up, and hear my mother's voice on the other end. She used to call me almost daily—right after Dad left her for Michelle about a year ago—but she's been pacing herself lately. Now it's more like once a week, if that. I realize this is the first time I've heard from her since my life fell apart. I'd considered calling but kept thinking I'd wait until things got better. She's had so much to deal with this year. I didn't want to add to her load.

"How's it going, Mom?" I ask, bracing myself for some of her usual sadness, feeling more empathetic than ever. I mean, I've been devastated over a three-year relationship. My mom and dad had been together more than ten times that long when he dumped her. Poor woman. No wonder she's been so depressed. I should've been there for her more. What was wrong with me?

"I'm doing okay," she says in a surprisingly cheery voice, which I'm sure is for my benefit. "I even sold a house last week. I think life's turning a corner."

"Well, I'm glad for you," I say, although I don't quite believe her. She must be putting up a strong front. Maybe if I tell her more about what's going on with me, she'll loosen up some. "My life hasn't been going that great lately."

"What's wrong?"

So I tell her a little about what I've gone through, sparing her some of the gorier details, but I do tell her about the credit-card fraud.

"Oh, dear," she says. "That's not good."

"I wondered if I should get a lawyer," I say.

"I don't know, sweetie. An attorney's fees could be as much as what you owe."

"If I wasn't so mad at Dad, I might consider calling him for some legal advice."

"I heard that he's retiring his practice," she says, her old sadness returning. "He and Michelle bought a condo in Arizona. I think he plans to golf every day."

"Lucky him."

"Well…"

"Sorry, Mom," I say quickly. "I didn't mean to depress you."

"So what are you going to do, Cassie? Any new job prospects?"

"I haven't really looked."

"Do you have enough money to live for a while?"

I consider this. "Well, I got a severance package, but if I have to pay off that bogus credit-card account—"

"You are responsible for it, Cassie," she warns me. "Now, if it were a Visa card, you might be able to get off. But this card's in your name, and unless you can find that girl and prove she did it, you'll be held accountable."

"But what if I skip town and don't pay it?"

"Then they'll get a collection agency after you and ruin your credit score. Really, it's better to take care of it before it comes back to bite you."

"Well, that'll pretty much take care of my severance package then."

"That's too bad. Do you have savings?"

I sort of laugh. "Not much."

"Well, as I've always told you girls: if you ever need to come home, the door is open."

Okay, I've heard this a lot during the past year. Good grief, there were times when Mom begged me to come home. And every time I came up with a great excuse not to. My job. My boyfriend. My life.

"You know what, Mom?" I say suddenly. "That's not such a bad idea."

"Really?" she sounds seriously shocked.

"Really!"

"Oh my, well, I don't know what to say—"

"I mean, I haven't seen you since last Christmas. And I need some time, you know. I need to think about where I want to go from here. Figure out my life."

"But I thought you liked working in marketing. I'm sure there must be more job opportunities there than here."

"I thought I liked it too. Apparently I was wrong—about everything."

"Well…"

"So that settles it. Thanks, Mom," I say brightly. "I'm so glad you called today. I'll start packing stuff up, and I'll be home by Sunday."

"It'll be so good to see you, Cassie!"

"Yes!" I say happily. "I can't wait to see you too." I hang up the phone, instantly unsure. Is this totally crazy? I've heard about people my age moving home and how it can backfire on them. Another expression my grandma would use comes to mind, one that I thought was pretty funny when I was little. "That's like jumping out of the frying pan into the fire," she'd warn someone who seemed to be making a rash decision.

Well, I'm sure this is exactly the opposite of what she meant. If anything, it feels like I've been walking on hot coals these past couple of weeks. Maybe a frying pan would be a relief.

Five

W hat's up?" asks Will as I use my foot to shove a packed cardboard box out into the hallway, where a small gathering is already waiting. I've rented a U-Haul that's parked on the street, and already it's starting to fill up.

"I'm leaving," I tell him.

He frowns. "And I was just starting to like you."

"Sorry." I set a smaller box on top of the others.

"I was thinking about what you said to me the other night," he continues. "And I think you're right. I guess I need to take some control over my life. I'm just not sure where to begin."

"Well, I happen to have an idea," I tell him. "It came to me while I was packing. I'm not sure if it'll work or not, but I'm willing to try."

He looks puzzled. "Huh?"

"You see, I have the rest of this month paid up, and I know there's no such thing as a refund. How about I ask Mr. Snyder if I can let you finish it out for me?"

"You'd do that?"

"I'll try."

"And then if I can get a job, maybe I can stay here."

"That's what I was hoping," I tell him. "But it's up to Snyder. It's not like people are lining up to rent these apartments." I point down the hall. "Mrs. Emery moved out last summer, and her place is still vacant."

"Well, tell Snyder that I'll have Monica's apartment cleaned out and spotless by tomorrow, okay?" He nods back toward the door. "I was feeling so energized that I started on it yesterday, and I've made great strides. I was also hoping that maybe he'd let me have the cleaning deposit back."

"Or maybe he'd let you apply it to my apartment?"

"Yeah, sure. I was heading out for a newspaper right now. I want to go over the classifieds. I was even considering doing some cold calls."

"You mean just walk up to some cool restaurant and tell them you want a job?"

"I've heard that works sometimes, especially if they're short-handed."

"And maybe if you cut your hair," I point out.

"I've got scissors," he says. "You any good at that sort of thing?"

"I can give it a shot," I tell him. "Hey, let's do dinner again tonight. I'll call for takeout, and we can—"

"No," he tells me, "I'll fix dinner tonight. I'm going to turn in my beer bottles for refunds, and whatever I get from that I'll use for groceries, and then I'll cook."

"You sure?"

"Yep. I could use the practice."

So we both keep at it, cleaning and packing up our apartments, and I experience this very bizarre sense of camaraderie with Will. Oddly enough, we have much in common. And as strange as it seems, I think discovering that is part of the answer to my prayer. I mean, when I realized I'd lose those weeks of rent, I almost called my mom back and told her that I'd just stick it out here and see if I could find a job. Maybe even at Starbucks. But then I thought of poor Will and how he would be homeless and how this could be his big chance to get on his feet. I would help someone else—and maybe as a result God would help me. Okay, it smacks just slightly of legalism, but it got me off my hind end and packing boxes. That's something.

I finally track down Mr. Snyder at the trash cans out back. I explain my situation and how I'd like to share the remainder of my month with Will.

"Well, we don't normally do—"

"Will is getting Monica's apartment totally cleaned," I point out. "And that's not even his responsibility."

Snyder seems to accept this. "Tell you what, if that's true and his place looks okay, I might agree. But if anything goes wrong at your apartment, it'll come out of your deposit."

"You mean I won't get my deposit back?"

"Not until the end of the month, and only if Will has rent money. Then I'll write up a new agreement for him."

I'm not sure I like the sound of this, but right then Will comes around the corner holding up two bags of groceries. "I got dinner," he says with a bright smile.

"I just talked to Mr. Snyder about my place," I tell Will. Then I explain the details to him, and we all shake hands on it.

Of course, I'm having serious doubts as I go up the stairs with Will trekking along behind me, happily talking about how he thinks he might have a lead on a cook's job. I nod as if I'm listening, but I'm really thinking, *How crazy is this? Will's girlfriend (okay, ex) takes me for nearly five grand, and now I think I can trust him with my apartment? This is nuts.* I pause by his door and am almost ready to tell him to forget the whole thing when he invites me to come in and inspect his cleaning.

"See," he says proudly, showing me his handiwork.

"Wow," I say as I examine the clean countertops, shining sink, and spotless floor. "If the cooking thing doesn't work out for you, you might try getting on with Merry Maids."

"My mom was a cleaning freak," he admits. "I guess it always bugged me that Monica never seemed to care about housekeeping. Sometimes I'd clean things up, but by the end of the day, it'd be a mess again."

"It sounds like Monica really took advantage of you," I point out. "What'd you get out of it anyway?"

He looks slightly embarrassed.

I roll my eyes. "Oh yeah, duh." Of course. Monica was a babe. Wrist candy. Gorgeous. "I'm sure you guys had some good times together."

"Yeah, but the good times were getting to be less and less."

"Hey, I'm impressed with your cleaning, Will. And if you can cook too, well, I might ask you to marry me."

He laughs, and we go our separate ways. What a totally lame thing to say! Seriously, how pathetic can I get? Flirting with a loser dude like this—Monica's castoff even. Oh, just shoot me!

I have most of my things packed by the time Will asks if it would be okay to cook dinner in my apartment. "So I don't make any more messes to clean up," he adds.

"Oh, yeah," I say. "I hadn't thought of that. But I've already packed all my pans and stuff."

"No problem. Mine are easy to get to."

"I guess you might as well put them in my cupboards," I say, thinking again about how strange this is. "But I haven't cleaned anything yet."

"You don't have to clean," he says. "I'll take care of it."

"Oh."

"Need help with that?" he asks as I bend down to pick up a big box.

"Thanks," I tell him.

"You want it in the van?"

"Sure, thanks," I say.

"Then I can help you move the big stuff out in the morning," he says, nodding toward my futon.

"That'd be great."

As Will starts bringing in his boxes, setting up the kitchen, and fixing dinner, I take a quick shower and put on a decent outfit. I take time to put on some lip gloss and mascara, even blow-dry my hair. I know it's silly, but I actually want to.

When I emerge from the bathroom, I can smell garlic and something else, maybe herbs. "Wow," I tell him as I check out his heavy-gauge cookware, "this looks like a real kitchen now."

He holds up a wire whisk as if it's a trophy. "That's because a professional chef should have professional tools."

He pours me a glass of wine, explaining that it's Pinot Gris and perfect with the halibut fillets he'll encrust in hazelnuts, then bake on paper.

"Sounds fancy," I tell him. Expensive too. "You must've had a lot of beer bottles to return."

"Thanks to Monica," he says. "Actually, I'm more of a wine guy."

So much I didn't know, never would've guessed. Oh well.

We've been leaving the doors open between our apartments all day, taking things in or out, and now a lot of Will's things are already making themselves comfortable in here. He even brought some candles, which he arranged on a small card table that's set with his dishes, which are way cooler than the ones I have.

"I'm impressed," I say. I sit at the breakfast bar, leaning on my elbows as I lazily watch him work.

"What's going on here?" asks a deep voice.

I nearly drop my glass of wine as I turn to see Eric standing in my open doorway. At first I feel guilty, like I've been caught doing something I shouldn't, and then I just want to laugh.

"What are *you* doing here?" I ask without even getting off the stool.

"I came over to talk to you, Cassie." He's looking around my apartment now, obviously taking this whole scene in and obviously not pleased by it. "I tried your phone, but it didn't seem to be connected."

"That's because it isn't." I nod to where the phone used to be plugged into the wall. "Anyway, what could *we* possibly have to talk about, Eric?" I don't even sound like myself as I say this. I sound light and disconnected, kind of like my phone at the moment. Maybe it's the wine. Or maybe it's just me. But I am no longer intimidated by this smooth blond guy wearing neatly pressed khakis and a navy sweater along with some very expensive shoes.

"Who are you?" Eric asks Will.

"This is my neighbor, Will," I say, finally getting off the stool and approaching Eric, who is standing like a rock in my doorway.

"You mean Monica's Will?" Eric's upper lip curls into what looks like a snooty little sneer. He's heard me talk about Monica and her down-and-out boyfriend. He knows how I tried to help Monica, how I prayed for her, hoping I might get her to come to church with me someday or at least dump her good-for-nothing boyfriend. Guess everyone is wrong sometimes.

Will wipes his hand on his apron, then sticks it out. "Actually, I'm not Monica's anything," he says. "Will Sorensen. You must be Eric. I think I've seen you around." Is it just my imagination, or is

Will standing a little straighter now? "I'm cooking dinner for Cassie."

"And he's an excellent chef," I say as if I've eaten his food on a regular basis.

Eric frowns. "Cassie, I need to speak to you in private."

I glance around the tiny studio apartment. "I guess we could go out—"

"Use my place," offers Will. "There are still some chairs in there."

So we go into Will's fairly stripped-down apartment and sit down. Eric takes the big recliner, and I sit on the edge of an ottoman that looks like a castoff from someone's grandma's house.

"Can you make it quick?" I say to him. "I don't want Will's dinner to get cold."

Eric just shakes his head. "I can't believe I was worried about you, Cassie. Seems like you have no problem whatsoever picking up with the first guy who happens along."

"Like it's any of your business."

"It's not?" Now he looks slightly hurt, and this makes me glad. "I still care about you, Cassie. I don't want you to throw everything away just because we broke up. I mean you haven't been to church or the singles' group or anything lately. I've been worried about you—about your faith."

"Don't worry," I say sharply. "I haven't given up my faith, Eric, if that's really what's freaking you." I have to bite my tongue to keep from swearing at him. What an arrogant jerk.

He nods in a self-satisfied way. "Well, good."

"So is that it then? You came over here just to make sure I hadn't tossed aside my faith because of you?"

"No, of course not." He looks a little sad now. "I do care about you. I was concerned—"

"Look, Eric," I say in a surprisingly calm tone. "You hurt me a lot, okay? I won't pretend you didn't. I know that you and Jessica had sex, and that hurts a lot too. But there's nothing I can do about any of it, and I know that I'm going to have to forgive you, okay? But I'm just not ready to do that yet."

He nods and looks down at his hands. "Okay."

"And, now, if you don't mind, there's a lovely dinner waiting for me." I stand up.

"So what's the deal with you two?" he asks as I head for the door.

"We're friends," I say as we go into the hallway. "We have some things in common."

Eric follows me back to my door, obviously burning with curiosity about this whole thing. I can see the wheels going around in his head. How long has this been going on? How serious is it? Was I seeing Will while dating Eric? But I am not going to give him the satisfaction of telling him. I may be a Christian, but that doesn't make me a doormat. "And that's all?" he asks.

"Well, that and he's moving into my apartment," I say lightly as I go inside. "See ya around, Eric." And then I close the door and lock it.

"Guess we showed him," says Will as he sets a pair of amazing salad plates on the table.

"These are like art," I say as I admire an arrangement of delicately placed vegetables and a swirl of what must be dressing.

And the whole meal is like that. By the time we're finished, I want to hug Will, but I restrain myself. "You really are an artist," I tell him. "And I so want you to find a cooking job." Then I start listing some of my favorite restaurants and even mention people I know who work there.

"Want to write me a recommendation?" he asks.

"Yes," I agree. "My laptop computer's packed, but maybe when I get to my mom's, I could do that and send it here." I sort of laugh. "Not that it would help."

"Might not hurt." He smiles. "This is so weird, Cassie."

"What?"

"Well, I always thought you were...well, you know..."

"No," I tell him, "I don't know."

"I don't want to insult you."

"Hey, go ahead, and then I can tell you what I thought of you." I give him my best evil eye.

"Well, the truth is, I thought you were this boring stick-in-the-mud. I knew you went to church, and then you're sort of conservative in your, uh, you know, your appearance. And I just never thought of you as very interesting."

I laugh. "Actually, that's probably just about right."

"No," he says quickly, "I was wrong. I'm not sure how to say it, but..." He squints as he tries to conjure up the right words. "I know what it is. You have a heart."

"Well, that's good to know," I say. "Maybe it's showing more since it's been broken."

"You're a nice person," he says, "and I wish you weren't moving."

"Well, we're both moving," I remind him. "We're moving on with our lives. We're taking control, right? We're becoming the people we were meant to be." I glance around the slightly messy kitchen. "And it's obvious you are an artiste in the kitchen, Will. I hope someday you own your own restaurant." Then I point to his hair. "Weren't we going to cut your hair?"

"You still want to?"

"Sure." I pick up some plates. "Let me start cleaning this up while you dig out those scissors."

Before long he's back and seated on the barstool, and I am cautiously snipping away at his shaggy brown hair. "I don't want to cut too much," I say. "I mean, you don't really seem like a button-down kind of guy. But I'll try to neaten it, okay?"

"Sounds good."

As I'm cutting, I can feel a serious attraction to this guy—I mean, it's like electric—and so I hurry up with the haircut. When I'm satisfied, I step back and think I need to go take a nice cool shower. "Go look," I tell him, pointing to the bathroom.

He comes back with a smile. "Great job. Thanks."

Then we both clean up the kitchen, but I'm careful to keep a safe distance. Not that I think Will would try anything on me. I mean, this guy is used to the looker Monica Johnson. The problem is that I don't trust myself. Finally we finish up, and I say it's been a long day and I have a long drive ahead of me tomorrow. Hint, hint.

"Thanks for making dinner," I tell him. "It was truly unforgettable."

"Thanks for everything," he tells me. "I'm thinking that you're an angel."

I laugh. "I can assure you that I'm not." Then I think of something. "But I will be praying for you, Will. I'll pray that you find the perfect restaurant to work in and that life starts going in a really great direction."

"Do you really believe in prayer?" he asks with a frown.

"You mean, do I believe that you can pray for things and they just magically will happen?" I shake my head. "But I do believe that God is listening, and sometimes when we're listening to him and getting it right, we manage to pray the kinds of prayers that God can say yes to."

He nods slowly as if he's trying to wrap his head around this.

"The problem is, I'm not sure I can pray like that for my own life right now," I admit. "But I know I can for you."

He frowns. "Man, I wish I could pray for you too, Cassie. I really owe you big time, but I'm not really, you know, into that kind of thing."

"I know." I smile. "And I actually understand."

Six

The next morning Will helps me load my remaining things in the U-Haul. There doesn't seem to be much to say as we stand outside in the crisp autumn air. "Thank you," I tell him, throwing my arms around his neck in a spontaneous hug. "Believe it or not, you have been a real godsend."

He throws back his head and laughs. "First time anyone said anything like that about me."

"I'll be sending that letter of recommendation," I tell him as I walk over to the driver's side. "Not that my seal of approval will help much. And you don't really need it, Will. You are a pro. You just need to believe in yourself and go for it."

"You too," he says. Then he frowns. "By the way, what exactly are you going for?"

I make a face and shrug. "Good question."

"We talked so much about me and my future, but you never said what you want to be when you grow up, Cassie."

I laugh. "Maybe it's because I haven't grown up yet." Then I hoist myself into the cab. "Hey, maybe I'll become a truck driver and drive one of those big old semis cross country and smoke big cigars and learn how to cuss."

He shakes his head. "Nah, I can't really see that."

"Stay in touch," I say as I start the engine and adjust the mirrors, sitting up straighter.

"You too."

Then I pull out, and the last thing I see as I drive away from Part One of my adult life is Will, Monica's ex, waving at me in the side mirror. So surreal.

I quickly realize that I need to focus here. For one thing, I don't drive all that much anymore. I gave up my car when I moved to the city. And this is a pretty big truck. But soon I'm on the freeway and haven't run over any little old ladies. Finally I slip into a comfort zone of sorts and randomly wonder if I might actually make a good truck driver. It could be interesting to see the country from this perspective. But before long I feel bored with the three lanes and fast-moving traffic. I turn the radio to an FM soft-rock station and replay Will's question in my mind. What do I want to be when I grow up? *What do I want to be?* Have I ever really known?

I was one of those kids who never make up their minds about a career. I liked so many things, and my attention span was about as long as a TV ad. For a time I wanted to be a ballerina and even took lessons for a couple of years, until I realized my slightly chunky body wasn't exactly cut out for it. Then I wanted to be a teacher, until I overhead my favorite teacher talking in the teachers' lounge, sounding so grumpy and unhappy. Next I thought I'd be an artist when I got attention for some of my works in junior high. But shortly after that, I discovered drama and wanted to be an actress. And on it went. I changed my mind with the seasons. As high-school graduation approached, my dad tried to get me to follow his example and go into law. And for a short while (probably to please him, since that had always been such a challenge), I considered it, but academics was never my strong suit.

The brains in the family belong to my younger sister, Cammie. Her SAT scores blew everyone away—even my dad. But being a healer at heart, she decided on med school. When she graduates in June, she plans to go to Uganda, where she will help thousands of AIDS orphans and probably become the next Mother Teresa. I can just imagine people calling my petite baby sister Mother Camilla (although we're not Catholic). But Cammie really is an angel.

On the opposite end of the angel scale is my older sister, Callie. Not that she's a devil exactly, but she has always been pretty self-centered, looking out for the big number one. And what Cammie got in the brains department, Callie got in looks. Tall, blond, classy, beautiful.

In some ways Monica Johnson reminded me of my older sister. Well, other than that little lying-and-stealing thing, because Callie can be obnoxiously moral. She got even worse after having kids. The only thing I can imagine Callie lying about would be her looks, like if she secretly got lipo or a tummy tuck. Last Christmas she complained about how much her body changed after giving birth to the twins three years ago. And unlike Monica, Callie has no need to steal. Her husband is an executive with a big recording company in Nashville, and they live in this humongous house in Brentwood. I suppose if I could switch lives with either of my sisters, I'd choose Callie, which I know is pure selfishness on my part. To be beautiful *and* rich, ahhh… But to be perfectly honest, I'd probably choose a trade that would make me a combination of my sisters. I would like to be rich and beautiful like Callie and have the brains and generous spirit of Cammie—which might make me into something that resembled God himself, and then I'd be in big trouble.

Instead, I am just me. Cassie in the middle. And right now, as I drive down the middle lane of this freeway with cars passing me on both sides, I feel so lost. Not lost as far as my destination goes. My turnoff is only fifteen miles ahead. I feel lost as in I really don't know who I am or who I want to be. Even Will seems to have a better handle on his life than I do. What is wrong with me?

And this is nothing new. Good grief, it took me four years to declare my major, and by then my options were getting limited. I settled on an MBA with a minor in art and didn't graduate until I was nearly twenty-six. When I got hired at the marketing firm right after graduation, I felt pretty proud of myself, and I thought I had life all figured out. I mapped my course, deciding that I would work hard and be successful in my career. Then I would meet and marry a nice Christian guy with a really good job that paid well enough to support both of us, plus our three lovely children—two girls and one boy—along with two golden retrievers and a calico cat, in a nice house in the suburbs. Out of that dream, all I have right now is a cat, and he's not even a calico. Nor is he happy at the moment. Poor Felix has been making his grumbling sounds all morning. I glance over at his crate and wonder how he'll adapt to living at my mom's house. At least he'll have room to roam there. And maybe he'll cheer Mom up. She always did like cats. Especially those big black-and-whites like Felix.

This thought encourages me some. I remind myself that I'm not just going home because I have failed at my life. I'm going home because Mom needs me. She's needed me for a year now, but I've been too busy to notice. All three of us girls have been too busy to notice: Cammie with her last year of med school, Callie with the twins, and me ruining my life by being totally oblivious. Poor Mom, all alone, rattling around in that big old house as she tries to survive a broken heart. Shortly after Dad left, Mom confessed to me over the phone that she usually slept in until noon or later. I told her it was probably just depression and suggested she watch *The First Wives Club*. But the last time I saw her, she was still in the thick of it. She tried to act cheerful for the sake of the rest of us, and she promised to renew her real-estate license, but I could tell she was tired and depressed and that she'd put on even more weight. Her usually light brown hair had turned gray. It was as if she'd aged ten years in just a few months.

I imagine her now as I drive. She's probably schlepping around in her old, plaid flannel robe, if she's even up yet since it's barely past noon. Maybe she's in front of the TV putting away a box of

Russell Stovers. Chocolate is pretty much her drug of choice. I'm guessing the drapes are still drawn. She also confessed that she pretends she's not home if anyone stops by. "They all act like they come here to cheer me up," she told me. "But I think they just come to gape. They want to see how fat I'm getting, like I'm some sort of sideshow freak."

"What about your good friends?" I say, listing the ladies I remember her spending time with while I was growing up.

"Well, Barbara Berg moved to Florida last year," she told me. "And you know Cynthia died of cancer. And Phyllis and Harold Abraham, well, they were one of our *couples* friends, so that's no good." On she went, listing all her friends and all the reasons they don't come around anymore. Really, I was depressed by the time she finished. Poor Mom.

"Here I come," I say aloud. I feel my spirits rising now, like maybe I will be Supergirl to the rescue—just me and my little cat, Felix. We'll get Mom out of her blue funk and back into the functioning world again. Maybe we can take walks together. Maybe we'll start a new hobby. It'll be fun. And who knows, maybe I'll find myself along the way.

My excitement builds as I drive into the mountains, slowly getting closer to my hometown. Just the sight of those magnificent ponderosa pines along the highway and the clear blue sky stretching overhead, well, feels almost like a welcome-home hug. Although I complained about it as a kid, I know I was blessed to grow up in the small mountain town of Black Bear. It might not be the biggest or fanciest place, but it's friendly and pretty and situated only minutes from Black Bear Butte, a small but popular ski resort. All three of us girls learned to ski at an early age, and Cammie even took up snowboarding in high school, which infuriated my dad since he believed that boarders were rebels. The town has grown since my sisters and I left home, but for the most part it feels the same. To my astonishment, I really feel like I'm coming home. I also feel like my tail's between my legs at the moment, but I'll get over that. Besides, I remind myself, I'm here to help Mom.

When I get to her house, no one is home. That doesn't surprise me, and I know where she hides the key under the flowerpot (so original). Anyway, I suspect she's at Warner's Groceries, stocking up on things we'll need because my homecoming has caught her totally by surprise. She probably got up early this morning, straightened things, aired out my room, and suddenly realized she needed groceries.

I decide to take advantage of her absence by emptying out the moving van into the big three-car garage. It's funny seeing it empty like this, though. I remember when all three of us girls were at home and driving, and how we fought over parking spaces. I back up the truck and start unloading. Today I'm thankful for my Spartan ways, since the heaviest thing I own is the futon frame, which slides out fairly easily. I scoot things around, working up a sweat as I shove everything up against one wall, making sure Mom will have plenty of room to park her old Suburban.

My sisters and I have been telling her to get rid of the old gas hog, but she insists it's still handy for getting plants and mulch and things from the nursery. "I don't drive much anyway," she told me the last time we talked about it. I felt so sad when she said this. She sounded forlorn, as if she were some little old lady who should just give it up altogether.

Finally I get the last of my big stuff out, then I take Felix's crate and my personal luggage into the house. I'm surprised to see that a few things have changed in here, but maybe that's good. Maybe it's Mom's attempt at starting over. I have to admit that big white sectional really brightens up the great room, although it needs some colored pillows to cheer it up. Maybe she and I can work on this later, I think as I haul my bags upstairs to my old bedroom. My sisters and I always stay in our old rooms when we're home. Mom's made changes to them over the years, and I know other people have stayed in them, but we still call them *our* rooms.

I'm a little dismayed to open the door and smell how stuffy my room is. But I figure Mom was busy getting other things ready. It's a crisp, clear autumn day, so I go ahead and open the windows wide, letting the fresh air waft in. Then I get Felix set up, deciding to confine him to my room for starters so he can get used to the change. And then I wander around the house.

I'm pleased to see that Mom's allowed some of our old family photos to return to the walls. I know she hated seeing my dad's smiling face among the rest of us, but how do you erase all those years without erasing the whole family? I study the last one taken. It was at Christmas shortly after Callie's twins were born. We think

Dad was already involved with Michelle by then. Thirty-five-year-old Michelle, who graduated from high school just ahead of Callie. We couldn't believe that she and our dad had really hooked up. She could be his daughter—such a scandal in a small town like Black Bear.

I study this family portrait of mostly smiling adults and two chubby baby boys, thinking how odd it is that the age gap between us and our parents somehow narrowed over the passing years. My parents were relatively young when they started their family. Not that they ever spoke of this much. It always embarrassed Mom to admit that Callie was born only six months after their first anniversary. She blamed it on Dad, the tall, handsome law student who seduced her when she was only a junior in college. And he blamed it on her for being "too darned pretty." Who would've thought those two would ever part? Even thinking of it now puts a lump in my throat. Poor Mom. I'm so glad I came. It's almost four o'clock, and I wonder where she is.

I decide to go ahead and return my U-Haul to the rental place in town. They close at five, and I don't want to get charged an extra day. I leave Mom a note, saying that if she gets home in time, maybe she could pick me up. But after I turn in the truck and try her from my cell phone, I realize that's not happening. I leave her a message, saying I'll grab a quick cup of coffee at The Butte (Black Bear's best coffeehouse) and maybe start walking home, since it's only about twenty minutes anyway.

I am barraged with worries about my mom as I sit down with

my latte. What if she's been in a wreck of some kind? I think she'd fare well in that old, heavy Suburban of hers. Or what if she's stressed over my unexpected visit? She could be having some kind of meltdown or breakdown or something. But that doesn't seem likely. She probably just had a lot of errands to do, things she's neglected and is embarrassed to let me see. Although Sunday doesn't really seem the best day for things like that. I hope nothing's wrong.

I realize I'm pretty grimy and dusty and develop an instant worry that I'll see someone I know. So I pick up the local newspaper (the *Black Bear Bulletin*) and do my best to hide behind it as I drink my latte. I try to focus on the small-town news. Most of the stories this week are about the Black Bear Blues Festival and the big names the organizers have managed to attract, which actually are fairly impressive. I'd totally forgotten this event was in late October.

When I'm finished with the news and my latte, I try calling Mom again, but there's still no answer. Feeling a little worried, I decide to hurry on home. It's a beautiful day, and the exercise won't hurt me. I just hope I don't run into anyone I know as I pop on my big sunglasses and take the back streets, going as fast as these chubby legs will take me.

I'm actually huffing and puffing and freshly sweaty when I turn down the street to our house. I really must get into shape. All that sitting around on my big rear end and eating junk food has taken a serious toll. As I approach Mom's house, I notice a car that I don't recognize parked in her driveway—a red Jeep Wrangler. As

I get closer, I notice a tall guy leaning against it. He has on khakis and a light blue shirt, and his legs are casually crossed as he talks into a cell phone. Something about this guy seems familiar to me, but I can't quite put my finger on it. He closes his cell phone as I cut across the front lawn, and suddenly I get it. I know who he is.

It's Todd Michaels from Black Bear High. He was a year ahead of me and one of the coolest guys around—smart, athletic, really good looking—the kind of guy I used to daydream about, imagining him inviting me out for a Coke, later taking me to the prom, and eventually being the father of my children... Of course, none of that ever happened. Not even close. I can see that he's changed a bit, probably for the better if that's even possible.

As the full realization of who he is hits me, I also remember how disgusting I look right now. I'm wearing my too-tight jeans, which are also too short, my run-down tennis shoes, an old gray sweatshirt—your basic loser-chick apparel. I want to turn around and walk the other way. But it's too late. He's already waving, and to my horror and despite my sunglasses, it's as if he recognizes me. Good-bye, incognito.

"Hey," he calls out, "is that you, Cassidy Cantrell?"

I try not to look like a shrinking violet as I nod and say an embarrassed "Yeah, it is." Is it possible that he's actually here to see me? I cautiously approach him, wishing I could rewind the clock and do this totally differently. I mean, this could've been one of those big moments in life—one of those times you dream of, hope for, fantasize about later. But maybe it's not too late. I force a smile as I stand across from him. I think I can smell his cologne—and it smells expensive.

"Your mom told me to look for you. She thought you would be here by now." He looks curiously at me as if he's not quite sure who I am. "You really are Cassidy Cantrell, right?"

"Of course."

"But your mom said you were driving from the city, and I don't see a car."

I laugh nervously. "No, I actually came here in a U-Haul truck. I just unloaded all my stuff into the garage." I point down at my grungy attire. "As you can see, I still have on my moving clothes. I just turned the truck in and decided to walk home." I really wish I could shove my hands into my pockets right now. I'd like to play up the sporty sort of fun girl who's not afraid to drive a U-Haul truck or walk across town, but my jeans are too tight for this little gesture.

He looks surprised. "So you are moving back to town?"

I shrug, then shyly smile again. "Yeah, I guess so."

"Your mom said it was just a visit."

"Mom doesn't know everything," I say a bit slyly.

He turns at the sound of a car coming down the street, and we both watch a sleek silver sports car slow down and pull into the driveway. I wonder what's going on here and why Mom's driveway has suddenly turned into Grand Central Station.

"Speaking of your mom…" Todd nods toward the pretty

blond driver, who's now climbing out of the car, as if this should all make some kind of sense to me, which it totally doesn't.

"Huh?" I study the tall, thin woman in the stylish denim jacket and belted, low-rise jeans. She smiles at me, then removes her sunglasses. For a split second, I almost think it's my sister Callie, only this woman seems a bit older.

"Hey, Audra," says Todd, using *my mother's* first name, as he goes over to greet this woman. He gives her a quick hug followed by a peck on the cheek. Reality hits me like a baseball bat to the side of the head. *That woman is my mother!*

odd," says the slender, pretty woman standing in my mom's driveway, "did you meet Cassidy already?" She uses a voice that sounds strangely like my mother's. Can this really be true?

"Yes," says Todd. "She just walked up, and I assumed it was your daughter."

"You assumed right," she says as she walks toward me.

Todd laughs. "But I forgot to introduce myself."

"I already know you who *you* are," I tell him in a chilly voice. My mom, who really looks nothing like my mom, has her arms opened wide and is grinning at me as if she thinks this is all very funny.

"You already know Todd?" she says as she hugs me tightly, the same way she always has, but there's so much less of her for me to hug in return.

I give her a reluctant squeeze, then step back and study her closely just to make sure it really is her. And it is; the eyes give her away. "Yeah, Todd was a year ahead of me in high school," I say pointedly. As in *He could be your son, Mom.*

She just laughs, then gently punches him in the arm. "You didn't tell me that, Todd. You gave me the impression you were older."

Todd looks slightly embarrassed as he peers at me. "Really? We were in school together?"

"Yes," I tell him, not taking my eyes off my transformed mother. When did she lose all that weight? More important, how did she? "I'm sure you don't remember me."

"Well, that was a long time ago," he says, smiling at my mom.

"But you told me you were older than my girls," she teases.

"I just figured I must be," he says. "You never mentioned their ages, and judging by you, I could only assume they were much younger."

She smiles even bigger now. "Thanks for the compliment, but I distinctly remember your telling me that you were pushing forty."

"I am pushing forty, just not too hard. It was the only way to get you to go out with me, Audra. I figured if we were *both* in our forties…"

My mom says nothing, which makes me wonder if she's been lying about her age too. What else might be going on here?

"I looked all over town for you, Cassie," she says in a slightly scolding tone, sounding more like Mom. "I read your little note about the U-Haul place and ran over there to get you, but the guy said I just missed you. So I assumed you were walking home, and I drove around and around and looked and looked, but—"

"I left phone messages," I point out.

She slaps her forehead. "Silly me, I forgot to check my voice mail. You see, it's been a busy day. I'd left to check on a new listing earlier, and then I showed a house, and one thing led to another… and by the time I got back home, you'd already come and gone. And then I was meeting Todd here at five thirty and—"

"Audra told me to be on the lookout for her long-lost daughter," Todd fills in as though they're some happily married old couple. "That's why I figured out who you were when you walked up." He scratches his head. "But I still can't place you in high school. Maybe I should get out the annual and have a—"

"Don't bother," I say sourly. "I'm sure you wouldn't remember me anyway."

"You might remember Callie," suggests Mom. Of course she would think so. *Everyone* must remember the beautiful Callie.

"Callie was like three years ahead of Todd," I point out. "Remember, she's your *oldest* daughter, four years older than I am, and then there's Cammie, who hasn't hit thirty yet, and she's—"

Mom laughs. "Yes, yes, well, you know me and numbers, Cassie. It's a wonder they trust me to sell real estate."

"That's how we met," says Todd. "Your mom recently sold me a house."

"He bought the Barley place on Alder Street."

"But I refused to sign the offer until she promised to go out with me," says Todd. "And I had to pretend to be pushing forty just to get her to agree to that." He winks at me as if this was all quite clever on his part. "I always did like older women."

"I forgot to tell you," says Mom, glancing at her watch. "I was so surprised when I spoke to you the other day, I didn't mention that Todd and I are going to a concert tonight. The Black Bear Blues Festival is this weekend, and he had already bought tickets for really good seats. I've tried all over town to find you one so you could join us, but everything seems to be sold out."

"That's okay," I say quickly. "I'm tired after the long drive anyway."

"Do you want to join us for dinner?" offers Todd, although I'm sure he's hoping I'll decline. I pause for a moment, almost wanting to say yes just to rock his boat a little. Maybe I could even call him Daddy.

Mom nods eagerly. "That's a great idea. We're heading over to the resort for a special dinner that's to benefit—"

"No, I'm not even hungry," I lie. "You guys go ahead. I'll be fine."

"You sure, honey?"

"Of course I'm sure. Go on. Have a good time." I head toward the house, waving as I go up the steps. "Have fun, kids," I yell just before I close the front door. Then I stand to one side of the big front window, lurking in the shadows as I spy on them. They're totally oblivious to me, in their own world as they appear to be discussing which vehicle to drive. But I just stand there numbly watching. I feel like I'm in serious shock as I scrutinize these two strikingly attractive people, who look like they could be posing for a car commercial. They seem as if they're younger than I am, and

I find this very disturbing. I still can't believe that's really my mom out there. What happened to all the gray hair and the frowzy haircut? And what about all that weight and the dumpy, frumpy old clothes she used to cover it with?

They finally decide on Mom's car, which is another unsolved mystery in this *Twilight Zone* episode that's actually a day in the life of Cassie Cantrell. Naturally, Mom lets him drive. I want to scream.

Instead I retrieve Felix from my bedroom, turn on the TV, then search the entire kitchen and pantry for some form of junk food, only to discover that my mom has turned into a total health nut. I can't even find chocolate—in any form. So I eventually settle on some "butter flavored" rice cakes and some pink premixed drink that she's got in the fridge. It has fake sweetener, which makes it taste disgusting.

I can't take it anymore. I pick up the phone and call information to see if there's still a Domino's Pizza in town, and when I'm connected, I order a giant with the works. I think I shall simply eat myself to death.

As I'm porking out on pizza, I wonder about my sisters. Do they have any idea what's going on with Mom? I decide to take advantage of her long-distance and start with Callie, hoping that she's put the twins to bed by now.

"Cassie?" She sounds surprised, probably because I rarely call. "Is something wrong?"

"Yes," I say as I set down a half-eaten piece of pizza. "Do you know what's going on with Mom?"

"What do you mean? Is she okay? Tell me, what's wrong?"

So I pour out a very dramatic retelling of my afternoon, leaving out no details. I finally pause to catch my breath.

"Is that *all*?" she asks in a bored-sounding voice.

"What do you mean, 'Is that all'?" I repeat, stunned. "It's like the *Invasion of the Body Snatchers,* Callie. It's like Mom doesn't live here anymore."

Callie just laughs. "Calm down, Cassie. This is old news, okay?"

"Huh?"

"Mom's lost a little weight, and that naturally requires some new clothes. And, yes, she's gone blond. I actually happen to have been the one who suggested that change after I saw how gray she was. Good grief, Cassie, she's five years younger than Goldie Hawn. It's okay if she looks like it. I even asked my hairdresser to help her pick out the color." She pauses. "The young boyfriend thing is news to me, but, hey, who can blame her?"

"So you *knew* about all this?" I am incredulous.

"Mom and I talk," she says casually. I can imagine her filing a perfectly shaped nail, giving it a little puff, checking it out.

"So do we," I say defensively. "Why didn't she tell me this stuff?"

"Mom thinks you've been having a hard time," she says in a more gentle tone. "I think she thought it made you feel better to know that her life's not so perfect either."

"What do you mean I'm having a hard time? What did she tell you?"

"Oh, you know, Cassie. You tell her about Eric and his inability to commit and how your baby clock is ticking away and how your job's not all that great and how you've put on some weight and—"

"Wait a minute," I say quickly. "Mom told you all that?"

"She worries about you, Cass. And she thinks you cheer up a little when she tells you about her troubles. It probably started innocently enough, since Mom really was miserable and you had time to listen. It's that old misery-loves-company thing. She told me how you started opening up to her more after Dad left and how you guys talked on the phone all the time. And then when things started turning around for her, well, she just couldn't bring herself to tell you."

"How long was she going to hide this?" I ask.

"She wanted to surprise you and Cammie at Thanksgiving this year. Remember that Cammie asked her to have Thanksgiving at home since it'll be Cammie's last one in the States before she goes to Uganda next summer?"

"Yeah."

"Well, Mom just wanted to surprise you guys then. She thought it would be fun."

"So it was just a big secret between you and Mom?"

"Hey, if it makes you feel any better, I wormed the weight thing out of her after I sent her some size twenty sweats for her birthday in June. She admitted they were a little baggy."

"She must've been swimming in them," I say. "She looks like she's lost fifty pounds since last Christmas."

"Seriously?" Callie lets out a happy little squeal. "Good for her! I wish I could see her right now. Hey, send me a picture, okay?"

"Sorry, you'll have to wait for Thanksgiving," I tease. "And who knows, maybe she and Todd will be married by then, and we'll have a new stepdad who is younger than you. But don't worry, I won't tell."

"Oh, come on, Cass. Don't take everything so personally. Be happy for Mom. I'm sure this Todd thing is just a phase."

"It's like both our parents have lost their minds."

"No," says Callie in a firm tone, "Dad lost his mind when he cheated on Mom. But Mom's finding herself now. It might take some time, but we need to be supportive of her. She's been through so much."

I almost start to tell Callie how much I've been through recently, but I feel too tired. Besides, it's so humiliating. I'll save it for another day. "Yeah, you're probably right. Sorry." I'm trying to think of a way to cut off our conversation now. I just want to go to bed.

"So what are you doing at Mom's anyway, Cass? She never mentioned you were coming."

"I kind of took her by surprise," I admit.

"I'll bet."

"Well, I should go." I'm tapping my toe, ready to hang up before I get some big-sister, my-life-is-so-perfect, be-more-like-me lecture.

"All right, but take it easy on Mom, okay?"

"What did you think I was going to do? Beat her up?"

"She's just getting on her feet, Cass. She doesn't need anyone stomping on her right now."

"I'm not stomping on anyone."

"You sounded pretty mad."

"More like stunned, okay? I was in a state of shock. I mean she's our mom, for Pete's sake. I expect parents to act like parents. First we go through this with Dad, and he checks out, living his own party-boy life like we don't even exist anymore. Then almost exactly a year later, it's like we're losing Mom too. I just can't take it." My voice breaks, and I actually start to cry.

"We're not losing Mom, Cass."

"But all these changes, and she's been so secretive, with me at least…"

"She's kept secrets from me too. I hadn't heard about the new car, although it sounds pretty cool. And you know we've all bugged her to lose that horrible, gas-eating Suburban. So really it's a good thing, right?"

"I guess. I just need time to adjust to all this." I wipe my nose on the sleeve of my sweatshirt. "Anyway, I should probably let you go."

"Tell Mom I said hey."

Then we say good-bye and hang up. I can't help it. I am so ticked that Callie knew and I didn't. I'm halfway tempted to call

Cammie and tell her the whole story. But knowing Cammie, she'd probably be very sweet about it. She'd take the high road and side with Mom.

"Let's go to bed, Felix," I say, bending down to hoist my cat. As I trudge upstairs, I know I should feel relieved to be here, back in the old family home. This place should feel like a refuge, especially after all the crud in my life lately. A great little escape. Even Eric doesn't know I'm here. Not that he'd care. And, hey, it's free rent, no pressure. I can take time to figure out my life without worrying about things like going to work or buying groceries or stopping by the dry cleaners. It's like a paid minivacation, right?

Even so, I am seriously worried. Maybe I've made another dumb mistake. Maybe I really did just leap from the frying pan into the blazes. Or maybe I'm just tired and beat-up. Hopefully it'll all make sense in the morning. I yawn as I flop onto my old twin bed, not even bothering to change into pajamas. Everything that's happened in the past few weeks feels like a really bad dream. If only I could wake up, be back in my old life, go to my old job, see my old boyfriend, I would be ever so thankful. Why didn't I see how good I had it while everything was still in place? I close my eyes and pretend that I've been stuck in a nightmare. When I wake up, all will be well.

But when I get up the next day, my back aching from the hard mattress that my dad always claimed was designed for good posture, I know that nothing has changed. My whole life is a living, waking nightmare.

"Good morning, sunshine," my mom sings from the kitchen. "I'm fixing us both some high-fiber hot cereal for breakfast."

I sit down at the island, lean on my elbows, and frown at her. "When did you become such a health-food freak?"

She laughs. "It was my New Year's resolution, the first one I've ever kept."

"So is that how you lost the weight? Eating nothing but health food?"

"That combined with yoga and spinning and walking." She hands me a bowl of some brown muck. "I try to work out every day."

"*Every* day?"

She nods. "Spinning on Mondays and Wednesdays. Yoga on Tuesdays and Fridays. And I walk for an hour on the other days."

I stick in my spoon and take a tentative bite, then make a face. "You really eat this stuff?"

"I actually like it."

I try another bite, suppressing my gag reflex.

"Want some blueberries to sweeten it?" She goes to the fridge. "They're loaded with antioxidants, you know."

"Whatever."

"I know you're really surprised by the changes in me," she says as she shakes some frozen berries onto my brown muck. "The heat should soften those berries right up."

I try another bite and attempt to look as if I like it this time. Hot brown muck with crunchy, icy blueberries. Yum, yum.

"Anyway, I was hoping to surprise you girls at Thanksgiving," she continues between bites. "I still have a couple of pounds to lose."

"A couple of pounds?" I stare at her already-thin body. "You're not becoming anorexic, are you?"

She laughs. "Not at all. I eat all the time. I just watch what I eat, and as I said, I exercise." She studies me now. "You could do it too, sweetie."

I shove the bowl away. "Thanks."

"I'm not trying to hurt your feelings, Cassie, but sometimes when life kicks you in the teeth, the best way to respond is to kick back. After several months of wallowing in self-pity, I realized I needed to pick myself up off the couch and kick myself down to the gym." She smiles and puts her hands on her slim hips. She's wearing this fitted brown jacket that shows off her trim figure. "And you can do it too."

"I don't think so."

"You *can*, Cassie. I know you can."

I just shake my head. "I don't think you really know me at all, Mom." My voice is breaking. "And I don't think I really know you either." Then I lower my head and try not to make ugly crying noises. I don't think I've ever felt so alone.

"Oh, sweetie." Mom comes over to my side of the island and puts her arms around me. "It always seems darkest before the dawn. Believe me, I know this personally. I've been there too."

I look up at her with tears running down my cheeks. "It just feels like my life is over. Like, why try?"

She nods, then glances at her watch. "But it's not over. You're only thirty-one. Your life has barely begun. Now, I hate to leave you, but I need to get some things done around here. Then I promised to meet a prospective buyer at the office at ten. But spinning class starts at noon, and I want you to come. Okay?"

"I don't think so."

"Please, Cassie, I want you to try it. Meet me there a little before noon. I want to treat you to a minimembership, just to see if you like it."

"Mom." I can hear the whine in my voice.

"Come on. You'll be glad if you do this, Cassie. Really, it makes you feel so good. It's energizing, and it's not hard at all. You just sit on the bike and ride—burning lots of calories."

"That's all there is to it?"

"Yes!" She smiles happily. "You know where the fitness center is, don't you? Same place as before, but they've totally remodeled, and it's really uptown. You're going to love it."

"What do I wear?"

"Just sweats." She looks at the grubby things I'm wearing and appears to have a revelation. "I happen to have a brand-new set of sweats that I'm sure will fit you. Callie gave them to me for my birthday last summer. They're very nice but a little big."

I nod knowingly. "Right."

"I'll set them in your room before I leave. And don't forget to bring a bag with a fresh change of clothes. Maybe we can have lunch afterward."

And, like a skinny whirlwind of energy, she does about twenty-seven quick chores and then is out of there, driving down the street in her new car like a silver flash.

I, on the other hand, am moving at the speed of a constipated tortoise on Xanax. And, oh yeah, I feel like sleeping for about a year.

On the way back to my room to escape, I remember the promise I made to Will. Even if I feel unable to help myself at the moment, I think perhaps I can help him. I don't want to dig out my laptop, so I go into Mom's office, turn on her computer, and attempt to write a letter of recommendation. After several feeble attempts, which assure me that a fiction writer I am not, I come up with a fairly decent letter that is mostly true. I may be stretching it a bit when I compare Will to Emeril Lagasse, but he's the only chef I know. Anyway, it's done. I put it in an envelope and will drop it in the mail later today. Right after my nap.

Eight

I sleep for about thirty minutes, until Felix leaps onto my stomach, punching me back to my senses. I sit up in bed, feeling skanky and foul. I briefly consider taking a shower, but why bother if I'm just going to get all sweaty anyway? That is, *if* I go to spinning class. I'd rather just go back to sleep. Well, after I eat something. I crawl out of bed and go poking around Mom's healthy-choice kitchen. I wish I'd thought to put some of the left-over pizza in the fridge last night. Obviously, Mom found my little mess and disposed of the contraband before I got up. I'll have to be smarter next time. Maybe I can sneak food into my room. Dad used to get furious if any of us girls ate in our room. It might be a nice way to get back at him. Ha! Who am I fooling here? Dad couldn't care less about his daughters—least of all me. He has Michelle to play daddy to now.

I pick up the sweats that Mom set neatly at the foot of my still-unmade bed earlier this morning. They're a little rumpled after having been kicked onto the floor, and it looks like Felix might've taken a nap on them. I shake traces of his fur from the dark peri-winkle blue velour, noting the neat white stripes down the sides of the sleeves and legs that are probably supposed to be slimming. The sweats look like something Callie would pick out. The tag says Elisabeth, as in Liz Claiborne, but obviously from her plus-size line. I read the size, which is printed in large letters as if Liz thinks that large women must need large letters in order to read. But seeing the number twenty there in big, bold print makes me feel slightly lightheaded. I have never worn a twenty anything in my life. Okay, sure, I had some challenges zipping my fourteens and recently upgraded my jeans to sixteens. But that's where it ends. Of course, it was the pockets of my sixteens that my hands couldn't fit into yesterday.

Anyway, I decide to try on the sweats just to see what they look like. To my surprise they feel pretty comfortable. And a little roomy, which makes me feel slimmer. I check myself out in the mirror, standing up straight and sucking in my cheeks, and I actually think something about this design works. I think those slender white stripes really do elongate.

Maybe Mom's right. Maybe I do need a fitness routine to help get me into shape and out of my slump. I move around my bedroom, putting clothes and things away, and I start to think that I can already feel a little spring in my step. It's so springy that I nearly step on poor Felix, and I decide that perhaps it's time to set the beastie free to explore the greater world of Mom's house. So I move his cat box and things down to the laundry room, and while I'm there, I even do a load of clothes. This is real progress.

By eleven, I'm still moving, and by eleven thirty, I decide that I'm going to do this thing. I'm going to the fitness club to work out! This also means I must walk to town to get there. Mom must've known this. But then I consider all the additional calories the walk might burn, and I figure maybe Mom's onto something. Besides, I think as I pull my hair back into a tidy ponytail and put on some lip gloss and mascara, I don't feel that worried about seeing someone I know today, because I really don't look too bad in these new sweats, which I've decided are rather sporty. The color's not bad on me either. I've also decided that they have been mistakenly sized. Really, they must be smaller. So I dig an old gym bag out of my closet, stuff a change of clothes in it, put on my sunglasses, tell Felix to be a good kitty, and head out the door. I *can* do this!

I'm a little winded by the time I get there, but then I was walking pretty fast. I'm surprised to see the changes to the fitness club, which used to be fairly Podunk. I'm also surprised that I made it here a couple of minutes before noon. I go inside and look around a bit, and I realize that someone has sunk some serious bucks into this place. For Black Bear it really does look uptown. I feel a little self-conscious as I hang out in the lobby, which is cozy with a large stone fountain and a rock fireplace. But I'm not really sure what to do now. I hope Mom hasn't already gone to her class without me.

"Cassidy Cantrell?" says a woman's voice. I turn to see a slim brunette with big brown eyes. Okay, something about her is familiar, but I can't quite place her.

"Yes?" I say curiously. "Do I know you?"

She laughs and comes closer. "Penny Grant."

I blink, then stare at this petite woman in her form-fitting pants and tank top. "Penny Grant?" I repeat like a dummy as I remember my plump friend from high school. "No way."

She laughs harder now. "I know, I know. I get that all the time. But it's me. I just shed a few pounds these past few years. Our ten-year reunion was hard on me. It seemed like everyone else had gotten better looking, and I was so, well…" She stops talking and looks more closely at me, then seems uncomfortable. "So, Cassidy, what are you doing in town?"

I sort of shrug, wondering how much I want to tell her. "I just thought I'd come home for a while. I wanted to spend time with my mom."

"Oh, I just saw Audra; she was heading to spinning."

"That's where I'm going," I say.

"Me too." She glances at the front desk, then at her watch. "You're supposed to sign in, but that'll take too long. Let's just go to class, and you can do it later."

So I follow Penny to the locker room, and she shows me where to put my stuff. Then we both get little white towels and head down a hallway.

"You didn't bring water," she observes as she pushes open a door that leads to a room filled with stationary bikes.

"Water?"

"Yeah, to replace your fluids."

"Oh." I force a smile. "I'm sure I'll be okay." Or not. I notice the people already in the room. Some are on their bikes, pedaling and visiting with others. Some seem to be making adjustments to the mechanics of the bikes. It's a mix of men and women and ages, but the one thing they all have in common is that they look fit. Whereas I am immediately aware that I do not. We're still standing by the door, and I'm ready to turn around and walk out.

"Have you spun before?" asks Penny.

"Well, no."

"Cassie!" says Mom happily. She's already seated on a bike and immediately calls out to the instructor, Gretchen, telling her that I'm her daughter and new to class and might need some help. The instructor, a buff-looking blonde in very tight sweats, tells me to come down to the front of the room so she can set me up on a bike. The bike she chooses, of course, is in the very front row where everyone else can watch. Great. But finally I'm on the bike, and everything seems to be working okay. It sort of reminds me of being a kid, and I think maybe it's not so bad.

"Now let's get going," says Gretchen as she turns up some fast-paced music.

No problem. You just sit here and pedal. No big deal. But then Gretchen tells us to tighten the resistance on our bikes, and even though I don't do the full turns that she dictates, I can feel my thighs now, and I'm having a hard time keeping up with the beat. Still, I think I can do this, and I remind myself that I am burning calories. Lots and lots of calories.

Soon I'm feeling winded. I think I need to loosen my resistance, but as I reach for the knob, I see that Gretchen has other plans. She wants us to stand and pedal now. For a few brief seconds, this new position is a relief, because my buns were getting seriously sore on that tiny, hard seat. But we keep standing and standing, pedaling and pedaling, and I think maybe I'm going to have a heart attack. I can't help but glance around the room to see if anyone else is in dire need of medical help, but everyone is just smiling and bouncing as they pedal to the music. Do they enjoy this kind of torture? Then it's time for sit and stand, sit and stand, and it feels like my thighs, not to mention my lungs, are going to burst.

"Breathe in through your nose," yells Gretchen. "Out through your mouth."

I try this technique, but it feels like all I can do is gasp and puff, gasp and puff, and I really don't know which part of my body the air is escaping from!

Finally we are seated again, doing what she calls "seated sprints," and we're supposed to have our resistance "way up there." But I turn mine to nothing in the hope that maybe I won't need a paramedic quite yet. Just as I can almost breathe, Gretchen changes the game again.

"Jump!" she yells as if she thinks we're a bunch of trained monkeys. "Jump! Jump! Jump!" I attempt to do these jumps, but my legs are so weak that I'm afraid I may flop to the floor in a big sweaty mess. So I just sit and pedal. The sweat is dripping down my face and trickling down my back. I notice the others taking regular sips from their water bottles, and I am so thirsty I want to swipe the bottle from the gray-haired guy who's happily jumping next to me. I wonder if he'd notice.

The class is merely half over when I decide that the only thing to do at this point is sit on this rock-hard seat and slowly pedal with absolutely no pressure on the resistance dial. Everyone else is rocking and rolling and even laughing and talking to each other as if this is a walk through the park. I wonder if they're showing off for my benefit or just being their regular selves. Whatever the case, I feel like the class dummy. The fitness failure. At least I'm not giving up completely. It would be so embarrassing to climb off this bike in the front row and slink out of here with my tail between my legs. I so wish I could just vanish now. Really, right off the face of the planet would be perfectly fine with me.

By the end of the class, which must've lasted at least six and a half hours, my head is throbbing, my legs feel like whipped noodles, and my buns burn so badly that I'm not sure I'll ever be able to sit down again. Plus I am soaking wet with sweat. I can actually smell myself!

"How'd it go?" asks Mom as she and Penny join me after the stretching exercises, which I barely pretended to do.

I wipe my face with my already soaked towel. "Okay," I mutter.

"Wow, your face is really red," observes Penny. "Are you okay?"

"And your lips are white, Cassie," says Mom with concern. "That can't be good. Maybe you should sit down."

"I'm okay," I say as I attempt to walk in a straight line toward the door. But my head is actually starting to buzz, and I think I might pass out. That would be so embarrassing. *I can do this.*

We're barely outside the door when I start staggering. I feel Mom's hand securely beneath my arm. "Sit down, Cassie," she insists, leading me to an area with several comfy-looking chairs by a window. I don't resist. I collapse into the closest one and lean back and try to breathe slowly.

"Get her some water, Penny," orders Mom.

Soon they are trying to pour water down me. While that sounded good earlier, now it makes me want to puke.

"Should we call for help?" asks Penny.

"No," I mutter, "I'll be okay."

"You don't look good," says Mom.

"Thanks." I close my eyes and wish I were dead. Maybe I will be before long.

"Go get her one of those fitness drinks," commands Mom. "You know, the ones with electrolytes and things."

"I'll be right back," yells Penny, taking off running, which amazes me. The building could be going up in blazes, and I couldn't possibly run. I couldn't even crawl out to save myself—not that I'd care at the moment.

"Breathe in and out slowly," says Mom. "Just relax."

"I'm okay, Mom," I say slowly without opening my eyes. "I just need to rest."

Penny returns with a blue bottle of something slightly sweet, which I do manage to slowly drink. And after a few minutes, I feel strong enough to walk to the shower room with them. They set me down on a bench, and Penny even retrieves my bag for me.

"Feeling better?" she asks sympathetically.

"I guess." I twist the handle on my worn gym bag. It looks so shabby next to the sleek bags the other women are using. But they're regulars to this whole fitness thing. They obviously know all the secrets. Not only that, they're totally comfortable undressing, showering, and dressing in front of other women. But then maybe I would be too if I were as slim as these women. Of course, the older ones sag here and there, but all in all they look pretty good. Even my mom looks pretty good. And they all look better than I do, which brings me to my next dilemma. No way am I going to strip in front of these women. I stand with my bag, looking for a place where I might disrobe discreetly, and finally decide that the bathroom stall is my only option.

"Where are you going?" asks Mom as she removes her bra.

I look down at the floor with embarrassment. When did my mom turn into such a floozy? Okay, *floozy* isn't the right word, but standing here naked with a bunch of strangers... Okay, maybe not strangers.

"I need a place to change," I say quietly.

"Oh, Cassie." It sounds like the same voice I've heard since I was toilet training and not quite getting the hang of it. "You're among girls. You don't have anything we haven't seen before."

Several other women make some comments and jokes, but I

just roll my eyes and head for the john. It's a little awkward, and I keep bumping my sore gluteus maximus on the door, but finally I've peeled off the sweaty clothes and am ready to hit the shower. I forgot to grab a towel. For Pete's sake! Holding my stinky sweats in front of me, I emerge from the stall and hurry/waddle over to the towel rack, grab a towel, which doesn't look very big, and try to wrap it around me while still holding on to my sweats.

"Cassie," says Mom as she comes around the corner on her way to the showers, "you're making this way too difficult."

I suppress the urge to swear at her as I go to dump my work-out clothes by my bag. As I'm coming back toward the shower area, I happen to catch a glimpse of something that looks like a pink and white spotted pig walking on her hind legs. And then I realize it's me. I turn and take a good, long look—reacting almost the way you would at the sight of a horrible car wreck where you know someone's been hurt and you want to look, but you don't want to. What I see right now is truly horrifying. Even with the towel partially covering my body, it's obvious that I am really, really out of shape. How did it get this bad? And the red and white blotches don't help. Plus my face looks swollen, probably from the strain of the workout. All in all, I look sick.

I turn away from the mirror and hurry to the showers. At least there are a couple of private stalls so I don't have to do the group thing with the women from class. I can tell they're whispering about the new sideshow freak. Maybe they feel sorry for me. If I weren't so stinky and sweaty, I would probably skip the shower altogether. I turn the water on lukewarm and stay in there for a long time. I'm hoping all the women will be finished and gone by the time I come out. And maybe some of this redness will fade.

"Cassie?"

I jump. I have no idea how long I've been in here.

"Huh?"

"It's Penny. Your mom was getting worried, so—"

"I'm coming out," I say as I turn off the spigot and reach for my towel.

"Are you feeling better?"

"Yeah, sure." I force lightness into my voice.

"We'll be out at the snack bar, okay?"

"Hey, you guys don't have to wait for me."

"It's not a problem," she says. "We're getting fruit smoothies."

"Okay," I say, still standing behind the shower curtain. "I'll be out in a few minutes."

"Take your time. And I set another one of those drinks by your bag. Your mom thought you might need it."

"Thanks."

When it's quiet, I carefully emerge. I've wrapped the towel around me as best I can, and—sweet relief!—the dressing room is almost empty. Just a couple of women drying their hair and doing makeup as they chat. I decide to chance it by getting dressed in a corner behind the lockers. It sounds easier than the john. But just as I'm tugging on my jeans, which seem to be adhering to my swollen thighs, I hear someone approaching. Not wanting to be found partially dressed, I tug and tug, nearly falling over with the effort. But it's too late. As I stand there, hunched over and huffing and puffing in my quiet little corner, a fairly overweight woman appears, and I'm afraid I surprised her.

"I'm sorry," she says, turning away. "I didn't mean to—"

"It's okay," I puff. "I'm almost done."

I finally get my jeans in place and zipped, and I decide to vacate my private corner for this woman. I'll put on my shoes and socks in the open area.

"It's all yours," I say as I come around the corner. The woman is just standing there looking a little uncomfortable, as if she's not sure what to do. She seems about my age, but I think she might be heavier. And I hate thinking that. I don't remember ever being as body conscious as I am today.

"It's silly, I know," she says. "But I like a little privacy when I'm changing."

"Hey, I'm with you there," I say.

"This club should consider some dressing rooms."

"I agree."

"Are you new here?" she asks.

So I explain about my mom and that it's my first time.

"You went to spinning class on your first day?" She looks shocked.

I nod. "Yeah, pretty stupid, huh?"

"Or brave."

I tell her they were probably about ready to call in the paramedics, which makes her laugh.

"I'm Emma," she says, "Emma Carpenter."

"I'm Cassidy Cantrell," I say. "Or just Cassie."

"Is your mother Audra Cantrell?"

"Yes."

"Oh, she's been my inspiration."

"Inspiration?"

"Yes. I met her about a year ago through a mutual friend. Then I was shopping for a house recently, and I met her again. Wow, has she changed!"

"So I've just found out."

"Isn't it amazing?"

I nod without commenting.

"Anyway, I asked Audra what her secret was, and she told me about changing her eating habits and joining the fitness club. So the next day I joined. I've only been coming for a month now. But I've lost almost ten pounds."

"Congratulations," I tell her.

She frowns now. "I have about ninety pounds to go."

"But you're on your way," I point out.

She nods. "Yes, I'm hoping that I can take it off in a year. I've heard about others who've done it."

"Good for you," I say. "Now you're an inspiration to me."

"You look like you're in pretty good shape," she says.

I guess compared to her, I am. "It sure didn't feel like it in spinning class," I admit.

She shakes her head. "You should start slowly, like I'm doing. I set things up with a trainer. I'm on a program that's designed just for me and my body type and my needs."

I nod and make a thoughtful face, as if I'm actually considering this—which I am *not*. I plan never to shadow the doorway of this place again. "I'll have to think about that, Emma," I say, "but I should get going since my mom is waiting."

"Oh, yes, don't keep her waiting. Tell her I said hi."

"Nice to meet you," I say as she goes around the corner.

"You too," she calls. "Maybe we could work out together."

"Maybe," I call over the lockers as I put on my socks and shoes, huffing as I bend over to tie the laces. Then I pack my gym bag with my sweaty things and go out and examine myself in the mirror by the sinks. I still look as if someone's been slapping me around, and even my eyes are bloodshot. I splash cold water on my face and realize that it's useless. I brush out my hair and pull it back into another ponytail, which is really unbecoming now that I'm so red and swollen looking. What does it matter? If I had any pride when I came in here, I surely have swallowed it by now. In fact, I think I can feel it lumped together in my throat—I will probably choke on it before I get out of this place.

Nine

I feel so bad," says Mom when I finally join them. "Penny was just reminding me how hard it is to get started in a fitness program after you've been out of the game for a while."

"Uh-huh." I take a sip of the fruit smoothie that Mom ordered for me. It's called the Fat Burner. Nice.

"I guess I just thought because you're so young…well, that you'd have no problem jumping into the spinning routine. I'm sorry, honey."

"It's okay."

"Maybe you'd rather do yoga," says Penny. "It's a lot slower and more about stretching than aerobics."

"Right." I nod as if this makes sense, but both these women are nuts if they think I'm coming back here.

"I met one of your fans in there," I say to Mom, hoping to change the subject.

"A fan?" She looks confused.

"Emma Carpenter. She said she met you last year when you were, well, you know, out of shape. Then she met you recently and—"

"Oh yes, Emma. She wanted to buy a house, but her offer was rejected."

"Anyway, because of you, Emma has joined the fitness club."

"Really?" Mom smiles and sits straighter. "Well, good for Emma." Then she turns her attention back to me. "And if Emma can do it, so can you, Cassie."

I let out a long sigh, then take a sip of my Fat Burner.

"Well, I need to get back to work," says Penny, "but it's great seeing you again, Cassie. Let's get together and catch up, okay? Some of our old friends like to meet on Fridays for happy hour at Black Bear Brewery. You should join us."

"Black Bear has a brewery?" I look at Mom. "This town has been really growing recently."

"Yes, and the forecast is for even more growth."

Penny nods. "A lot of the kids who grew up here are starting to come back. It's been fun meeting up with old friends again. I can't wait for you to see Gary Frye."

"You mean the jock who thought he was God's gift to women?"

She nods and chuckles. "He's bald and fat and trying to get me to go out with him."

"No way!"

"Exactly!" She stands and slings her pink Nike gym-bag strap over one shoulder. "No way." Then she waves. "See you around."

"I can't believe how much Penny's changed," I say as I watch her walking away. "She's like a different person."

"I didn't realize you hadn't seen her," says Mom.

"It's been a few years."

Mom smiles. "See? Lots of people change, Cassie. It's not such a big deal."

I consider this. "Well, you need to respect that you changed when you were ready for it, when you wanted to change. I doubt you let anyone push you into it."

"I don't mean to push."

"I know. You're a mom; you can't help yourself."

"But you should consider your health, Cass."

"I'm perfectly healthy," I say. "At least I thought I was until you guys tried to kill me in that stupid spinning class."

She nods. "I am really sorry, sweetie. I just didn't think it was that hard. I didn't start spinning until I'd lost most of my weight. I guess I was in pretty good shape by then."

I finish my drink, then look at Mom. "You mentioned lunch."

She nods and points to our drinks. "That was it."

I frown. "That?"

"It's a complete meal in a drink, honey. It has protein and antioxidants and fiber and three servings of fruits and vegetables."

"Oh." I nod, still frowning.

"And it was 475 calories," she points out. Like I care. "And I have to meet a client in a few minutes. Sorry if I wasn't clear."

"No no," I say. "That's fine."

"Do you want me to drop you at home?" She's looking at her watch now, and I suspect she's in a hurry.

"No, that's okay. I think the walk will do me good."

She smiles. "That's the spirit."

"By the end of the day, I bet I'll have burned off about a thousand calories."

"Good girl," she says, standing. "That might almost undo all that pizza you ate last night."

I nod, but I'm thinking it probably won't put even a dent in the pizza I plan on eating as soon as I get out of this torture chamber of a fitness club. Or maybe I won't do pizza at all. Maybe I'll head over to Mountain Burger and get a deluxe cheeseburger basket *and* a chocolate shake. But after hearing what Penny said about a lot of classmates moving back to town, I'm not so sure I want to be spotted at Mountain Burger scarfing down several thousand calories while looking all red faced and puffy, as I know I must. I can still feel the heat throbbing out of my face and the top of my head. So as I slowly walk toward the café, I call on my cell phone, place a to-go order, and then slip in, wearing my sunglasses, and discreetly pick it up.

Worried that it might get cold, I stop in the park on my way home and quickly eat it. Okay, I feel just a little bit bad as I realize that I'm undoing all my hard work and exercise today. But a bigger part of me simply doesn't care. I don't think I'll ever care.

It's about two o'clock when I get home, and all I can think of is a nice long nap. It looks like Felix has found the best napping spot. He's contentedly curled up on the old, faded brown corduroy couch in the sunroom. I scoot him over to make room and join him. And that's where Mom finds me when she comes home around four. I don't admit that I've been here for nearly two hours. But I do tell her that all that fresh air and exercise probably wore me out.

"Then maybe you won't miss me if I go out tonight," she says.

"Another date with Todd?" I ask in a slightly sour tone.

She laughs. "No, this is a chamber meeting at the Den."

"You're on the chamber now?"

"Yes, Ross Goldberg talked me into it."

"Ross Goldberg, as in the Goldbergs who own Black Bear Butte?"

She smiles in a funny way. "Yes, Ross has sort of been flirting with me lately." She shrugs like she's in middle school and unsure of herself. "I don't know why. But he's nice."

"And rich."

"Oh, Cassie, I have no interest in the man for his money."

"How old is he anyway?"

"Does it matter?"

"I'm just curious. If my mother is becoming known as the town cradle robber, I'd like to have a heads-up."

"Cassie!" She frowns at me. "That's not very nice."

"Well, it's kind of shocking to see your mother going out with men you went to school with. So how old is Ross?"

"Older."

I blink. "Older than you?"

"No, I meant older than Todd. If you must know, Ross is forty-six."

"Only nine years younger than you."

"Really, Cassie, you make too much of this age thing. Someday when you get to be my age, you might figure it out."

"Figure what out?"

"Well, for one thing, men age more quickly than women. That makes Ross more like my age. And people have told us that he looks older than me."

"So you've been going out with him for a while?"

"Just off and on, nothing serious. At least not on my part. I think I'm just a handy date for Ross. His wife died a few years ago, and his son is off at the Air Force Academy now. Ross has been lonely. And we've always been friendly to each other."

"So how does poor Todd feel about this?"

She giggles like she's fifteen. "Todd? Well, he knows that I have no intention of getting seriously involved with someone his age. I only went out with him because we had that silly deal. And…"

"And?"

"And, well, it sounded like fun."

"Was it?"

Now I think she's actually blushing. "As a matter of fact, it was."

I frown. "Why?"

"I don't know, Cass. I guess he made me feel young…and special…and maybe it has something to do with your father…"

"Oh."

"Anyway, it's just silliness. I'm sure Todd won't ask me out again. I made my age perfectly clear to him last night."

"So you lied to him before?"

"No, of course not. I was just evasive. What woman my age wants everyone to know it?"

"Especially when you can pass for much younger?"

"I'm not trying to *pass* as anything, Cassie. I just want to have a little fun before I retire to my rocking chair, thank you very much."

"Sorry, Mom." Now I peel myself off the comfy sofa and give her a hug. "I guess I'm just jealous."

She laughs hard now. "Oh, darling, that's perfect nonsense."

"Seriously, Mom. You look great; you have a life. Why wouldn't I be jealous?"

"Well, don't be. I've been through a lot to get to this place. I hope you and your sisters never have to go through what I have."

"But I thought your life was pretty happy. I mean, until Dad ran off with Michelle."

"It's a long story, Cass. And I want to change my clothes and put my feet up for a few minutes, if you don't mind."

"I'll take a rain check on that story," I call after her as she heads for her room. She has me curious now. It's also curious to imagine my mom with Ross Goldberg, sitting together in the back meeting room at the old Bear's Den restaurant on the south end of town. Life sure takes some funny twists along the way.

Mom's ready to go a little before six. She's wearing a smoky blue pantsuit tonight. It looks expensive and brings out the color of her eyes. I tell her she looks pretty, and she actually seems embarrassed by the attention.

"Have fun," I call as she goes out the door. I watch as she backs her sporty little car out of the driveway. I want her life.

I also want food. But I'm feeling guilty for my indulgence at lunch. I think I should make up for it by eating some of Mom's healthy stuff. But everything I find looks like it's made of cardboard and hay. I finally settle on one of the green boxes in the freezer. I've seen their ads, which make it look like the finest cuisine around. So I follow the directions and give it a try. And while I'm waiting, I munch on some crackers, which after a while don't seem to taste so bad.

I'm just sitting down to my boxed meal when the phone rings. I'm tempted to let it go, except that I've been secretly hoping Eric will find out I've left town and get concerned enough to look for me. Maybe he's tired of Jessica and has realized what he lost. I just wish Mom had caller ID.

On the third ring, I pick up.

"Audra?" says a sexy male voice.

"No," I answer flatly.

"Oh, is this her daughter, uh, Cammie?"

"Cassie," I snap.

"Oh, it's easy to confuse all those *C* names."

"Yeah, our parents thought it was cute at the time, but they've been sorry ever since. Who is this?"

"Sorry, this is Todd. Remember? From last night?"

Like I needed a reminder. "Oh yeah, Todd, the guy who went to school with me but doesn't remember—"

"I do remember you now," he says quickly. "I looked you up in the annual."

"Oh, wow, I'm impressed." I'm staring at my dinner, which had looked somewhat tasty but is quickly getting cold.

"Sorry," he says. "I probably offended you last night."

"Yeah, whatever. Look, my mom's not here. She's out with Ross Goldberg. Do you know who he is?"

"Of course."

"Oh, well, did you know they were dating?"

"Sure. Audra told me she's been dating several guys."

"Several guys?" I drop my fork.

"Yeah. I know she's not serious about me, *Cassie*." He pronounces my name like that's supposed to mean something.

"Yeah, that's what I heard too."

"She told you that?" Now he sounds slightly hurt, and I feel a tiny bit guilty.

"Sort of. I guess she just thinks you're too young."

"But that's where people are wrong," he says. "I mean, it's okay for an old guy, like your dad, to take out a young girl."

"Okay by whom?"

"You know what I mean. Our culture accepts it when old guys and young women hook up. You see it in the movies all the time. But when the roles are reversed, everyone gets all bent out of shape. They start calling the women cougars."

"Cougars?" I pick up my fork and actually get some food on it. "I've never heard of that. What does it mean?"

"They see older women as predatory, like they're prowling around for young guys. Then they'll devour them and spit out the bones and go hunt for more. Cougars."

"That's creepy."

"Not to mention unfair. You don't hear people picking on older men like that."

"Or younger ones," I point out. "I mean, they can do the same thing: go out on the hunt, have their fun, dump the girl, and go find someone new."

"Sounds like you've been hurt, Cassie."

"Sounds like none of your business," I shoot back at him, then take another bite. This stuff is really pretty good, at least while it's still warm, which it won't be for long if I don't get off the phone.

"Ouch."

"Sorry," I say. "But why are you keeping me on the phone when you obviously called to talk to my mom, the *cougar*?"

"Don't call her that, Cassie. Your mom is a sweet woman."

"And old enough to be your mom."

"That doesn't make her a cougar. I'm the one who pursued her, remember?"

"Are you still pursuing her?"

"Maybe."

"Well, like I said, she's not home. She's out with Ross Goldberg." Okay, I know I already said this, but I'm trying to make a point. Like get a clue. Give up already.

"At the chamber meeting, right?"

"Yeah." I take another bite.

"That's not exactly a date, is it?"

"I don't know. I guess it depends on what they do afterward. She took time to dress nicely."

"Your mom always looks nice."

I consider telling him about the days when she wore the same cardigan sweater until it looked like it was falling apart but think better of it. Instead I use this pause to eat a couple more bites.

"You could take a lesson from her, you know."

I quickly swallow a lump of chicken. "Thanks a lot."

"Sorry. But I was looking at your pictures in the annual, and you were a cute girl. I actually remember you from a creative-writing class. I had one last English requirement to take, and you were in the class that Mrs. Hornby taught. Do you remember?"

I feel my cheeks flushing slightly as I swallow the rest of that bite. "Yeah, I sort of remember." The truth is, I totally remember. Todd sat right in front of me, and I would sit there and daydream about him.

"Mrs. Hornby was always saying you were such a good writer, and one day she read one of your stories, and I was pretty stunned that a junior girl wrote it. I remember turning around to look at you and kind of scratching my head."

"That's probably the *only* time you looked at me," I say and suddenly wish I hadn't.

"Well, the school year was almost over, and then I graduated. But I remember thinking that this girl has something going on, and if I had been around another year, who knows? I might've asked you out."

"Well, isn't that nice." Even so I'm sitting up straight now, I've pushed the food away, and I'm listening as if my life depended on it.

"I probably would've."

"You're just being nice to me because I'm Audra's daughter," I tell him, thinking I've probably nailed this one on the head.

"No, that's not it. I just looked up your photo, and I remembered you and how you caught my eye. You know I can't make up something like that."

Okay, my memory is that Todd turned around and looked at me, and we locked eyes. I felt certain that he was falling in love, that he'd ask me out, that we'd be married by now with three children playing in the backyard. But I always figured it was just me.

"I'm sorry," he says. "I'm sure I've offended you again. Look, Cassie, all I wanted to say was that I think you've gone through some hard stuff. Your mom told me a little about it at dinner last night. And I think it's taken a toll on you. And I really hope you can get it together. You're a cool girl with a lot going on, and I know that Audra's worried about you. That's all I wanted to say."

I barely nod, still unable to speak. "Well, thanks," I finally mutter. "I appreciate it."

"Sure."

"Do you want me to tell my mom that you called?"

"No, that's okay."

"Okay." Now I really don't want him to hang up, but I have absolutely nothing to say. In fact, I feel as if I've been rendered nearly speechless. Todd Michaels actually noticed me in high school. He thinks I have a lot going on. He actually knows my name. Well, go figure.

"I should let you go," he says.

"Yeah. Thanks for calling…I mean, for saying those things." I pause to compose myself. "That was nice. Really."

"Okay, you take care."

Then we hang up, and I'm suddenly not hungry. I try another bite just to see. Nope. I throw the rest of it away.

Ten

I'm in something of a daze for the next few days. Mom bustles about in her busy life and jam-packed schedule, and I don't do much besides hang out at the house and take long, long walks. At first Mom bugs me about not coming back to the fitness center, but I explain I need to get to a place where I have more endurance, which I plan to do through walking for at least a week. To my surprise, she thinks this sounds like a good idea. I'm sure she's also relieved that I won't embarrass both of us by passing out at any of her classes.

But I'm finding that walking is therapeutic in many ways. Not only is the fall weather perfectly delightful, with things like autumn leaves and honking geese and pumpkins on porches, but it's also slightly inspirational. I remember other autumns when I had just started school and had great hopes for the year ahead, imagining how I would do something significant that year, how I'd learn what I was good at and then really excel at it—the way I saw my sisters doing. Autumn always felt like a second chance, a time of renewal and rebirth, of hope and expectation. That's how

I feel as I walk now. I think about the things Todd said about me Monday night, about my potential and how I have "a lot going on." I feel optimistic again. I realize I am only thirty-one, and if my mother can reinvent herself at fifty-five, I should be able to do equally well. I can do this, I tell myself. I'm a can-do kind of girl. Really, I am!

By the end of the week, I have something of a can-do plan. One: I will pay off my stupid credit-card debt and contact the police or proper authority with information about Monica. It's just plain wrong that she does things like that and gets away with it. Two: I will look for a job that suits me and has real potential. Three: I will join Mom's fitness club, if she is still willing to foot the bill, but on my own terms, which will not include spinning class. Four: I'll look into buying an inexpensive car. This walking thing is okay for now, but winter *is* coming.

By Friday, I'm actually starting to feel stronger, both physically and emotionally. After walking from ten until almost one (okay, I did stop for coffee), I decide to take Penny up on her invitation to come to happy hour at the new brewery this afternoon. I have a nap, then take a nice, long shower, and even shave my legs—something I hadn't done since I lost my job. Then I actually curl my hair and put on some makeup. Not too much, because I don't want to look desperate, but enough that I think I look presentable. Then I sit on my bed in my bathrobe and try to think of something cool to wear. Of course, the coolest things I own are my Valentino boots. But maybe that's a bit much. I don't want to look like I'm trying too hard. And the last time I wore those boots, things didn't go too well for me.

Even so, I try on several outfits with the boots and finally settle on a denim skirt, which actually looks pretty good. But it still looks like I'm trying to impress someone, which I am not—well, unless I thought Todd would be there, which I doubt. Consequently, I decide to go more casual. I mean, it's not like this is a class reunion or something.

I kick off the boots, which are already hurting my feet, and try several more combinations until I finally settle on my best jeans, which although just washed seem to fit better than they did last week. I top this with an olive green cashmere sweater that Eric once told me looked classy. Leaving the boots for another day, I go for my old-faithful Dansko clogs. They might not be chic, but they're comfortable, which reminds me that I'll be walking to the brewery. Another good reason to pass on the boots.

I try several pairs of earrings, but nothing seems quite right. Then I remember the pair of mossy green stone earrings that Callie gave Mom for Christmas last year, and I know they'd be perfect. I doubt Mom would mind my borrowing them, especially since she's been worried about my lack of a social life.

So I peruse her jewelry box the way my sisters and I used to do when we were kids, and I try on several old things that I remember Mom wearing as we were growing up. She might not have been a fashion diva back then, but she always had good taste in jewelry. Finally I find the dangly green earrings, and they are absolutely perfect. Feeling only a little guilty, I write a quick note explaining what I did and that I'm going out with friends. "And feel free to borrow anything of mine too—ha-ha!" I write with a smile face. Then I leave this on her jewelry box and head toward town.

I get to the brewery just a little before five and am not sure I want to go in just yet. Something about making an entrance when you don't know who will be there is unnerving. I wish I'd thought to call Penny and arrange to arrive with her. But standing out here on the street feels a little conspicuous too. I can't lean against the lamppost like I'm some kind of hooker. So I brace myself, give the big wooden door a push, and walk in as if I own the joint.

Okay, I feel a little weird going into a place like this without a date, but it's not like I'm going in a bar to pick up men. This is simply the hometown brewery, where I'll be meeting old friends. No biggie.

I glance around and don't see anyone I know. In fact, the place is pretty quiet. I wonder if I made a mistake, if I misunderstood Penny. I wish I knew her phone number. I'm about to walk out when I hear a guy call my name. And for no explainable reason (well, other than the fact I've been obsessing over him), I think it might be Todd Michaels. But when I turn, all I see is a middle-aged, bald dude wearing a Seahawks T-shirt that's stretched over his beer belly, waving at me. I have no idea who he—

"Gary Frye," he calls out, motioning me over to his table. "Bet you don't remember me."

I sort of smile as I approach him, deciding to play coy. "Not exactly," I say. True, I remember the name, but as Penny warned me, this guy has really gone to the dogs.

"We graduated together. I played some sports in high school," he says modestly. He chuckles as he pats his head and then slaps his belly. "But I guess I've changed some."

I nod. "Yeah, we all have."

"I missed our last class reunion," he says, pointing to the barstool across from him like he wants me to sit down.

"Oh."

"But I ran into Penny, and she told me that you'd moved back to town and that you might come to our little gathering sometime." He grins. "And here you are."

I sit down but feel like running. "Here I am."

"What'll you have?" He hands me a list of the beers. "They have some great little microbrews here, and everything is two fifty until six o'clock. My buddy Brian Stuart—he was a little older than us—started this place up a couple of years ago. He asked me to go in with him, but I thought he was crazy to try to make this work in our little one-horse town." Gary holds up his hands and makes a goofy face. "Guess I was wrong."

"It's a nice place," I say as I browse the list and try to think of an excuse to leave.

"Don't know where everyone is tonight," he says, glancing around as if he expects someone to pop out of the pinewood paneling.

"I thought Penny would be here."

"Me too. She usually is."

Suddenly I feel bad about being rude. It doesn't really fit with my new can-do attitude. "Hey, I do remember you," I say as if I've just had a revelation. "You were a real sports jock, weren't you?"

He grins and raises his mug like a toast. "That was me."

"I'm surprised you know who I am." I look curiously at him.

"No, I remember you," he says and actually sounds sincere. "You were that quiet, brown-haired girl in geometry. Kind of kept to yourself."

I force a smile. "Sounds about right."

"Looks like you've come out of your shell." He waves to the waiter. "Bring the little lady a beer, will ya, Tony?" Then he studies me. "You look like a pale ale sort of gal. My treat." And before I can protest, he hollers at Tony to bring me a Black Bear Pale Ale. When Tony drops off my drink, Gary orders some wings to go with it. "Happy hour special," he reminds me.

"So what do you do now, Gary?" I ask, thinking I can at least be nice.

"I've got a small landscaping business."

"Uh-huh?" I take a tiny sip of my beer and try not to wrinkle my nose. I'm not much of a beer drinker.

"Gets a little slow in the winter, so then I do some snowplowing. I also sell firewood."

I'm trying not to judge this guy, but it sounds like he's probably barely making ends meet. Must've been a comedown after being the big guy around town in high school.

"Did you ever marry?"

He nods. "Yep, you probably don't remember Mollie Peterson."

I laugh. "Maybe if I'd lived under a stone back then. Mollie Peterson was homecoming queen, cheerleading queen, prom queen—she must have a whole trophy case of crowns. Did you really marry her?"

"Yeah, right out of high school."

"So, are you guys still together?"

He looks down at his nearly empty mug and sadly shakes his head. "Mollie took the kids and left me about five years ago."

"Kids?"

"Yeah, Jennifer and Jackson."

"You have two kids?" I don't know why, but this astounds me. I mean, this guy seems a little like a kid himself.

"Want to see their pictures?" And before I know it, he's pulling out his wallet and showing me photos of two half-grown kids.

"How old are they?"

He chuckles. "Well, we had Jenny right out of high school. It was one of those shotgun weddings, if ya know what I mean. She'll be thirteen in December. Jackson came along right after, and he'll be twelve in April."

"Wow, where are they living?"

"Seattle. We all moved up there for a while. Then our marriage hit some bumps, and Mollie hooked up with a guy from her work. My dad was having health problems, and I decided to come home and help out. He passed away last year."

"I'm sorry."

He nods and downs the rest of his beer. "Yeah, my dad was a good guy. But I live with my mom now and try to keep things up for her."

The idea of this grown man still living at home doesn't really help his image much. Then I remember I'm in the same position myself.

"Do you see your kids often?"

"Oh yeah. I get them for most of the summer and some holidays. They'll be here for Christmas. I promised to teach Jackson how to snowboard."

"So you snowboard?"

"Oh yeah. I love it."

"That's cool."

He orders another beer and talks about snowboarding and his kids and his mom and his business, and I manage to drink a little beer without talking too much about my own life, which is nothing to brag about. But his easy manner helps me relax. I'm feeling like there's more to Gary than meets the eye. I wouldn't want to go out with him, but he'd make a good friend. Plus, he sounds like he's handy when it comes to fixing things.

"So how about you?" he finally says. "What've you been doing since high school?"

I start out with my normal answers, designed to impress. How I got my MBA and a great job in marketing, blah, blah, blah. Then I decide to drop the mask, and I tell him that I recently lost my job, broke up with my boyfriend, and moved back home to figure out my life.

"Man, I know how that feels," he admits. "It wasn't easy coming back here and starting over, having to tell everyone about my failed marriage, no education, and no great job experience. I felt like a real loser."

"But you don't now?" As soon as I say this, I wish I hadn't. Fortunately, it seems to go right over him. Or maybe he's just a gracious guy.

"I'm really starting to feel good about myself," he says. "I know I'm not much. But I'm happy."

"There's a lot to be said for being happy," I say a little too longingly.

"And you're not going to believe this," he says in a conspiratorial tone.

"What?"

"I've started going to church."

"No way!"

He nods. "Yep. I haven't told anyone except my mom. The idea of old party animal Gary Frye going to church…" He chuckles. "Some people are gonna be shocked."

I'm thinking most people probably don't really care, but I don't say it. "So what church are you going to?"

"It's a nondenominational church." He grins. "I'm not really sure what that means, but it sounds important. Anyway, Mountain Fellowship started up last year. I'd been doing some landscaping for this woman who goes there, and she kept inviting me to come. When the weather cooled off and the business slowed down, I decided to give it a try. And I like it."

"Well, I think that's very cool."

"Really?" He looks surprised.

"Really. In fact, I've been thinking I need to find a church here."

"So you go to church?"

"I have in the past."

"Well, come try our place. We meet in the old Lutheran church—you know, that little chapel out on the highway."

"Oh, I always liked the looks of that church."

"It got too small for the Lutherans. They built a bigger one on the other end of town. Anyway, service is at ten thirty on Sunday morning. They have other things going on, but I don't know too much about all that yet." He slaps his thigh and gives a hoot. "I've only been twice myself, and here I am, inviting newcomers. They should give me a gold star or something."

I laugh at this and am surprised to realize I'm actually having a good time. I notice a guy coming into the room—and then my heart seems to skip a beat when I see that it's Todd, who's looking extra handsome in a golden-colored suede jacket that goes great with his hair. He sees me and waves. This is too good to be true. But then I realize I'm sitting here with Gary Frye, local lawn man, and I'm sure Todd will assume we're on a date. So I'm formulating what I'll say to him, something like, "Hey, are you here for Black Bear High happy hour? I heard there were supposed to be lots of old friends here, but so far it's just Gary and me." Yeah, that ought to work.

But it looks like he's waiting. Then I see that he's with someone. And when the two of them come fully into the brewery, I can see that this particular someone is a pretty woman who happens to be my mom. I try not to fall off my barstool as the two of them approach us with warm smiles.

"Cassie," says Mom, "fancy meeting you here."

"Small town," I say, then I notice her footwear. "Nice boots, Mom."

"That's your mom?" says Gary in a shocked voice.

"Yeah, *my* mom wearing *my* boots," I add.

"I got your note," she reminds me. "I like your earrings."

"How's it going?" asks Todd politely.

"Great," says Gary. "Cassie and I've been getting reacquainted after all these years. I think I even talked her into going to church with me on Sunday."

"Good for you," says Todd, winking at me. "I think the girl could use some religion."

I am speechless. So the three of them talk and joke about some of the local happenings, and then Todd and Mom excuse themselves to a booth in the corner where I can't see either of them. I am fuming.

"Wow," says Gary, "that's one hot mama you got, Cassie."

"Yeah, right," I say, rolling my eyes.

"Bet the apple don't fall far from the tree," he says to me.

I'm sure he means it as a compliment, but all I can think is *Get me outta here.* "Wow, look at the time," I say, glancing at my watch. "I really need to get going."

Gary looks sincerely disappointed. "You have someone to meet?"

I nod. "But I've really enjoyed getting to know you again—" I force a laugh. "Well, again for the first time."

He smiles now. "You'll think about coming to church?"

"I sure will."

He stands as I stand and actually shakes my hand. Then I thank him for the beer, which is still half there, and the buffalo wings, which I did indulge in and weren't half bad, and then I leave. It's getting dusky outside, but if I hurry, I think I can make it home before dark. I button my jacket to my chin and wish I'd thought to bring a wool scarf and gloves tonight. Although it's not even November, I can feel winter in the air. Winters here can be brutal. I walk down the quiet streets, the cold sting of the wind numbing my face and chilling my tears as they trickle down my cheeks. So much for my can-do optimism.

Eleven

I can't believe that it's Halloween today. Consequently, I will be wearing my happy mask for the entire day. I've already given myself several lectures regarding Mom and Todd. For one thing, their relationship is really none of my business, and for another, Mom saw him first—or at least dated him first. So what if she's just having a little fling with him? He knows the score. And even though the whole thing about the boots really had me steamed, well, I asked for it by borrowing her jewelry and leaving that stupid note. If I hadn't wanted her to take me up on my offer, in particular with my boots, I should've hidden them. From now on, I will! So, anyway, I'm trying to act all cheerful and fine. I really don't see the point in pouting.

For some reason, Mom seems to think I've really turned a corner. If she's right, I'm pretty certain it will just lead to another dead-end street. Still, in trying to regain my optimism, I told Mom about my plan to get a good job in town and to join her fitness club. She was ecstatic about this and insisted on taking me to the club to sign up today. So I ride with her in her pretty car, then fill out the forms, which include questions about height and weight and general health and "regular workout routines." I add an inch and subtract ten pounds. What're they going to do, arrest me? Anyway, it looks better that way, and I always did like looking good on paper. Mom pays the fees, and I am an official member of Black Bear Fitness Club. I just don't look like it.

"Now you'll have to come to the big shindig tonight," says the receptionist, a perky redhead named Cindy. "It's a costume party, and it's going to be a real hoot. I heard the mayor is dressing up like Batman."

"That's right," says Mom. "I almost forgot about the Halloween party. Oh, you'll come too, won't you, Cassie?"

I shrug. "I guess I could. Although I don't have a costume."

"I haven't got one either," says Mom. "But we can forage in the attic and throw something together. You girls always had lots of dress-up things. It'll be fun."

I nod, catching some of her enthusiasm. "Yeah, maybe so."

"See ya tonight," calls Cindy.

Then Mom and I head for the locker room. Part of the fitness-club agreement was that I'd work out today. "No time like the present," Mom chirped as we ate our bark-o-mulch cereal for breakfast. But, as I reminded her several times, I am going to do my own thing at the fitness club. Today *my own thing* consists of riding a stationary bike with this electronic panel that gives me several options. I choose the beginner option and monitor my own speed, hill incline, and whatnot. I keep it low—like a beginner-beginner. Even so, I can feel my heart pumping hard by the time I finish my twenty minutes. Mom is still doing the elliptical machine, whatever that is, smiling and chatting with people. While she's distracted with the grade-school principal, I slip out of this part of the facility and go downstairs to peek at the swimming pool.

To my huge relief it is empty! Despite my body-image problems, I really do love to swim, and the idea of working out in the water is extremely appealing. I just hope that I can get into my swimsuit and out here before anyone else comes along. So I hurry back to the locker room, peel off my sweaty clothes, and wrestle into my one-piece, slimming, black Calvin Klein swimsuit that I paid way too much for several years ago. I pause briefly in front of the mirror, tugging on the suit here and there. Didn't this fit me better the last time I wore it? When was the last time I wore it?

I wrap a towel around me like a sarong—well, almost—then hurry back out to the pool. Naturally, there are several lap swimmers in it now: two athletic men who seem to be racing each other and a stocky, white-haired lady who's just getting in. The woman, who must be in her seventies, gives me hope as she slowly eases herself into the water. She chooses to swim in the only "slow" lane, which leaves one unoccupied "fast" lane. *Okay,* I think as I get into the open fast lane, *I should be able to outswim this granny.* I begin to do an easy backstroke, keeping my head up because I'm not sure I want to get my hair wet. I slowly move through the water, watching as grandma puts on her swim goggles, adjusts them, then ducks under the water and pushes herself off the side of the pool. With surprising grace and speed, this old lady slices through the water like a fish. I'm halfway through my first lap when she meets me on her way back—still swimming in the slow lane. Yeah, right. She smiles at me as she takes a breath and another smooth stroke. Or maybe she's laughing.

After twenty minutes of trying to keep up with granny, who has swum at least twice as many laps and probably more, I decide to quit. My hair is soaking wet, and I can tell my eyes are going to be red. I need to get some goggles. But when I climb out of the pool and scramble to get my towel wrapped around me before anyone looks up, I realize that my legs feel weak, like they are seriously tired. I was actually working pretty hard in there.

I go back to the locker room, where I have things partially figured out. With my swimsuit on, I can head straight to the showers without having to disrobe in front of everyone. It's not so crowded today, since there wasn't a class, but I can hear my mom in there now. She's still chattering with the grade-school principal, and I have no desire to strip in front of them. Getting dressed after the shower might prove more of a problem, but hopefully the little corner will be free, or maybe they'll be gone by then.

"There you are," says Mom as I return to the locker area wrapped in two towels. She introduces me to the principal, Linda Moore, who's topless at the moment, and although she looked fairly trim in her sweats, she seems to be sagging a bit now.

"Didn't you know you're supposed to use only *one* towel?" she says, sounding like a principal.

"Oh?" Am I supposed to drop one of them? Forget it.

"She's new," says my mom. "Her first day as a member."

Linda Moore nods. "Well, we don't want them raising our dues. Just one towel from now on, Cassidy."

I resist the urge to say, "Yes ma'am," as I grab my bag and retreat to my corner.

I hurry to dress and then go to the mirror, where I attempt some damage control on my face and hair. Today I remembered to bring a bit of moisturizer and makeup so that I don't look quite as devastated as last time. Still, it's not good, and my eyes are really red. I'm thinking goggles and Visine. I will get this down eventually.

"Ready to go?" chirps Mom as she does a quick fluff to her blond hair, then applies some lipstick from what appears to be a Chanel tube. Very impressive. It's a perfect shade of peachy pink that looks fantastic on her. I stand there just staring at her for a moment. Her hair looks great, her skin tone is perfect, her eyes are clear… She's so together that it makes me want to scream and pull my wet hair out by the roots.

"You look so unreasonably good, Mom," I say as I shove my lip gloss back into my bag. "How do you do it?"

She laughs. "Oh, I've put some work into it, Cassie, don't kid yourself."

"What kind of work?"

She doesn't answer right away, and I wonder if she's had some plastic surgery. "Well, after losing the weight, I decided I needed a makeover. I read about this place in the city where they do a total redo, and I made an appointment."

"You were in the city?" I say. "And you never called?"

"It was during the week, sweetie, and I knew you'd be at work."

"But you never even called?"

She smiles. "I didn't want to bother you. And I had a pretty full day with my little makeover."

"So what did they do to you?" I ask in a flat voice, not sure I even want to know now. Who is this stranger?

She glances over her shoulder like she's worried about eavesdroppers. "Oh, lots of things. How about if I tell you over lunch?"

I look at the mirror, seeing my mom next to me, and I try to imagine us pleasantly sitting together at lunch. She looks hot, and I look, well, *not*. Still, it's not like I should care about such things. I mean, it's not like I have a life or a job or a boyfriend or anything. Besides, despite my hurt feelings about being snubbed in the city, I am curious—has Mom actually gone under the knife?

"Sure," I agree. "But let's not go anyplace fancy. I'm not really looking so great right now, and my hair's still wet."

"You can dry it," she says, holding up the hair dryer.

For whatever reason, this just irritates me. "I don't *want* to dry it," I snap.

She nods. "Sure, whatever. How about if we go to Claire's?"

"Sounds good." Claire's is a tiny deli on the quiet end of town, and as I recall, the lighting is rather dim in there.

After placing our orders and taking our drinks to the table, I ask Mom to tell me about her makeover. She proceeds to tell me that she got "the works," which included a little Botox, a little collagen, a chemical peel, and some kind of electronic treatment that's supposed to tighten sagging jowls.

"Really?" I lean forward to look at her more closely. "Any surgery?"

She shakes her head. "No, I wasn't too sure about that. I worried that I might come out looking like someone else."

"You *do* look like someone else," I point out. Someone who's not my mom.

"Well, that has a lot to do with losing the weight and changing my style as much as anything." She takes a sip of her white tea. "Also, I changed my eating habits, which can greatly affect your looks, especially at my age. Of course, I had a makeover with my hair and makeup. That helps. And I almost forgot, I go in for tanning now too."

"You do a tanning bed?" For some reason the idea of Mom cooking herself in a hot tanning bed totally astounds me.

"No, not at all. I get sprayed."

"Sprayed?"

"Yes, you know. You stand in the booth and get sprayed with a tanning solution."

"Seriously?" I vaguely remember seeing an ad for this once, but it sounded ridiculous.

She giggles. "I know it sounds terribly vain, but last summer I wanted to wear shorts, and my legs were ghostly white. The spa in town had just gotten a booth for this very thing, so I thought I'd give it a try. I go in twice a month now."

"No kidding?"

She nods. "And I always have an exfoliation treatment before the spray-on. I keep thinking I'll stop doing it when winter comes, but it just feels so good to have tan legs. Do you want to see?" She actually bends over now like she's about to pull up her pant leg.

"No, Mom," I say quickly, "that's okay."

Fortunately they bring our food at that moment, so I'm not forced to view Mom's tan and slender legs. Oh. My. Word.

"I felt silly about all this," she admits as she forks a piece of salad, "then I thought, why shouldn't I have some fun? I may be fifty-five, but I'm still alive!" She laughs at her little rhyme.

I take a bite of my turkey sandwich and think that I'm thirty-one and I'm no fun. But I don't say this. I just chew and watch my mom daintily picking at her healthy-looking salad.

"I was thinking, Cassie, that maybe you'd like to have a makeover too."

"That's okay," I say, still chewing. The truth is, I would *love* a makeover. I would absolutely love to go someplace far away and have talented professionals totally work me over until I emerged looking like—like Cameron Diaz. The problem is, I just don't want my mother involved. I can't handle that right now.

"My treat."

"No thanks," I say firmly.

"It's fun," she says in a tone that she must think sounds tempting to me.

"Look, Mom." I set down my sandwich. "All that foo-foo nonsense might work for you, but I am not you, okay?" So what if part of me wishes I were her?—not that I'll ever admit it to her or anyone. It just irks me that she's so obsessed with fixing me right now—as though a makeover is going to change my life. Okay, it probably wouldn't hurt. But not like this. I don't want to be Mom's little project. No thanks!

She looks down at her salad. "Sorry, Cassie, but you just seem so unhappy. I wish I could help."

"I'm unhappy because I lost my job. I'm unhappy because I got dumped by my boyfriend. I'm unhappy because my finances are a disaster. A makeover isn't going to change any of that."

"But it might not hurt."

"Mom. Stop."

She returns to eating her salad, and I can tell I've hurt her feelings, which makes me feel horrible. Why am I so mean to her? It's not her fault that my life's a mess and that hers is starting to look up. Still, it seriously irritates me that she's dating a guy young enough to be her son, a guy I happen to like and who might even like me, or so it seemed the other night on the phone. I remember what Todd said about that whole cougar bit. Although he made it clear that he didn't think my mom was a cougar per se, I'm beginning to wonder. As if to answer my thoughts, an attractive, forty-something man pauses at our table and leans over to smile at my mom.

"Hey, Audra." His eyes crinkle at the edges as he puts his hand on her shoulder. Other than having a little gray at the temples, he has a youthful, boyish look that's quite appealing. In fact, I'll bet he's not even ten years older than I am.

"Hey, Phil." My mom beams up at him in a way that I can only describe as…as flirtatious! I mean, she's literally sparkling! My mom is sparkling!

"I noticed you have the listing for that house on Park Side."

"I do!" She beams even brighter now.

"Well, you and I should get together," he says in a slightly seductive voice that makes me feel like gagging on my partially chewed bite of turkey sandwich.

"We should." Then Mom seems to remember she's not alone. "Phil, have you met my daughter Cassidy?"

He turns and smiles at me now. But I don't think his smile is as big for me as it was for my sparkling mom. Or maybe I'm getting totally paranoid.

"Nice to meet you, Cassidy. Are you just visiting Black Bear?"

"Actually, I've moved back."

He nods. "Good for you. This town is getting to be quite the hot spot." Then he laughs as though he thinks that's very clever. He turns back to Mom. "Call me, okay?"

"You got it." She beams him another bright smile. *Mom, show a little restraint, will you?*

"Another boyfriend?" I ask after he's out of earshot.

She giggles. "Goodness, no. Phil is a happily married man with two small children."

"Lucky him."

"He's a Realtor too. He works for the competition. But if he's got buyers, I won't complain if he brings them my way."

"What if he insists you go out with him first?" I try to make this sound like I'm being funny, but when I see her expression, I can tell that I'm not.

"Oh, Cassidy." She shakes her head. "That thing about going out with Todd—at first, well, it was mostly a joke. You must know that."

"So you're not serious about him?"

"Serious?" Her Botoxed brow almost creases but not quite. "I don't think so."

"But you were out with him again the other night," I point out, trying not to remember how humiliating it was to see Todd while it appeared I was on a date with Gary Frye.

"He happened to call after I got home from work. I'd been planning a quiet evening at home, but you'd already gone out, and I thought, *Why not?*" She laughs. "I was so surprised to see you and your date—"

"Like I already said, Mom, Gary was not my date."

"Yes, yes, I know."

I try to shake the image of my mom wearing my Valentino boots as she and Todd paraded into the brewery. Instead, I see my mom as a cougar in Valentino boots, dragging in her poor victim as she prepares to devour him. "So you're not serious about Todd?"

"I'm not sure I'll ever be serious about a man again." She sets down her fork and looks evenly at me. "I don't know if I have that in me anymore, Cassie."

"Really?" I feel skeptical. "Did Dad hurt you that much?"

She sighs. "It's hard to explain…without getting all weepy. But I'm sure it must be a little like how you felt when Eric broke up with you. Especially if you didn't see it coming. Sort of like being blindsided. It can shatter a person."

I nod. "Yeah, I suppose so. So you really didn't see it coming? Dad didn't give you any clues or anything?"

"Looking back, I'm sure there were clues. But I recognize them only because of hindsight. I never figured that after all those years, after all we'd been through—and I put up with a lot of things, things no one ever knew about, Cassie—I just never thought he'd leave me. I thought we'd been through the worst of our trials. I figured we'd grow old and gray together. And suddenly I was old and gray and by myself." She shudders as if the memory still stings.

"You really loved Dad?"

She blinks as if she thinks I must be kidding. "Of course I loved him. He was everything to me." And now she picks up her napkin and uses it to blot the corners of her eyes, and I realize I've hit a sore spot. I can't believe I was thinking my own mom was a cougar. I'm such a thoughtless daughter.

"I'm sorry, Mom." I shake my head and want to slap myself. "Let's not talk about Dad anymore. What's important is, you're doing really great now. You're making a life for yourself, and you'll have to excuse me if I look envious sometimes."

"Oh, it's okay, sweetie. I know you're going to be fine too. But it might take time, and I've probably been rushing you too much. I'm sorry." She wipes her nose. "And if I pressured you into going to the Halloween party and you really don't want to, well, I'll understand. You'll have to remind me not to be so pushy."

"No no. It's okay," I assure her. "I probably need some pushing now and then. And I think a Halloween party sounds sort of fun. If I dress up, maybe no one will know who I am."

"That's right," she says. "You could pretend to be anyone."

"It could be fun."

She reaches over and takes my hand. "Yes, it'll be lots of fun. Now let's get home and find something cute to wear."

e're in the midst of dusty cardboard boxes and foot-lockers, trying to figure out some clever costumes for the party tonight, when the phone rings. Mom, still wearing Callie's old black and gold cheerleading skirt, hurries down the steep attic stairs to answer it. I can hear her chattering away, then she calls up, "Cassie, I have to run to town to show Phil's buyers that house. I should be back in an hour or so."

"No problem." I pick up the Ralph Lauren jeans that she left on the floor when she tried on the skirt. The jeans look to be about a size six (not that I'm actually looking). "You going out dressed like that?"

She laughs. "Now wouldn't that make an impression!"

So I toss her pants down to her, then I continue perusing the weird clothes and hats and props. Most of the old costumes are way too small for me. I'm about to give up when I find an ancient-looking box that's tied up with a string, and to my surprise there's an old baseball uniform inside. Then I remember that Dad played semipro ball on a farm team one summer. He was only nineteen when he got scouted off his college team, but a shoulder injury cut his catching career short, and to his parents' relief, he returned to college in the fall. Now, my dad's always been a pretty hefty guy, and I think it's possible this baseball uniform might actually fit me. It might even be big. Here's hoping.

So I take it downstairs and give it a try. I don't know whether to be pleased or ashamed when the uniform actually fits, albeit a bit snugly in the rear and the bust. If I wear my sports bra to hold the girls in and try not to bend over too much, it might just work. Besides, I think I look sort of cute in the cap.

By five o'clock, trick-or-treaters are starting to come to the door. Mom's fake electric jack-o'-lanterns are lined up on the porch and glowing, and her big pumpkin-shaped candy bowl is full of Snickers and Three Musketeers and M&M'S—the tempting kinds of candy we've both tried to avoid all afternoon. I asked her why she couldn't have gotten something besides chocolate. "What would be the fun in that?" she said.

At first it's kind of fun handing out the goodies to these minia-ture princesses and superheroes. This is something I hardly ever did in the city, since kids rarely came to the apartment house. For the most part, these little ones are accompanied by parents, who linger on the sidewalk. After a while I think I recognize some of the par-ents as kids I once went to school with. So far no one has recog-nized me. Or maybe they're just too preoccupied with their kids. I feel sad to think that people my age are out there, happily married with kids of their own, trick-or-treating and having fun doing parental kinds of things, while here I am, living with my mom and being an overgrown kid with barely a life at all. It's so depressing that I eat several Snickers bars before Mom's car pulls into the driveway.

She's flushed and pleased when she comes inside. Tossing off her leather coat, she informs me that she might've just sold another house. "They spent two hours going over every inch of the place, then they wrote up an offer right there. I just dropped it off with the sellers, and we should know by tomorrow whether it's a go."

I give her a high-five. "So what're you going to wear to the party tonight?"

She slaps her forehead. "In all the excitement, I nearly forgot."

"The cheerleader outfit was sort of cute," I say, hoping she'll have better sense.

She makes a face. "Cute, but a bit much for someone my age."

I shrug, relieved that the doorbell is ringing again. Mom answers it, oohing and aahing over the costumes as she plops generous handfuls of chocolate into their bags and buckets.

"What are you going to wear?" she asks me as she closes the door.

"I'll surprise you," I say.

"Great. Then I'll surprise you too. Can you ride herd on the little goblins for a while?"

"Sure. It's kind of fun. And my costume's all ready to go anyway." So I continue to answer the door, and after about twenty minutes, Mom reappears, dressed in black.

"Is that it?" I ask as she shoos me upstairs to change.

"No, but I can finish down here and answer the door too. Hurry and get your costume on. The party is already starting."

"We'll be fashionably late," I call as I go into my room.

I wish I'd thought to air out this wool uniform. It smells strongly of mothballs, but I give it a misting of Poison perfume, hoping that'll help camouflage the musty aroma. First I button up the shirt, which is fitting better thanks to my constricting bra. Hopefully I won't faint from lack of oxygen. Then I put the short pants over the funny socks and pin up my hair and secure the baseball cap. For shoes, I decide on my Dansko clogs, since their dark color sort of makes them resemble old-fashioned baseball shoes. Or so I tell myself.

I study my reflection in the full-length mirror and decide I make a rather cute ballplayer, although a little on the feminine side. I'd really wanted to go incognito tonight, but short of a mask, which I don't have, I can't do much about it. Just the same, I try on an old pair of wire-rimmed sunglasses, which actually add something. Then I decide to use my eyeliner pencil to create a small, sporty mustache. There—I don't think anyone should recognize me now. Especially if the lights are dim.

I go downstairs and find Mom in the powder room, putting the finishing touches on her ensemble. When she turns around, I see that, like me, she's used an eyeliner pencil for whiskers, but hers are curly feline whiskers. She's turned herself into a cat. A rather sexy black cat with hot pink pouty lips and heavy blue eye shadow.

"Wow," I say as she turns around to show off her costume.

"These rhinestones are from your grandma," she points out, showing off her sparkling blue cuff bracelet and matching collar. She's a rich kitty.

"How about the ears and tail?" I ask.

"That was my inspiration. I think they were Callie's. Remember when her dance team dressed like cats for a competition one year?"

"Vaguely."

"Well, I found them in the attic and remembered I had these black velour sweats, and it all seemed so simple."

"You look great," I tell her, trying not to feel too envious of her cool outfit. I mean, I have some black sweats too—maybe not as elegant as her velour ones, which also fit her like a glove—but I could've been a black cat. Even if I was a plumpish cat, it might have been better than this dumpy ballplayer.

"You look great too," she says. "Or maybe I'm just being catty."

I make a fake-sounding laugh. I'm thinking I probably resemble Rosie O'Donnell in that women's baseball movie, *A League of Their Own*, when I'd really rather be Geena Davis. "And if the Halloween party doesn't work out for you," I say to Mom, "you could always go down to the Highball and offer to serve cocktails." Who's catty now?

She makes her hands into claws and actually hisses at me.

So it is that I (the cross-dressing ballplayer) appear to be escorting a sexy black cat in faux diamonds (is that really my mother?) to a costume party. Mom's the one who drives us there, though.

I try not to feel too dumpy as we walk up to the fitness club, which has been transformed into Halloween Central, complete with pumpkins and spider webs and skeletons and ghosts. We're barely in the front door when Todd, dressed like an old fighter pilot, comes up and starts talking—make that *flirting*—with Mom. When he finally notices me, it seems like an afterthought. "Hey, Babe," he says, gently punching me in the arm, "how's your batting average these days?"

At first I think "Babe" is a compliment, and I smile and joke back. But when he turns his attention back to Catwoman, I get it. Babe Ruth was pretty chunky too.

"Hey, is that you, Cassie?" says a guy in a bandanna. He has a black patch over one eye and a fake parrot on his shoulder. He, too, is sporting a fake mustache.

"Yeah?" I say, trying to figure out who this guy is.

"Aye, it's me, Gary Frye," he says, chuckling. "Aargh, I'm a pirate of the Caribbean, mate-tee."

"Hi, Gary," I say in a flat voice. I don't want to encourage him.

He slips his sword into his belt and fingers the fabric of my jersey. "Cool. This is the real thing, huh?"

So I tell him about my dad's one season in the minors.

"Yep," he says. "Same thing happened with me and football."

"What's that?" I ask, falling for it.

He launches into a long tale about how he had all these full-scholarship offers from some of the smaller Pacific Northwest schools and how he decided on Seattle Pacific, but then he injured his knee midway through the season and eventually lost his scholarship and had to drop out and get a job at Boeing to support his wife and kid.

"Tough luck," I say.

He nods, and his parrot nods with him. "Yep. All my NFL dreams straight down the toilet.

"Hey, Penny," he says when a petite belly dancer comes up. She has on a long, dark wig, and I can tell that Gary thinks she looks pretty hot in that outfit.

"Hey, Gary. Who's the cute ballplayer?"

"It's me, Cassie," I tell her.

"Oh, I actually thought you were a guy."

"That's the whole point."

She laughs. "Yeah, but I was going to ask you to dance."

"Why don't *you* dance?" says Gary in a suggestive voice.

So she actually does a little belly dance for us, complete with finger cymbals and jingling coin jewelry, causing a few others to stop and watch.

"Wow, you're really good," says Gary. "Where'd you learn to do that?"

"I've been taking a class at the rec center." She pats her toned midsection. "It helps to slim the waist."

"Maybe I should come," says Gary, patting his paunch.

While everyone is joking about the benefits of belly dancing, I decide to slip off to the sidelines, maybe even get something to eat. It figures, this being a fitness club and all, that most of the refreshments are healthy. I fill a paper plate with veggies and fruit and go to stand next to a woman dressed like a bowling ball, who turns out to be Emma Carpenter, the chubby gal who was inspired by my mom to join the fitness club. I tell her that I officially joined the club and plan to set up my own workout regimen, which won't include spinning.

"Maybe we could work out together sometime," she suggests again.

I glance down at her rotund costume, which is covering her rotund figure, and just nod. "Yeah, sure, maybe."

"I don't know why I came tonight," she admits. "I usually avoid things like this. But that Cindy at the front desk talked me into it. Then I went to the costume shop, and all she had left was this stupid bowling ball." She looks down at the three white spots, which I assume are the finger holes. "It's pretty bad, huh?"

I laugh. "Well, I'm not too thrilled about being taken for a guy. Penny, the belly dancer, tried to pick me up."

She laughs. "And then they don't have any real food here." She lowers her voice. "I mean, I'm trying to diet just like the next person, but I understood this was supposed to be *dinner.*"

I nod. "I know. I'm starving."

"Me too." Then she looks at me with a devious expression. "Want to go get something to eat?"

As tempting as this sounds, I'm not sure I want to be seen leaving with the bowling ball to go eat. "Let me think about it," I tell her. "I mean, I just got here, and I came with my mom. Maybe I shouldn't run off right away."

"Yes, I understand. I should probably stay awhile longer too. But if you change your mind, let me know."

I thank her, then set off to find Penny, the precocious belly dancer, again. I want to ask her why she ditched me at happy hour on Friday.

"Sorry," she tells me after I corner her at the drink table. "It was my nephew's fourth birthday. The party ended at four, but it took forever to clean up the house after the kids finally left. I should've called you."

"Well, no one was there except Gary and me."

She giggles. "Oh. That must've been fun."

I frown. "Actually, Gary's not that bad. But it was kind of embarrassing. I'm sure people thought we were on a date."

"Hey, are you two a couple or something?" asks Gary. He's got a guy dressed like a cowboy in tow.

"Yeah, we're lesbians, Gary," teases Penny as she links her arm through mine. "You going to leave us alone now?"

He looks sort of embarrassed, then his brows lift in curiosity. "Hey, no problem. I'm an open-minded guy."

She makes a face as she thumps his lopsided parrot, then introduces me to the cowboy, whose name is Bob and who's sort of cute in a nerdy way, although I notice right off that his teeth are crooked. I can also tell by the way he avoids eye contact that he's probably pretty shy. Probably due to those choppers. He seems to be trying to camouflage them with a big bushy mustache, which is slightly askew, but it only draws more attention to his mouth.

"We thought you girls might like to try out the dance floor," says Gary with his eye on Penny and her exotic getup. He elbows Cowboy Bob, who nods and says, "Yeah, sure. Wanna dance?"

So the four of us head over to the gym, which is improvising as a dance floor tonight, and when the DJ begins the next song, which I'm glad to hear is a fast number, we go out and attempt to dance. Despite those teeth, Cowboy Bob looks pretty good in his boots and leather vest, but he is not much of a dancer. Still, we make an attempt. By the end of the song (and a few dumb jokes from me), he seems to loosen up some. We dance another one, but when a slow song comes on, I tell him that I'd like a break, that I'm thirsty. He seems relieved.

"What do you do?" he asks as we sip some kind of green and ghoulish punch that Cindy, the red-headed receptionist, now disguised as Lily Munster, dipped out of a big, black cauldron.

I give him my minibiography about getting my MBA and working in marketing for a few years before deciding to reinvent myself. Eager to change the subject, I inquire about him.

"I'm a CPA."

"An accountant?" I say stupidly. Like what did I think—maybe he's certified public *astronaut*?

He nods. "Yes. I work for Warren and Wesley."

"The bookkeeping place," I say. "I've seen their office on Main Street."

"Most people think it's kind of boring work," he says, "but I like it."

I nod. "It's good to do what you like."

"What do you like?" he asks. "I mean, as far as work goes?"

"That's what I'm trying to figure out," I admit. Then I hear a fast-paced song starting, and I decide that dancing might be preferable to talking, at least with this guy. "Want to dance some more?"

He smiles shyly. "Sure. That was kind of fun."

I wave at Emma, the lonely bowling ball, as we head back to the gym. I'm surprised she's still here. Her offer of escaping this scene for food is starting to sound better than spending the evening dancing and chatting with Cowboy Bob, the accountant.

As we're dancing to a goofy disco tune, Bob's mustache tumbles from his upper lip and is about to be trampled underfoot. As he touches his upper lip with a worried look, I decide to rescue the furry little thing that resembles a fat caterpillar. I bend down to pick it up, and I hear a loud ripping sound behind me. This is not good. Nor is it good that this sound is immediately followed by a rush of cool air on my hind end. I stand up straight, putting one hand behind me to feel the seat of my dad's old baseball britches. Sure enough, they've split right down the middle.

I hand Bob his fake mustache and excuse myself, backing away from him with both hands holding on to the seat of my pants. Then, realizing that spectators might also be behind me, I turn around just in time to see Catwoman and the Flying Ace and several others loitering near the entrance to the dance area. And I can tell by their semishocked, semipitying expressions, they've witnessed the whole pants-splitting thing.

I'm sure my face is crimson as I shoot out of there still clutching my bottom. I spot Emma, the forlorn bowling ball, rolling toward the exit. I imagine the double doors turning into pins that she will knock down, with me barreling through right behind her. I rush toward her, still holding the seat of my pants, and call her name.

"What's wrong?" she asks as I practically shove her out the door.

"Can I catch a ride with you?" I ask breathlessly.

She catches her balance and stares at me in wonder as I explain my unfortunate incident in colorful detail. Before long we're both laughing about it.

"I'm guessing you don't want to get something to eat now."

"I just need to go home," I say desperately.

"No problem."

Once I'm safely in my driveway, I thank Emma for the ride, then go straight into the house and make a beeline to the full-length mirror in my room so I can survey the damage—not to the pants so much as to my ego. Is it even possible to still have an ego when your backside looks like this? The baseball pants have a vertical split that runs all the way from the waistband to the crotch. To make matters worse—or maybe not when you consider the coverage I was getting—I'm wearing an ugly pair of light blue granny panties. Why do I even try?

Thirteen

I spend all day Sunday lying low, hoping the town will forget about my granny-panties-clad derrière making such an un-expected appearance at the Black Bear Fitness Club Halloween party. My mother assures me that no one even noticed. Yeah, right!

But by Monday I know I need to get serious about my can-do plan. First I call and report the credit-card fraud. This takes longer than I expected and involves filling out some forms, which I arrange to have faxed to my mom. The woman I speak to says that these cases rarely get resolved and that I shouldn't assume that Monica's real last name is Johnson. Duh. Then, despite the pain of almost emptying my checking account and saying good-bye to my severance pay, I pay off the Valentino boots and most of the credit-card bill, telling myself that one way or another Monica Johnson is going to make good on this.

Thinking of Monica reminds me of Will. I wonder how he's doing, whether he got a good restaurant job, and if my little rec-ommendation helped at all. I wonder if he got his cell phone reconnected and am tempted to call the number he gave me, but what would I say? That I've managed to do practically nothing since I got home? Still, it would be good to hear his voice. Without giving it any more consideration, I punch in his number. To my utter surprise, he answers.

"Uh, Will," I say, wishing I hadn't done this. "Hey, this is Cassidy."

"Oh, hi, Cassidy. What's up?"

"Not much. I just wondered how you're doing."

"Great, actually. But I'm at work right now. Not a good time to talk."

"So you got a job?"

"I did. Thanks for writing that recommendation."

"I'm so glad for you."

"Life going well for you too?"

"Uh, sure. Things are great."

"It's good to hear your voice. I wish I could talk—"

"That's okay, Will. I'm just glad to know everything worked out for you."

"Thanks, Cassidy. Catch you later, okay?"

"Yeah, sure."

I hang up and try not to feel envious that Will has a life. I mean, really, I'm glad. He's a great guy. It's very cool that he has a job. I don't know why I assumed that he'd be like me, stuck in a slump. His life is on track. He's moving on. Well, good for him.

Staring at my sorry bank balance drives home the point: I need to follow Will's example and get a job too. So I set up my laptop computer and printer and update my résumé, which is pretty impressive, if you ask me. Then I pour another cup of coffee and sit down to scour the classifieds in search of something that suits my educational training and experience. But all I find are ads like "wait staff needed for weekends and evenings" or "cashier for convenience market, experienced only" or "money-making opportunity for motivated salespersons," which smells like telemarketing to me. Finally I fold the newspaper and decide I must try another tack. I get out the skinny local phone book and start to list any businesses that might need a marketing guru, which is what I've decided I am. Of course, my list is pitifully short and not very promising. Eventually I wad it up and toss it into the trash. What was I thinking when I moved back here? How can I possibly make a decent living in a town this size? And I can't keep living with Mom. Not only is it humiliating to have to admit that I live with my mother, but it's frustrating to witness her social life, which is much more highly evolved than mine.

Despite my optimistic can-do plan, I'm afraid that it's useless to attempt to accomplish it in this town. And even if I did get a job here, I still don't have a car to get me back and forth from work once the weather snaps, which it will soon. Oh, Mom would probably loan me the down payment, but what's the point if I end up working at the Dairy Queen or 7-Eleven?

To fight off the gloomy cloud of depression that's settling over me, I decide to at least stick to my regimen of walking. I even consider walking to the fitness center and having a nice long swim, but the idea of seeing someone who saw my behind at the costume party deters me. I wonder if I'll ever be able to show my face there again. Maybe I should take Penny up on her offer to work out with me. If I stick around, that is, which seems increasingly unlikely.

It's crispy cold outside, but the air is invigorating. I walk briskly, striding down familiar streets and crunching autumn leaves under my feet. I could get used to this rural sort of lifestyle. As much as I tried to convince myself I was a city girl, part of me likes the slower pace here. Still, it's no good without a job. It's even less good without a social life. And it wouldn't hurt to have a boyfriend either! This leads me to think of Todd again, which is totally ridiculous. My chances of winning the lottery are probably better than my chances with him. And so, with all these things against me, I decide that it's pointless to stick around. As soon as I get home, I'll go online and do a national search on one of those job-finding Web sites, and I'll take the best thing that pops up, no matter where it is.

Even as I make this decision, I feel a lump growing in my throat. I feel so lost—more lost than I've ever been in my life. More lost than anyone should be at the age of thirty-one, an age when most people are really starting to get it together. The thirties are supposed to be the decade when your career takes off, the years you become financially stable, maybe even get a BMW or something along those lines. It's a time to buy real estate and settle down with the one you love and start a family. Of course, these sad thoughts are underscored as I walk through a quiet family neighborhood. I see neat little houses with bikes in the yards and moms loading complaining kids into minivans, and moms walking with strollers toward the little city park. And I feel so sad, so robbed. Life is so unfair. It's not that I want to be stuck at home with a couple of kids, but it's not that I don't either. Frankly, I don't know what I want. I just know that I don't want this. I don't want *my* life.

As I turn back toward home, I feel tears streaking my face again. I'm having a pity party of one. But it's my business, and if I want to cry, so what? There's no one around to see me. Even if there were, it couldn't be a worse humiliation than I experienced on Halloween.

I feel so desperate that all I want is to give up. I know the only thing that can really help me at times like this is to pray. I also know, despite the confident claim I made to Eric, that I've been pushing God further and further away since my life fell apart. Even though I thought about going to Gary Frye's church yesterday, I couldn't make myself do it. The truth is, I've been secretly mad at God. Maybe I subconsciously thought I could do a better job of putting my life back together than he would. It wasn't like he did such a great job before, when I was following his direction—at least that's what I thought I was doing. Suddenly I'm not sure. I'm not sure of anything except that my life has fallen apart, and I'm falling apart with it.

And so, feeling totally directionless, I decide as I turn the corner toward my house (really my mom's house) to ask God to intervene. I confess to him that I've been mad, that I'm hurting, and that I'm not doing such a great job. If he has a better plan, I ask, won't he please, please reveal it to me? I don't know what more to say. I know I'm groveling, but I figure God's used to that sort of thing. And maybe he wants us to grovel sometimes. Maybe we get too full of ourselves, and maybe he wants to remind us who's really boss.

It's noon by the time I get home, and Mom's pretty car is in the driveway. I'm not eager for her to see me looking so miserable, since it only seems to frustrate her. So as I go inside, I wipe my wet face and decide I'll tell her that the chilly air made my eyes water and turned my cheeks red.

"Cassie!" She looks happy to see me. "I was hoping I'd find you. You'll never guess what happened."

"You sold another house?"

"Well, possibly. But that's not what I'm talking about. This has to do with you."

"What?" I feel a faint flicker of hope.

"I had coffee with Ross Goldberg this morning." She smiles mysteriously.

"Let me guess," I offer. "He proposed marriage to you, and he wants to adopt me and give me a million dollars as a—"

"No, silly! But he might want to give you a job."

"Yeah, right." I roll my eyes as I remember the selection of low-level jobs at Black Bear Butte. "What, as a lift attendant? Or maybe I can work at the snack bar in the lodge. I can sling a mean bowl of chili."

"No, not anything like that, Cassie. He needs a marketing consultant. He said he's ready to take the ski resort to the next level.

He's made lots of improvements and wants to see some money coming back in. He thinks he needs a really good marketing campaign, and I told him you might be just the one to do it."

I feel my eyes light up. "Really?"

"Yes! Isn't that wonderful?"

I nod without speaking, remembering my prayer of moments ago.

"Of course, you'll have to interview with him and—"

"I just printed out my résumé," I tell her.

"Perfect."

"Uh, was Ross at the party Saturday night?" I ask uncomfortably. "I mean, do you think he saw the, uh, spectacle I made of myself?"

She laughs. "Really, sweetie, almost no one noticed. And Ross was not there. He doesn't even belong to the fitness center. He has this great workout room in his home."

"You've been to his home?"

She looks slightly uncomfortable. "Well, yes. At one point he was thinking of listing it. I think that's the first time I saw it."

"So you've been there more than once?"

"Well, we're friends, Cassie. You know that."

"So is it your friendship that made him think up this marketing job?"

"No," she says, "not at all. We were just chatting, and he mentioned needing to do something. And I told him about your background. He didn't even know."

"And he really wants to talk to me?"

"Of course."

"So what do I do? Should I call him or what?"

"Call his assistant." She pulls a business card out of her jacket pocket. "Her name is Marge, and she'll set it up."

I hug Mom. "Thanks! This is so cool."

"And, honey?"

"Yeah?"

"You should probably wear something nice—you know, businesslike. Ross is from the old school. He likes people to look professional."

I try not to feel insulted. "Mom," I say in a tone that sounds like I'm fifteen again, "I know how to dress for business. I have a pretty decent professional wardrobe that I haven't even unpacked yet."

"Well, you do have a nice pair of boots," she admits with a twinkle in her eye.

I scowl at her. "And I have some nice things to go with them." I don't tell her that those nice things have probably kept me from having a bigger savings account and a car. "Uh, Mom," I venture, "I'm guessing I'll have to go to Black Bear Butte for the interview, right?"

She nods as she thumbs through the mail.

"Well, I don't have a car."

She looks up at me and frowns. "That's right." She thinks for a moment. "I suppose I could loan you mine."

I can't help but grin at the thought of being behind the wheel of that hot little car. "I'd be super careful with it."

She nods but doesn't look totally convinced. "Maybe if you get the job, we should look into getting you transportation of your own."

"Well, if I get the job, I could probably afford a car."

By the afternoon I have an appointment with Ross on Thursday at two. This motivates me to swallow my pride and head to the fitness center. My short-term goal is to work out every day before this interview, as well as to eat right. I also plan to unpack my working clothes, do some laundry, and visit the dry cleaners, and I might even get my long hair cut into something more stylish and flattering. I'm not exactly ready for that makeover Mom would like me to have, but I plan to do everything I can to spiff up my image. At the moment, it's not terribly impressive.

I wouldn't say that I'm a new woman by Thursday, but I'm off to a pretty good start. With my mom's encouragement and financial backing, I made an appointment with her hairdresser, Crystal. On Tuesday I got my long hair cut into layers that curl softly around my face and stop at my shoulders. Then Crystal highlighted it with auburn, something I've never even considered. But I like it. I saw Emma at the fitness center yesterday, and she said my new do makes my face look thinner. Then, after my haircut, Crystal introduced me to a "beauty associate," Gloria, who's the local makeup guru, and I made an appointment with her for the next day. Gloria gave me some basic pointers and sold me some can't-live-without items, which I had to use my Visa to purchase, but I'm sure it's all worth it. The overall effect is quite an improvement. Plus it made my mom happy.

Thursday morning I meet the day with a brand-new optimism. I go to the fitness center as usual, then hurry home to get ready for the interview at Black Bear Butte.

Knowing that Ross Goldberg is a man of discerning taste, I realize I must dress as impeccably as possible. I'm going with businesslike chic. For the chic part, I choose the Valentino boots. The Ralph Lauren tweed suit should do the rest. I realize this combination could be risky because it rendered me jobless last time. But, really, I can't blame these innocent clothes for that. I'm not superstitious.

Even so, I feel anxious as I drive Mom's beautiful car up to the ski resort. My nervousness is partly due to the fact I'm not that great a driver. We had a dusting of snow this morning, and I'm worried the roads may be slick. Consequently I'm driving like a grandma.

Even more than that, I'm nervous about this interview. I'm a little inexperienced when it comes to interviews. I mean, I haven't interviewed since I got out of college. And then I had only two interviews before I landed my previous job. So when it comes to impressing a potential boss, I feel pretty clueless. On one hand, I could blow my own horn, but that might make me look like a conceited show-off. On the other hand, I could act teachable and eager to learn everything about the ski-resort biz, but I don't want to come across as ignorant. Finally I decide that a combo might be my best bet.

It also occurs to me that prayer can't hurt. After my little epiphany the other day, when I handed the steering wheel of my life back to God, I realized that I need to stick with it. So I pray. I ask God to open this door if it's meant to be open. Otherwise…well, I guess I don't really know what happens then. It's not like I have a backup plan.

When I get to the resort without a single fender bender, I'm impressed with the improvements I see. The Goldberg family really has sunk a bunch of bucks into this place, which looks stunning under its first thin blanket of snow. It's not enough to open the resort but enough to make it picture perfect. I find my way up to the administration area, and Marge, Ross Goldberg's assistant, invites me to wait in the recently redecorated lobby. I sit in a big leather chair that faces a tall rock fireplace. Impressive.

After about twenty minutes, Marge informs me that Mr. Goldberg can see me now. I can feel my palms sweating as I rearrange my bag, a chocolate brown Monsac that Callie gave me for Christmas last year. I thought it was a little old for me then, but now I think it looks rather sophisticated.

"Cassidy," says Mr. Goldberg, standing behind his desk as he leans forward and extends his hand to shake mine, "good to see you." Then he actually seems to look at me—I mean, *really* look at me, almost as if he's surprised at what he sees. And he nods with what seems like approval. "You are looking well."

"Thanks." I smile.

"Your mom told me you've gone through some hard times lately."

I nod and bite my tongue. Does the whole town know my history by now? What did Mom tell him about me?

"Have a seat, and let's talk."

I try to block out all negativity as I sit down, willing myself to forget about what Mom may or may not have said. *Just focus on this interview.* "The resort looks fantastic," I begin. "I'm so impressed with all the improvements. I hadn't been up here for a couple of years. But it's really coming into its own."

"Coming into its own?" he echoes with a thoughtful brow. "I like that." Then he thanks me for sending him my résumé prior to our meeting, saying that he's gone over it carefully and that he likes what he's seen.

"Thank you."

"So tell me, Cassidy, what can you do for Black Bear Butte?"

"I did a little research," I tell him. "I saw your Web site and picked up some brochures in town. To be honest, I found them, well, unimpressive."

He nods and leans forward slightly. "Yes?"

"And then I come out here and see that this place, for a small ski resort, really is impressive."

"It's even more impressive when we have real snow."

I smile. "Yes, I know." Then I launch into an off-the-cuff plan about how we could cross-promote with local businesses by offering free ski passes combined with a purchase, how we could take advantage of some online opportunities, and how a graphic designer I know in the city would be perfect to create a new logo and some promo materials. "I'm sorry," I finally say, pausing to catch my breath. "I didn't mean to get carried away."

"No, I like that," he says. "That's exactly the kind of enthusiasm I'm looking for."

"Really?" I shouldn't act so surprised.

He grins. "Yes. And I like that you're from here, Cassidy. You know what Black Bear is all about."

I laugh. "That's for sure. My sisters and I sort of grew up on the mountain."

"Do you still ski?"

"I haven't for a couple of years, but everyone knows it's a little like riding a bike."

"Well, if I hire you, you'll get a free season ticket that I'll expect you to use. Of course, you get a few other benefits too." Just then his phone rings. He answers it and says he'll be right there.

"Will you excuse me for a couple of minutes?" he says, standing. "Something came up in the mechanics department that needs my immediate attention."

"Of course," I say, leaning back into my chair.

"I'll be right back."

Then he goes, and I'm alone in his swanky office. It really is attractive with its large, lodge-style furnishings, a smaller stone fireplace with a gas fire that's cheerfully burning, and floor-to-ceiling windows that look out on the mountain. I notice several manila file folders neatly fanned out on his oversize desk and can't help but wonder if they are for other applicants interested in this job. And, if so, who are they? What are their qualifications? Are theirs more impressive than mine? I glance over my shoulder and see that Marge has left the area too. Then I stand up and casually glance down at the pile of files. Two of the names, both men, are completely unfamiliar, but then I see Suzanne Diessner's name, and I cringe.

Suzanne and I used to work at the same firm in Seattle. We started out in the same department about the same time. Actually, I think I was there a month before her. But she was one of those women who knows how to use "all her assets" to get ahead of the game. Consequently, she quickly climbed the corporate ladder, landing an enviable position above me. I didn't know her that well since she didn't usually give someone like me the time of day. Even so, I tried not to believe every rumor I heard, although I did question her scruples occasionally. Not verbally. But some of the things I saw made me wonder. Then, about a year ago, Suzanne suddenly left the firm. I never heard why. I suppose I could assume she was smart to get out of there before downsizing began. Still, it makes me wonder what she's been doing. And I'm curious why she's looking for a comparatively small-scale job like this now.

I've just flipped open her folder and am viewing an attractive cover sheet, complete with a gorgeous photo of Suzanne, when I hear the sound of a woman loudly clearing her throat. I drop the cover of the folder and turn around. My face is already getting warm.

"Can I get you anything?" asks Marge with highly arched brows. I know she saw me peeking at the folder. I can only imagine what she thinks of me.

"I, uh, no thanks," I say quickly, suppressing the urge to press my cold hands against what I'm sure are now blazing red cheeks.

"Coffee, tea, water?" she persists. "Mr. Goldberg might be a few more minutes."

"Sure, some water might be nice," I say, hoping to get rid of her. "My throat is a little dry."

"Yes, it can be very dry up here with the altitude and cold weather." But she just stands there, watching me as if she expects me to steal something. It seems my only hope is to confess.

"I, uh, I noticed the name of someone I know," I admit, pointing to the folders. "I haven't seen her in about a year, and I was surprised to see her name…"

"Ms. Diessner?"

"Yes," I say eagerly. "Suzanne Diessner and I worked for the same firm in Seattle. I'm sure it's on her résumé. And I just couldn't help but, well, be curious, you know, as to how she's doing and all."

Marge nods with knowing eyes. "She seemed like a nice young lady when she interviewed last week."

"She's very pretty, isn't she?" I say, certain I should be crawling out of here with my tail between my legs.

"Very."

"And she seemed very good at her work," I add, somewhat generously, I think.

"Her résumé is impressive."

I know my expression is desperate now. How do I get out of this? Should I just apologize and leave? I am such a fool. "I really wasn't trying to snoop," I say. "It's just that, well, the name was familiar, and I…was curious, and I'm so sorry. I must look terribly unprofessional."

She nods, but then she smiles slightly. "I'll get your water."

I seriously consider slipping out of this place while Marge is getting my water, but I'm afraid I'll just run into her or Mr. Goldberg, and then I'll have even more explaining to do. I have no doubt she will tell him of my faux pas. And I have no doubt that it will be a good excuse for him not to hire me. It makes no difference that he and Mom are friends. Except that he may tell Mom why he was forced to disqualify me. You don't hire someone who can't even make it through an interview without embarrassing herself. Besides, why shouldn't he hire Suzanne over me? Even if I hadn't been a snoop and a fool, Suzanne is everything I am not. Of course he'd pick her.

"Here you go," says Marge, neatly centering a glass of ice water on a coaster made of stone.

"Thank you," I mutter, feeling like I'm in the principal's office, waiting to be disciplined.

After several more minutes, Mr. Goldberg finally returns. But now he seems a little stiff and formal. I'm guessing that Marge already spilled the beans. Whatever.

"I'm sorry that took so long," he says without sitting back down in his chair. He just stands there looking at me in a way that I'm sure is meant to indicate that this interview, as well as my chances of being hired, is finished.

I stand too, picking up my purse and glancing at the door. "That's okay." I force a smile. "I totally understand."

"Thanks for coming in." His voice sounds stiffly polite, but I can't read his expression. During the interview he seemed fairly positive and somewhat interested in me. But now he's wearing a poker face. And as he shakes my hand, I have a feeling this is it. Just get me out of here.

"Thank you for considering me," I say, moving toward the door.

"Someone will get back to you."

I make a quick exit. I don't even look at Marge or say good-bye. I just want out of here. As I walk across the deserted parking lot to my mom's car, I can't help but replay the whole scene with Marge as well as some of the more stupid things I said during the interview. I know that it's hopeless and the best thing would be to forget about it. But I can't help but relive the whole, horrible thing again and again. It's like a form of self-torture. I said too much during the interview. You're supposed to hold some things back, but as usual, I let it all hang out. Then to top it off, I get caught red-handed snooping through the competition. How lame can I get? His last words hit me as I get into the car. *Someone will get back to you.* That means Marge will be very polite when she calls. She'll probably say something like, "I'm sorry, Ms. Cantrell, but we've decided to go with someone else." Probably Suzanne Diessner. And the idea of Suzanne taking the only job in Black Bear that might've been suitable for someone like me makes me want to pull out my hair and scream. And yet I have only myself to blame. When will I learn?

I turn on the ignition and pray out loud, "Dear God, please help me get smarter about life." Then I step on the gas with too much force, and Mom's car peels out over the icy parking lot, slipping sideways and totally out of control. My heart leaps to my throat as I slide straight toward a lamppost. I shut my eyes, not even daring to breathe until the car comes to a stop inches from the immovable iron. I breathe a prayer of thanks, then glance up to see Ross Goldberg looking down from a tall narrow window that overlooks the parking lot. I offer a feeble wave. Now he can be absolutely certain that he just interviewed a total idiot. I'm sure that cinches it.

Fourteen

uring the weekend I try not to obsess over the fact that I totally blew my chance at a good job. Concerned that he might've told my mom about how I nearly wrecked her car, I ask if she's seen Ross Goldberg lately, but she hasn't. Of course she tells me not to worry. And I tell myself not to worry, reminding myself that I did my best. Sort of. Even so, I know it's useless. I just hope Mr. Goldberg isn't the sort to share stories. It'll be just one more thing to live down.

On Sunday I decide to seek a distraction by going to Gary Frye's church. I feel pretty self-conscious at first, and it doesn't help matters when Gary comes over and greets me like his long-lost friend, then introduces me to everyone he knows. But I also find an old friend in the crowd. Okay, *old friend* might be an exaggeration. I went to school with Bridget Ferrington. We never spoke that much in high school. Mostly I just admired this tall, willowy brunette and wished I were more like her. We were in art together, and she generally kept to herself. Not in a shy way, as I would sometimes do, but in a way that suggested she was just slightly superior to the rest of us. We all knew she'd moved here from New

York, which sounded terribly exotic back then. Anyway, I'm surprised to find her at this church, surprised she's fairly friendly, and surprised she's a Christian, which she makes clear from the get-go.

"You really remember me?" I say after the service ends.

"Of course. Besides me, you were the most talented artist in Mr. Bevie's class." She laughs. "I guess that sounds a bit conceited."

"But Bridget's a real artist," says Gary, who seems to be stuck to me like glue now. He turns to me. "Have you seen her stuff?"

I admit that I haven't and learn that Bridget's art is usually available in a small gallery called Blue Pond.

"It has mostly my nature pieces," she explains. "My more modern work doesn't do too well in this town."

"I can understand that."

"But I have a rep in New York who is kind of a family friend. He gets my work into some East Coast shows."

"That's so great, Bridget. I'm really impressed. And it's encouraging to see someone who's doing what she really loves—using her gifts. That's so cool."

"Sort of like me," kids Gary. "I mow lawns and shovel snow for a living."

I feel bad now. "But you're kind of an artist too," I say. "I mean, landscaping is an art, isn't it?"

"That's right," agrees Bridget. "It's totally an art."

Gary smiles now. "Yeah, I guess so."

"How about you, Cassidy?" she asks. "What do you do?"

Without going into much detail, I give her the nutshell version of my education and work history, and without thinking, I tell her that I applied for a marketing job at Black Bear Butte.

"They could use some marketing help," she says. "They've put so much into that place, and yet the ski traffic last year was worse than ever."

"You can't even blame it on the snow," adds Gary. "We had tons of snow. I remember because I was backed up for plowing most of the time."

"I probably won't get the job," I say, wishing I hadn't admitted that I applied. When will I learn to keep my big mouth shut?

"Why not?" asks Bridget.

"Oh, I don't know. Just a feeling."

"Well, then there will be something better. How about your art?" she asks. "Do you still do it?"

This makes me laugh. "My art?"

"Yes. You were good."

"Well, thanks. I guess I never took it seriously."

"So you don't even dabble?"

"Nope. Guess I've been stuck in the corporate world too long."

"You're not stuck anymore."

"That's for sure," says Gary.

"But when it comes to art..." I just shake my head. "Good grief, I wouldn't even know where to begin."

"Well, maybe marketing provides you a creative outlet," she says.

I consider this. "Maybe."

Just then someone calls out to Gary, and Bridget takes the opportunity to quietly ask me if I want to get out of here and get some coffee. "Yes," I say, trying not to sound too eager. Then I confess my current carless state, and she offers me a ride.

"It's not that I don't like Gary," she says as we drive away.

"I know," I admit. "He's a nice guy and all."

"And as a Christian, I know I should love him…" She giggles. "But sometimes he makes me want to scream."

"I can't wait to see your art at Blue Pond," I say. "That's great that you're making it with your art. Very impressive."

"I'd offer to take you there, but they're closed on Sundays during the off-season."

We find a quiet table at the coffeehouse, and Bridget tells me about a failed marriage and several messy affairs and how she finally became so desperate that she took her grandmother's advice and cried out for God. "It was so amazing," she says. "It's like he answered. I don't mean audibly, but suddenly things began to change. I got back into my art and felt like I should move back to Black Bear. It's been about three years now, and I'm extremely happy."

"Wow, that's so cool."

"I still have down days, but not like before. It's like I have a purpose now. And I really love this church. I go to a home group on Wednesday nights. You might like it too."

"Does Gary go?" I know it's terrible. But the idea of being cornered by this guy at a home group is a little scary.

"No, I think he goes to a different one."

I nod. "Hmm."

We talk some more, and it occurs to me that of all the people I've gotten reacquainted with in Black Bear, Bridget seems the most interesting. As she drives me home, she tells me about a landscape she's been working on. "It's more like a mural really, and I have no idea what I'll do with it. It's too huge to go in Blue Pond, and because it's more of a Western theme, I can't send it to my rep." She laughs. "Like I can send it anywhere. For all I know, it may simply be for me. It fills an entire wall of my living room."

"Sounds cool."

"It's big anyway." She's pulling up in front of my mom's house.

"Well, if it's true that size matters…" I pause as I notice the familiar red Jeep in my mom's driveway, with a familiar guy leaning against it.

"Is that Todd Michaels?" she asks as she peers out the window.

"Yeah."

"Are you dating *him*? I mean, it's none of my business, but he is so hot, Cassidy. We're friends and all, but he's never asked me out."

"No," I say the words slowly, "I am not dating him."

"Then why is he here?"

"Well, he's sort of dating my mom."

"Your mom?" She laughs. "Are you kidding?"

"I wish I were."

"No way. Your mom?"

"Yes."

"That's just so kinky."

"Tell me about it."

As we sit there gawking at Todd from behind Bridget's tinted windows, my mom comes out the front door.

"Who's that?"

"That's my mom."

"No way!" Bridget leans over to see better. "I've seen her around town, but I thought she was new to the area. That's really your mom?"

"That's really my mom." I can feel my cheeks getting flushed now. And it figures that Mom is wearing her tight jeans and a little denim vest with rhinestones on it, plus those silly high-heeled cowboy boots. It's like she thinks she's Britney Spears.

"Wow."

"She's a cougar," I say quietly, almost under my breath, then wish I hadn't.

"What?"

"Sorry, I shouldn't say that."

"Did you just say she's a cougar?" Bridget is still leaning over and peering at the two of them. Totally oblivious to our presence, they get into Todd's Jeep. "What does that mean?"

"It's just a stupid term for older women who prey on younger men. And to be fair, Todd was the one who originally talked my mom into going out with him. Although she did give him the impression that she was younger."

"I'll say." We both watch as the Jeep drives away.

"I just don't know why she's still going out with him," I say, hearing the longing in my voice.

"Well, I know why. Todd is a hot guy. And your mom's not blind. But how old is she anyway? I mean even if she was only seventeen when she had you, she'd still be like forty-some—"

"Try fifty-five," I say, feeling like a tattletale. "And, as she says, still alive."

"That's obvious." She shakes her head. "Wow, fifty-five. I hope I look that good when I'm her age. Not that I'd be a cougar." She laughs. "Although you never know…"

I consider telling Bridget the rest of Mom's story, about how Dad dumped her for a younger woman and how Mom was overweight and frumpy and depressed, but I don't really see the point. Instead, I thank her for the lift and promise to be in touch.

"I'll be praying for you about the job thing," she tells me as I get out.

"Thanks."

"And if you don't get it, that only means God has something better in mind for you. Don't forget that!"

I thank her again, then walk up to the house. I know I shouldn't feel like this, but right now I'm exasperated with my mom. I am embarrassed by the way she's acting. So she's going through some kind of a phase. I wish she would get over it and start acting her age!

I try not to fume about my cougar mother as I feed Felix. Why can't she be a regular middle-aged mom—the kind I need right now? She should be home making cookies, watching the Home Shopping Network, and wanting to know how my life is going. Instead she's running around like a teenager, riding in Todd's Jeep and wearing tight jeans and little T-shirts. It just doesn't seem right.

I begin to wonder if this thing between Todd and her is more serious than I'd thought. I realize that some older women actually marry younger men. Look at Demi Moore and Ashton Kutcher. From what I've heard, they're pretty happy. Maybe I need to get used to this.

But when it's after eleven and they're still not back, I actually start to feel angry. I mean, Black Bear is a small town, and it's a Sunday night, for Pete's sake. Absolutely nothing is open at this hour! Well, besides some of the little ski motels. That thought totally grosses me out. I mean, it's one thing for them to date and act ridiculous, but what if they start sleeping together? Would Mom do that? What if Mom wants to invite him to spend the night here sometimes? Maybe she already has. Maybe he'd be here right now if I hadn't moved back home.

Does she feel like I'm intruding on her space? What if I'm the only thing keeping her from doing—well, who knows what? I refuse to think about that. I turn off the lights and stomp off to my room. So what if Mom wants to make a fool of herself and a mess of her life! It's really not my business. I'm not responsible for her. And there's no reason I should wait up for her either. I mean, who is the parent here?

I get ready for bed, scrubbing my face much too vigorously. I decide she really is a cougar. She's taking advantage of Todd, having her stupid little fling to make her feel young again. That thought makes me feel sick. More than anything, I wish I could get out of here. I need to get back on my feet again. As impossible as it seems, I need to find a place of my own.

Not wanting to see my mom's guilty face, I sleep in the next morning. I heard her tiptoeing up the stairs very late last night. I almost charged out of my room to accuse her—of what? Instead I just fumed and fumed until I finally fell asleep. And I knew better than to talk to her this morning. I knew I would probably lose it, probably say things I'd regret, probably make her cry again.

By the time I get up, she is long gone. I'm sure she looked cute and perky as she headed off to sell a house or something. I'm also sure that everyone who knows her is well aware of what's going on with her and Todd. Is it possible people make jokes about her behind her back? What if she's the laughingstock of the town?

I try to push these thoughts away from me as I make a cup of green tea. But I wish it were coffee instead. I'm so weary of Mom's healthy style of living. Maybe I should dig through my stuff and find my coffeepot. Then I could sneak it up to my room and enjoy it, my own personal contraband. But why bother? Don't I plan to move on and get out of here? I can't live with my mommy forever. But how do you move out when your bank account looks like mine? Oh, my life is so depressing. It's like a black hole that keeps getting deeper.

Certain that I'm not going to get the marketing job at the ski lodge, I peruse the classified ads again, but that scene is pretty much the same as before. November is not the best time of year to get a job in this town. Maybe I should go back to the city. But where would I live? This makes me think of Will. I wonder how he's doing and which restaurant he actually works for. I think about my old studio apartment with a longing that surprises me. I was so eager to get away from that place, and suddenly I would give anything to go back. Not that I miss the city. I miss having a life. I miss having my own space, even if it was small. I miss having a reason to get up in the morning.

I try to remember last week's resolve not to obsess over my life—or rather the lack of one. I remember how I was trying to trust God to lead me where I need to go. I also remember Bridget's encouragement and her saying that God has something special for me—something that will be fulfilling and just right for me. I'm still amazed that she's making a living with her art. I'm also a bit jealous. And it bugs me that I feel that way.

Telling myself to get over it, I get dressed and walk to town. My plan is to work out at the fitness center, get some real coffee, then go to see Bridget's art at the Blue Pond Gallery. That's like having a life. Anyway it's better than staying in my sweats, hanging out in my mom's house, and having a big old pity party.

So after my workout and coffee, I wander over to the Blue Pond and am impressed with the quality of Bridget's art—not to mention the prices. Once again, I feel jealous. How is it that everyone but me seems to have a handle on life? How do they figure these things out? More than ever I feel lost as I walk through the gallery, looking at the various pieces on display and wondering if I'll ever find myself and where I fit in. Just as I'm about to leave, Bridget comes in with what appears to be a covered canvas in her hands.

"Hey, Cassidy." She smiles as she sets the parcel down and leans it against the counter. "I'm just dropping off a new painting."

"Cool. Your other pieces are so awesome. You're really good."

"Thanks." She waves at the woman working on something in the back. "Hey, Sheila, here's that new landscape I promised."

"Want to put it behind the counter for me?" calls the woman.

"No problem." Bridget slips it back there and turns to me. "What are you up to today?"

I shrug. "Not much."

"No word on that job?"

"No."

"Want to get coffee?"

I nod without telling her that I just had coffee. It's not like a second cup is going to hurt.

"You seem down," she says as we carry our lattes to a table.

"I guess I'm a little discouraged." Then I admit that I feel lost. Seeing her success, while encouraging on one level, is kind of depressing on another. "I mean, I'm so happy for you," I continue, "but I think I'm never going to get to a place like that—doing what I really love and making a living at it. It seems like an impossible dream."

"What do you really love?" she asks, then takes a slow sip.

I consider this. "I'm not even sure."

"Someone once told me that if you think back to when you were about ten years old and what you loved doing then, it will be a clue as to what you'd love to do as an adult."

I try to remember what I liked to do when I was ten. At first nothing comes to mind. Then I remember the lemonade stand and smile.

"Aha," says Bridget. "You thought of something, didn't you?"

"Yeah, but I think I was actually eleven."

"Ten, eleven—I don't think it matters."

"Well, I don't think it'd work nowadays anyway." I cringe to imagine myself setting up a lemonade stand on Main Street.

"What was it? What did you love doing?"

I laugh. "It was a lemonade stand."

"Uh-huh?"

"I designed the stand myself and made my own lemonade from scratch, but it wasn't doing too well, so I added brownies to the menu. Then I started selling beaded necklaces too. By the end of the summer, I'd made quite a bit of money, and it was really fun. I would've done it again, but I entered junior high then, and it seemed a little juvenile."

"So you're a businesswoman at heart?"

"I don't know. Maybe I'm really a marketing person after all."

"What did you love most about your lemonade stand?"

"I think it was having a kind of control, you know? Running

my own business, calling the shots, figuring out what worked, and making it work better. That was fun."

"So what if you started your own business again?"

"How?"

"I don't know."

"It sounds fun, but the truth is, I wouldn't know where to begin. It sounds like an impossible dream."

"Maybe you just need to dream bigger, Cassidy."

My cell phone rings. "I should get this," I tell her without admitting what a rarity it is to get a phone call.

"Cassidy Cantrell?" It's a woman's voice, official sounding.

"Yes?"

"This is Marge at Black Bear Butte. Mr. Goldberg asked me to call you."

Okay, I know what's coming, and I brace myself for yet more rejection. I just hope I don't start blubbering in front of Bridget.

"Mr. Goldberg wants you to know that he'd like to offer you the position."

"Really?" Okay, I'm sure I sound totally shocked and not terribly professional. But I just find this very hard to believe.

"Yes. He'd like you to come in this afternoon if you can. He wants to go over some things, and of course there's paperwork to fill out."

So we arrange for me to come at four, and then I hang up and look at Bridget with amazement. "I got the job," I tell her.

She gives me a high-five. "Well, that's kind of like running a lemonade stand," she says. "A really big one."

I laugh. "Yeah, with lots of ice."

"And Ross Goldberg's not too hard to look at." She winks at me.

"He's going to be my boss," I point out, although I can't disagree with her. "I think it'll be wise to keep some professional distance, if you know what I mean."

"Well, why don't you arrange for your boss to meet your friend then?"

"You haven't met him?"

"Not officially."

"Well, give me time. I'll see what I can do." The truth is, I'm so stunned I actually got the job that it's all I can think about. What on earth caused him to change his mind? Not that I knew he'd made up his mind. But it sure seemed like a lost cause to me! Maybe it's just a God thing.

Whatever it is, I decide not to obsess over it as Mom drives me out to the lodge at a quarter till four. Okay, it's a little embarrassing having your mommy drive you to your new workplace, but it's better than hitching. And she promises to wait in the car.

"You sure you won't get too cold out here?" I ask.

"I'm fine," she assures me. "I have paperwork to go over, and I'll turn the engine on if I need to warm up."

"I don't think I'll be long," I say.

I feel pretty nervous as I approach Marge's desk. I'm sure she remembers my snooping episode. But she just looks up and smiles, saying, "I'll tell Mr. Goldberg you're here." I thank her and wait, and soon I am seated across from him again. I so want to ask if he knows about what I did, and yet I'm determined to act more mature this time.

He slides a paper across to me. "This is what we're prepared to offer," he tells me. "I know it's not as much as you were making in Seattle. But at least there's room to grow."

I take time to look over the offer, although I'm not sure I care much about the details. Right now I just really need a job. Even so, I don't want to appear too eager. And I don't want to stick my foot in my mouth and say something childish or regrettable. The salary is a little less than at my former job, but the benefits package is actually better. Finally I nod, and using my most grown-up, business-type voice, I say, "This looks acceptable to me."

He smiles and extends his hand. "So you'll take it then?"

I nod as I shake his hand. "I can't wait to begin, Mr. Goldberg."

"For starters, please just call me Ross. Marge is a little old-fashioned and insists on the *Mister*. But I try to get everyone else to lighten up a little."

"Okay, Ross. I'm looking forward to working with you."

He smiles. "I'll ask Marge to show you to your office, and you can start as soon as you're ready. As far as I'm concerned, tomorrow isn't a day too soon."

"I can't wait."

Fifteen

I'm amazed at how easily I slip into my new marketing role at Black Bear Butte. I have my own corner office at the resort, and by midweek I feel like I've got a real plan to begin executing. Mom lets me borrow her car for the first couple of days, and I drop her off at work on my way to the resort. But by Thursday morning I can tell she's having second thoughts about this little arrangement.

"How about I drive you to work today?" she says as she rinses her tea mug. "I need my car to show a house that's out of town."

"I know it's an inconvenience sharing your car."

"But you need a way to get to your job," she points out.

"I don't have much left in my savings," I admit, "but it might be enough for a down payment on a car, if it was a cheap one."

"A Realtor at my office has an old Subaru that belonged to her daughter before she went off to college. Anyway, she'd like to get it out of her driveway. It's not much, but it runs, and she only wants fifteen hundred dollars for it. Plus it already has snow tires."

"Wow, I could almost afford that."

"I could help you with the rest." Mom looks hopeful, and I can tell she's missing her sleek silver car, which I've been enjoying immensely. "How about if I arrange for us to look at it after work today?" she suggests. "I can pick you up and take you over to check it out."

So it is that I'm driving an old Subaru to work on Friday. With its dented left fender and scaly paint, it's nothing like my mom's pretty car, but it runs okay, and the CD player works. Life could be worse.

"I think I'll have a game plan to show you on Monday," I announce to Ross as I pack my things to go home. He's been out of town the past couple of days and stopped by my office to see how things are progressing.

"Really?" He looks suitably impressed. "That soon?"

"Well, there's no time to waste," I point out as I slip some folders into my briefcase. "Ski season is just around the corner, and we need to get the word out ASAP."

He nods. "I couldn't agree more, but I don't want this to feel or look like a rush job, Cassidy. I want a quality campaign, something we can all be proud of."

"I know that." I nod as I close my laptop. "That's what I want too."

He smiles as he leans against the doorframe to my office. "I can't wait to see it."

"I think you'll be pleased," I say. Of course, I won't tell him that I plan to work on it all weekend. Let him think I'm Supergirl.

"So do you have big plans for the weekend?" he asks.

I shrug. "Not really."

"Not even going to the art walk in town tomorrow night?"

"Oh, I saw the poster," I say. "But I guess I forgot about it."

"I thought I might go," he says. "Just to absorb a little of the local culture."

I nod. "That's probably good."

"You should come too," he says.

Now, I'm not sure what he means by "you should come." Is that supposed to be an invitation? No, of course not. "Yes, I should probably absorb some local culture too," I say.

"You want to join me then?" He actually looks hopeful, and I feel shocked. Is Ross Goldberg asking me out?

"I, uh, I don't know."

"It doesn't have to be like a date," he says quickly. "More like two business associates just doing something together."

I smile at him. "That sounds great."

"Shall I pick you up then?"

I blink. The idea of Ross Goldberg picking me up at my mom's house is pretty weird. It wasn't long ago that he was picking her up, although her involvement with Todd seems to have taken priority over Ross. "Sure," I say as I stand and pick up my briefcase.

"The walk is from five to seven," he says. "Maybe we could grab a bite to eat somewhere along the way." He gives me a sheepish grin. "I still haven't mastered the art of cooking. I tend to eat out most of the time, and it's not much fun to eat alone."

"Sounds great," I say as I get my coat.

"See you tomorrow night then." He gives me a nod, then turns away and heads back to his office.

I walk to my car, wondering what just happened. Ross said it's just two business associates doing something together, but I wonder if it could be something more. I can't help but be flattered by this unexpected attention. Still, I've always had a strict policy about dating fellow employees. Of course, Ross isn't an employee. He's the boss. He owns the place. Even so, I probably need to be careful.

As usual, I go to the fitness club after work. I do my regular workout plus an extra fifteen minutes of swimming. And as I'm getting dressed, I think I can see a slight improvement. I'm not nearly as svelte as my fitness-obsessed mom, but I'm not quite as flabby and out of shape as I was two weeks ago. I wasn't totally winded after doing the cross-trainer either.

Once again, Mom is going out with Todd tonight. They're just getting into her car as I get home. She tells me they're heading over to Keller for dinner and a new-release movie. I tell them to have fun and to drive safely. "There's supposed to be freezing rain tonight," I warn, feeling like the parent once again.

Then I go inside, and after heating and eating another low-cal frozen entrée, I go straight to work. Ross's concerns about this campaign not looking thrown together have me worried. I will put everything it takes into making this plan slick and cool and compelling. I work until well past midnight, noticing that Mom and Todd are still not home. I tell myself not to think about it. It's none of my business. Besides, I have a date tomorrow. Okay, not a date. But I don't have to tell Mom that. I wonder how she'll feel when she finds out that I'm going out with one of her male friends. Will she be jealous of me for a change? Probably not. As Ross said, it's just two business associates doing something together. Big deal.

I work nearly all day Saturday too, taking only one midday break for a walk to clear my head. The weather is really snapping cold now, and the low-hanging clouds make it look like it could snow. While snow would be great news for the lodge, I hope it will hold off until after the art walk.

Although I'm not going on a date, I take my time getting ready. I try on several outfits and finally decide on a caramel-colored DKNY cashmere turtleneck sweater and my favorite jeans, which despite having been in the dryer too long are fitting a little bit loose now, and that actually makes me feel thinner. I consider wearing my Valentino boots to make me look taller, then choose practicality, going with my lower-heeled Franco Sartos, also a caramel color, which looks perfect with the sweater. *Not bad*, I think as I check myself out in the mirror.

"You look nice," says Mom after we nearly collide in the hallway. "Going out tonight?"

"Just to the art walk," I say as I wrap a mossy green knit scarf around my neck. "It's supposed to be cold."

"Are you going with someone?" she asks.

"Just Ross," I say casually.

I see her brows lifting. "Ross Goldberg?"

"Yeah. We thought it would be fun to check out the local art scene."

"You're dating Ross?"

I smile. "It's not really a date, Mom. Just friends hanging together, you know. We might get a bite to eat. No big deal."

"Oh." But as she says this, I sense she's not pleased. Could she be jealous after all?

"Are you and Todd going out?" I ask.

"Not tonight," she says a little too quickly.

"Oh."

"Those late nights can be a little tiring," she admits. "I told Todd I needed a night to recuperate."

I nod, suppressing the desire to remind her of her age and how older folks should take it a little easier. "Have a good evening," I call as I head down the stairs, hearing my mom's footsteps coming right behind me. She hovers at the foot of the stairs as I peek out the front window just in time to see Ross's black BMW pull into the driveway. Then I slip on my Ralph Lauren brown wool car coat and pick up my purse.

"Have fun," says Mom in an uncertain voice.

"Thanks!" I call back as I open the front door. It's so great to be the one going out tonight! I suppose I'm feeling a little bit smug.

The art walk isn't terribly impressive. Most of the work being shown in the regular businesses is by high-school students, and although it's pretty good for their age group, it's not like what you'd see in the city. The galleries are a bit better, and it's fun to watch the artists actually at work. We save Blue Pond, Black Bear's premier gallery, for last. Of course, the featured artist there is Bridget.

Ross and I partake of the complimentary cheese and wine, then watch as Bridget dabs at a landscape of a mountain lake surrounded by autumn foliage.

"That's an interesting style," comments Ross, "sort of traditional with an impressionistic touch."

Bridget laughs. "I've never heard it put quite like that, but I guess that works." I remember my promise to officially introduce them and decide there's no time like the present. Even so, I feel a little reluctant. I mean, Bridget is gorgeous. She's an established artist. And I know that she already admires Ross—a lot. But she's cool with the introduction, and then she explains that some of her other pieces, the ones shown back East, are much more contemporary. But I can feel her eying me as she talks to Ross, as if she's trying to figure out if we're an item. She probably wants to know what her chances with him might be. I figure I can straighten her out tomorrow at church.

Another couple comes to talk to Bridget. They talk as though they might like to commission a piece for their home, so Ross and I use this opportunity to move on. I wave to Bridget as we head for the door, but I can still see the questions in her eyes.

"Hungry?" he asks as we go back outside.

"Starving," I admit, which is true since I skipped lunch.

"Good." He glances at his watch. "I actually made us a reservation."

"A reservation?"

He grins. "Yep. Have you heard about the new restaurant?"

"We have a new restaurant?"

"Yes. It's called Petit Ours Noir."

"Little Black Bear?"

"*Oui.* Your French is *très bien.*"

"*Merci!*" I laugh. "I took three years in high school, but I'm pretty rusty now."

"Well, maybe you can help me read the menu then. I've never taken French. All I know is from a little handbook. The last time I was in southern France, I made a complete fool of myself."

"I'm sure I'm not much better."

"The restaurant is in the old McNulty mansion on Tamarack Street."

"I noticed some nice renovations there, but I didn't realize it was for a restaurant."

"Yes, the owner has been keeping it under wraps, but he's my old buddy Alex Morgan. The restaurant is not officially open until next week, but he invited friends to come in and try it out this weekend. To get the kinks out. The restaurant is on the first floor, and Alex and his wife, Elise, who is the chef, live upstairs."

"This sounds like fun," I say, pulling my scarf more snugly around my neck.

"Well, I've tasted Elise's cooking before," says Ross. "She trained in Paris, and she's fantastic."

He pushes open an ornately carved wooden door. The name of

the restaurant is etched in the center of its oval beveled-glass panel. "Very chic," I say as we go into the warm foyer.

"Ross," says a man who comes over and shakes his hand, then hugs him, "so glad you made it."

Then Ross introduces me to Alex, who takes our coats and escorts us to the main dining area, where only a few tables are occupied. I take in the beautifully restored wooden floors, oriental carpets, and a welcoming gas fire in the large, ornate fireplace. Then Alex seats us near the fire at a small table complete with white linen and fine silver. I can tell this place isn't going to be cheap. Alex tells us that tonight's menu is somewhat limited and then goes over the features. If this list is limited, I can't imagine what they'll be serving a week from now.

We both decide to have the beef entrée, which is tenderloin beef medallions and chanterelles in burgundy sauce. Ross orders a bottle of Pinot Noir to go with it.

"I feel like I should've dressed up," I say after Alex departs.

"No, you look fine," says Ross. "This is a casual evening." He waves to a nice-looking middle-aged couple, who look vaguely familiar, and then to a younger couple who, like me, are both wearing jeans. Then he tells me who the other diners are. As he goes over the names, which I recognize, I realize they are the who's who of Black Bear.

"Impressive," I say.

"I hope they'll be impressed."

"How do you know Alex and Elise?"

"I went to college with Alex." Then he explains how his deceased wife, Gwen, introduced Elise to Alex, and how the couples became good friends over the years. I can see the sadness in his eyes as he talks about some of the trips they took together.

"How long has your wife…been gone?" I realize this is none of my business, but I'm curious.

"It'll be four years in the spring."

"I can tell you really loved her."

"You can tell?" He looks surprised.

"When you were talking about her and your friends, I could see it in your eyes."

He nods. "I've been told it should get better with time, but I still miss her." He sighs and takes a sip of wine. "I haven't really gotten back into dating yet."

This surprises me since I thought he'd gone out with my mom. He seems to read my mind.

"Oh, I've put on the appearance of dating. I've taken women to dinner. Even tonight, I'm sure some will assume this is a date."

I nod, thinking, *Yeah, I could almost make that assumption myself.*

"I guess it's pride, you know, wanting to look like I'm back in the swing of things. But the truth is, I'm not ready to seriously date anyone."

"So you and my mom weren't…"

He chuckles. "Audra's a wonderful person, but, no, we weren't really dating. She's fun to sit with during those boring chamber meetings, and sometimes we grab a meal together. But that's all."

I try to remember my mom's take on this. It seems to me she thought Ross was serious. She thought he was really into her. I suppose I thought he was too.

"After Gwen died, I put all my energies into Nathan's high-school years and renovating Black Bear Butte. Then renovations were complete, and Nathan got accepted at the Air Force Academy last year, and now I'm getting used to a change of pace." He holds up his hands. "I guess I feel a little lost."

"I know how you feel," I admit. Then I tell him a bit about my own situation and how I've been trying to find where I fit.

"Well, it looks as though you're going to fit into the resort just fine. I can't wait to see what you've put together for the new marketing plan."

For the rest of the evening, I tell him a little about some of my ideas. Oh, I don't give it all away—just enough to whet his appetite. By Monday, when he sees the whole thing laid out before him, he'll be impressed. I hope.

"That might've been the best meal I've ever had," I tell Alex as we're putting our coats on and preparing to leave. I don't like sounding all schmoozy, but it's the honest truth.

He's beaming. "I can't wait to tell Elise."

"I have to agree with Cassidy," says Ross. "That was absolutely fantastic. Give my regards to the chef." He winks.

"She'd come out, but she spilled beet juice down her front," says Alex. "She doesn't want to make a bad impression."

"Well, next time then," says Ross as he shakes Alex's hand. "And congratulations on what should be a great success."

As Ross drives me home, I think about how I could get used to being with a guy like this. He's got polish, manners, money, experience... What more could a girl want?

"Thanks for a great evening," I say as he pulls into the driveway.

"Thank you for joining me."

"And I love that it wasn't a date."

His smile looks relieved. "Really?"

"Sure. It's lots more relaxing that way. It's just like hanging with a friend." I point to his windshield. "Hey, it's starting to snow!"

"Perfect," he says. "Now if it will just come down hard for a whole week, maybe we can open by Thanksgiving."

"I know I'm praying for snow," I say as I reach for the door handle. "See ya on Monday."

"Can't wait to see that marketing plan!" he calls out before I close the car door.

I look up at the swirling snowflakes, illuminated by the street-light, as I walk toward the house. And I do pray that it continues. But as I pray, I wonder if I'm only thinking of the snow.

$\mathcal{M}$ y marketing plan is a hit! Ross is totally jazzed as he tells me Monday afternoon to begin implementing it immediately. He wants to pull out all the stops. "This could be Black Bear Butte's best year ever," he says as he looks over my presentation again. Then he nods to the big window. Outside the blanket of white grows deeper by the minute. "And if this keeps up, we'll be open *before* Thanksgiving."

"Then I'd better get busy," I say. "I've got a lot to do, lots of phone calls to make."

"Go for it."

"And I'll need to go to the city to set up some things with the designers."

"As I said, go for it."

I smile at him. "This is so fun."

He laughs. "That's what I like—a woman who enjoys her work."

I do enjoy myself as I make phone calls and set things up. It's fun having this kind of control—almost like my old lemonade stand—and as I pull things together and get all the pieces in place,

I think maybe this is what I was meant to do. Maybe I've finally found my niche in life.

The snow continues, and by the time I leave for the city Wednesday morning, the mountain has accumulated thirty-one inches of new snow. I feel exhilarated even as I drive through the dismal rain, knowing that rain down here means snow up there. My enthusiasm seems to be contagious as I meet with the graphic designers and ad people. At first they were shaking their heads and telling me it couldn't be done, but after a few more phone calls (and some silent prayers on my part), it begins to look like my marketing campaign might actually launch by the first week of December.

"You guys started this pretty late," says my favorite designer as he adjusts his calendar to schedule our project.

"I suppose it's late for this year," I admit. "But it's early for next year."

He chuckles. "You've always been one of those glass-half-full kind of girls, haven't you, Cassidy?"

"Don't I wish. Trust me, I've had my negative moments. Not that long ago either."

Somehow we work out the details and scheduling challenges, and I finish up my appointments around four. As I'm getting ready to head out of town, I decide to swing by my old apartment. I'm not even sure why. Maybe it's for old times' sake. Or maybe I'm curious as to how things have gone with Will. As I turn down the street, I wonder if that job he got made it possible for him to stay in my apartment. Or has he moved on? I'm surprised to feel a little sad that he never returned my call, and I second-guess my spontaneity. In the end, I don't really plan on stopping, but when I spot an empty space right in front, something that rarely happened when I lived there, I decide it's an opportunity. I park my old Subaru and get out. The rain has let up, but it's still overcast and gloomy. A wet day in the city used to depress me, but I remind myself again of the snow on the mountain. I'll bet another ten inches fell today.

As I go up the stairs, I start to feel irrationally nervous. What am I doing here? And do I really plan on knocking on my old apartment door? This is crazy. As I think back, my whole experience with Will was pretty odd. I mean, the short time we spent together was so strange and surreal. What was it—two days? three? And yet I felt so close to him then. It's like we connected. How weird is that?

I pause at the top of the stairs, rationalizing that what happened then was simply the result of two desperate people thrown together by another person's greed. Monica had hurt us both. We were vulnerable. We were brokenhearted, down on our luck, kicked in the teeth by life, and looking for a morsel of sympathy wherever we could find it. Why not just let it go? My life has moved on. Why come back here and wallow in old memories?

I stand on the landing and stare at the door of Monica's old apartment and wonder what has become of her. Is it possible that she's returned? What if she and Will are back together? Maybe even living in my old apartment, yukking it up about how they pulled one over on me. This thought makes me feel sick, and I realize it's nuts for me to be here. I'll go back downstairs, get in my car, and pretend I didn't stop by. What if I actually saw Monica Johnson right now? Who knows what I might do? I'm sure it wouldn't be pretty.

"He's not here," says a gruff voice from the hallway behind me.

I turn to see old Mr. Snyder leaning on a push broom and looking just the same as ever in his old, yellowed T-shirt topped with an unbuttoned, faded, plaid flannel shirt, tails hanging out. I wonder how long he's been standing there watching me. For whatever reason, I feel embarrassed.

"Oh, hello," I tell him. "What do you mean?"

"I mean if you're looking for Will Sorensen, he's not here."

"Did he move out?"

"No, I mean he's not here 'cause he's at work."

"And where would that be?"

"He's a cook over at that Italian restaurant—that Terrazio place."

"Do you mean Terrazzo de Giordano?" I ask in surprise.

"That sounds about right. It's that fancy-schmancy place over on First Avenue." He rolls his eyes. "Little too rich for my blood, but at least it pays the rent."

"That's great." I feel an unexpected thrill of happiness for Will. That's quite a place. Good for him.

"Ya want me to tell Will you stopped by?"

"Sure," I say. "Tell him hello for me."

He seems to study me, softening just a little. "And you're doing okay too?"

"Yes." I smile at him. "I'm still living at home with my mom in Black Bear. But I got a good job, and things are looking up."

He nods, then returns to his sweeping.

Although it makes no sense, I decide to take First Avenue on my way out of town, slowly cruising by Terrazzo de Giordano. I've eaten there only once, but it's an impressive restaurant, both on the outside and within. I try to imagine Will working in the kitchen there, and I hope he's happy. I hope his life has really turned around. I'm tempted to stop in and say hello, maybe even order something light on the menu. But for some reason I can't. Even so, I think about Will as I drive away. I remember that dinner he made for us and that amazing evening we spent together. It still seems surreal—sweetly yet disturbingly weird. And something that's best forgotten.

To distract myself from these unsettling thoughts of Will, I decide to stop at the mall. I've been so good about not spending money since returning to Black Bear that I think maybe I'm due for a few new things. Also, thanks to losing some weight, I could use a smaller pair of jeans and maybe some winter clothes for my job at the resort. I realize this will mean using my credit cards, which I've paid down some, but I also know that I'll have a paycheck at the end of the month that should cover this expense. Plus,

I remind myself, my image as the director of marketing at Black Bear Butte is important. In a way, any wardrobe improvements should be considered a work expense.

By the time I'm done shopping and loading my bags into the car, I've decided that living in Black Bear might be a real blessing to my pocketbook. Especially if I avoid any unnecessary trips to the city and particularly to the mall. Still, I found some good sales, and I tried to shop sensibly. I avoided the overpriced designers like Armani and Gucci in favor of Liz Claiborne, Ralph Lauren, and DKNY. Even so, it all adds up. I don't even want to think about what it actually adds up to, but I know I'll get statements by the end of the month. But I'll look stylish in my new job. And my jeans will fit. Also, I got a couple of really great coats that are perfect for the ski resort. One I can even use for skiing—a navy-blue North Face parka—and it came with some slimming ski pants that match. All in all, I think I made the right choices.

I will start saving for my own apartment as soon as my bills are paid off.

Life at home isn't intolerable, and it does save me money to stay there. In the following weeks, Mom and I are both busy with work and life, and we seem to call a truce. Not that we were fighting exactly. But there has definitely been some tension in the air, especially when I do something with Ross, which is fairly often. To be fair, I probably get a little uptight when I see that she's still going out with Todd. Not that I want a chance with Todd. I've decided the poor boy probably has an Oedipus complex, which I find rather pathetic. But the idea of my mom being a cougar still doesn't sit well with me.

At least life at work goes fairly well. My marketing plan hits a few snags, but I just consider these challenges as opportunities to prove myself. When I work hard enough, I usually find a way around problems that often turns out for the best. All in all, I think I'm seriously on track. And that feels pretty good.

We have a big celebration at the lodge just two days before Thanksgiving because the resort is officially open. We're not especially crowded, but that's the way Ross likes it, for the first couple of days anyway. It gives the employees time to get up to speed. By this weekend, the place should be running like "a well-oiled machine," or so Ross assures us all as we lift glasses of champagne at the end of a busy day.

"Fifty-one inches of snow is a record for us this time of year," he tells everyone. "I think it's a good omen for the season. Mother Nature is being kind to us." Then he winks at me. "Of course, I've also heard that certain people have been talking to the big guy upstairs about the snowfall as well. I guess we should give credit where credit is due." He talks a bit more about projections for the season and how there will be bonuses for everyone if things go as planned. The general spirit of this crowd is upbeat and optimistic. I just hope that it will continue throughout the season.

"Is Nathan coming home for Thanksgiving?" I ask Ross as I pull on my coat at the end of the day.

He frowns and shakes his head. "They're in the midst of some special training right now. I won't get to see him until Christmas."

"Do you have plans for the holiday?"

"To be honest, I've been so obsessed with the mountain that I haven't really given it much thought."

Well, I know the lodge is closed for Thanksgiving Day, and the idea of this sweet guy sitting at home by himself is just too sad. So without really considering the ramifications, I invite him to come to our little family get-together. I actually expect him to decline.

But his eyes light up. "Hey, that sounds great. What time?"

I give him the details, hoping that Mom won't be upset. "It's just my sisters and Callie's family," I explain. "No big deal."

"Sounds good to me."

To my relief, Mom is perfectly fine with this. "Of course you should've invited Ross, Cassie. No one should spend the holiday alone." As it turns out, she's already invited Todd too.

By Wednesday afternoon, Callie and Andrew and the twins have arrived. With Jack and Joe running around like wild things, Mom's house suddenly seems to have shrunk in half. Later that night Cammie arrives with a nice-looking young man in tow! She introduces us to Clay Hartford, a young intern who graduated from med school two years ago. Then she shyly holds out her left hand to show us a small diamond ring, and we all let out the appropriate squeals and congratulations. Cammie informs us that

a small Christmas wedding is in order and that she and Clay still
plan to head off to Uganda following her graduation.

It's so good to be with my sisters again, but I'm disappointed
that Cammie is a bit preoccupied with her beau. Of course Callie
is distracted by the rambunctious twins, who seem to suffer from
some undiagnosed hyperactivity disorder. So my time with them
seems rather secondary. However, we all gather to help Mom in the
kitchen the next day. Meanwhile Andrew and Clay ride herd on
the twins and try to watch a little football.

"I can't believe how great you look, Mom," says Cammie for
like the hundredth time. "It's so amazing."

"Don't you think she could pass for forty?" says Callie.

"You girls," says Mom, but I can tell she loves it. Then she
looks at me. "Doesn't Cassie look great too?"

Cammie and Callie look over at me and nod and smile, but I
can tell they're not impressed. However, they didn't see me a month
ago. They don't realize how far downhill I'd gone.

"Cassie is dating Ross Goldberg," continues Mom.

"You mean Ross Goldberg, as in his family owns Black Bear
Butte?" says Callie with wide blue eyes.

"Mom," I say, "I'm not dating him. Ross is my boss, for Pete's
sake."

Mom gives me a sly look. "He might be your boss, but he's also
taking you out a lot lately."

"Well, you should stick with that guy," says Callie. "His family is loaded."

"He's my boss," I say again.

"Isn't he pretty old?" asks Cammie.

"He's forty-six," says Mom.

"Wow," says Cammie. "Fifteen years' difference. That seems kind of old, Cassie."

"I know," I tell her. "I'm not going out with him. Okay? We're just friends. And as I've mentioned several times, he's my boss."

"Cassie invited him to join us for dinner," says Mom as she slides the turkey into the oven.

Why do I feel like screaming just now? Instead, I take a deep breath. "And Mom invited Todd Michaels to join us today too," I say. "Callie, you might remember Todd. Or maybe not. He's about three years younger than you. Todd and Mom have been dating for a while now." I give Mom a teasing poke, and Callie gives me a warning look, but I can tell I've got Cammie's attention.

"You're dating someone younger than Callie?" says Cammie.

"Oh, it's nothing serious," says Mom. Then she goes into the cute little story of how she sold him a house and he insisted she go out with him. "We just have fun together, that's all."

I nod with raised brows. "And sometimes it's pretty late-night fun."

Mom tosses me a sharp look, and I'm pretty sure I've hit pay dirt. Not that I'm trying to go there. But her jabs about Ross were getting to me.

After this, Cammie and Callie take over the conversation. Callie wants to plan Cammie's wedding and already has dozens of ideas, most of which Cammie vetoes.

"We want to keep it simple," she explains. "Clay and I are both more focused on helping people than on having the wedding of the century. We think big weddings are a waste of money."

"But it's a once-in-a-lifetime event," persists Callie. "You want something you can remember forever."

"Making it expensive doesn't make it memorable," points out our ever-sensible Cammie. Then she tells about her friend who had a fifty-thousand-dollar wedding and divorced less than a year later.

"Just because you have a nice wedding doesn't mean you'll get divorced," says Callie, exasperation showing in her voice.

"Hey, it's Cammie's wedding," I say. "If she wants to keep it simple, why shouldn't she?"

"Fine," snaps Callie. "She can get married in sackcloth and ashes for all I care."

"Oh, Callie," says Cammie, putting her arm around her oldest sister. "I want your help with this. Really, I do. But you have to promise to keep it simple. Okay?"

Callie sniffs indignantly.

"We can do that," Mom assures her.

By two o'clock everyone is here. Ross mixes easily with the other guys and seems glad to be part of our family gathering. Todd actually seems to fit in fairly well with everyone too. But it does look just a little awkward, at least to my eyes, when we all sit down at the table and Todd is seated next to Mom. I, naturally, am seated next to Ross. No one else seems to notice the discrepancies in ages, though, and the friendly chitchat prevails. As we're finishing, the focus is on Black Bear Butte and what a great season it promises to be.

"I'm surprised you aren't open on Thanksgiving," says Andrew. "Most of the places out our way are open on all major holidays."

Ross nods. "Yes, I've considered this recently. It's been my family's tradition to close on holidays, but there's a lot of lost revenue. And now that my folks have pretty well checked out of the whole thing, living the big life in Hawaii, well, I guess I could change things if I wanted to."

"And it's always cool to hit the slopes after gorging yourself on turkey all day," says Clay. "Cammie and I are both snowboarders."

"Hey, I have an idea," says Ross. "We could sneak up there after this great meal and run the red chair for an hour."

"No way," says Todd. "You could do that?"

Ross laughs. "Hey, man, I own the place."

So it's settled. We quickly clean up the food, grab our ski stuff, hop into our cars, and head up there. Before long, we're all riding in the red chair, laughing and hooting over the lack of holiday lines, and then sailing down. It's not a challenging slope, but the idea of being up here like we own the place—well, that makes up for a lot.

"You need to hang on to this guy," says Callie as she and I ride up together.

I roll my eyes. "Like I said—"

"You're not dating…he's your boss…yada-yada-yada, blah-blah-blah. *So what?* He likes you, Cassie. You need to hook this guy and land him before someone else does." She practically smacks her lips. "Now there's a wedding I'd love to plan."

I try to explain that I'm just enjoying being friends with Ross and that we have a mutual respect for each other, but she refuses to get this. She wants Ross Goldberg as her brother-in-law! The more she talks, the more I begin to wonder if she might not be onto something. I watch as Ross glides effortlessly down the slope ahead of me, racing Todd, I think. He might be fifteen years older than I am, but he's youthful at heart. He's a great guy. And we have fun together. Well, I seriously doubt that Ross sees me as someone he'd like to settle down with. But Callie's planted a little seed in me. What would it be like to be Mrs. Ross Goldberg?

he next couple of weeks of ski season break all records for Black Bear Butte. Sure, this is partially due to the great snow, as well as Ross's renovations, but it's obvious that my marketing campaign hasn't hurt business either.

"If this keeps up, it'll be our biggest year ever," Ross tells me as we meet to grab a bite at Mountain Burger after work.

"And we're not officially into Christmas break yet," I point out as I set my half-eaten burger back into the basket, then push it aside.

"You're not going to finish that?"

"Do you want it?"

He laughs. "No, but that wasn't much of a dinner."

"Well, I didn't work out tonight either," I point out.

"I don't understand women," he says. "Always trying to lose weight. As if they think we guys like skinny chicks."

"You don't?"

He shakes his head, then grabs one of my fries. "I like a woman who looks like a woman."

I can feel myself blushing now. But I don't want to let on that this is making me uncomfortable. "What does that mean? What do you think a woman should look like?"

"You know…" He does a wavy motion with his hands. "Curves. Give me a girl with curves over a stick-thin, lettuce-eating, weight-obsessed woman any day. And I think most guys agree."

I laugh. "Well, too bad the media hasn't caught on to this yet. We keep getting anorexic models thrown in our face."

"Girls like that don't have staying power," he points out. "Have you seen them on the slopes? A couple of runs and they're winded. They look good hanging out by the fireplace while they sip their diet drinks, but I just don't get it."

I smile at him, remembering Callie's observations. Maybe he is into me. "Well, I think I'll take that as a compliment, Ross. Thanks."

He nods. "Now, you gonna eat the rest of that burger?"

I take another bite, then set it aside again. "The truth is, I don't really want it." I consider this. "I think I put on weight last fall because I was overeating to compensate for how unhappy I was."

"And you're happy now?"

I consider this. "Yeah, I am."

"I'm happy too," he says. "Things are kicking into gear and really working at the lodge. And I know you're a big part of that, Cassidy. I appreciate what you've brought to the team."

"I appreciate just getting to be on the team."

We talk about things that still need some attention, and I help him do some troubleshooting, and I wonder if that really is the way he sees me: just another team player, a buddy. Sure, he gave me an offhand compliment about looking the way a woman should look. But that was probably because he thought I'd quit overeating for the wrong reasons. As we part ways, I think I need to call Callie and ask her what exactly she suggests I do to hook this man. If that's even possible.

"For one thing you need to dress differently," she tells me later that night.

"Like how?"

"More feminine. Show off your girlie side, Cassie."

"My girlie side?" I imagine myself in a fluffy pink dress and want to gag.

"Yes. Try wearing skirts more often. And spice up your makeup."

I sigh. "Thanks, but that's not really the kind of advice I was looking for."

"Well, that's just the beginning. Then you need to learn how to play coy, sort of hard to get. If you keep being Ross's buddy, always available to hang with, what's going to make him want to take this relationship to the next level?"

"But he's my boss, Callie. What do you—"

"He's your boss right now, but that doesn't mean things can't change. Lots of people fall in love in the workplace."

"But isn't that wrong? I mean, what about sexual harassment and employment ethics and—"

"I'm not suggesting you sleep with him, Cass."

"Well, obviously." I try not to sound too shocked.

"I'm just saying that things can change. You could get him to see you in a whole new light."

"How do I do that?" I frown. "That is, if I even want to, which I'm not sure I do." It might be wrong or even stupid, but I am curious.

"For starters, be a little distant, a little mysterious…"

"Yeah, right." I roll my eyes and wish I'd never got her going on this.

"The next time Ross asks you to do something, make an excuse. Better yet, tell him you already have a date."

"But that's mean. Not to mention dishonest."

"If you want to bag a big boy, sometimes you have to bring out the big guns, Cassie."

I groan.

She goes on with more "helpful" hints that sound so corny I think she must've read the stuff in a teen fashion magazine.

"Well, thanks," I finally say, knowing that I'm not going to use any of these ideas. Besides sounding dumb, they don't seem right or fair.

"Good luck," she says. "Maybe by Cammie's wedding, you'll be engaged too."

"Fat chance," I tell her. "New Year's Eve is only three weeks away."

"Did you get your dress yet?"

"Uh, I think I have it narrowed down." Okay, this is a lie, but I do not want to risk the wrath of Callie right now.

"E-mail me the photo first," she says with big-sister authority. "I have to approve it, you know."

"I know."

As I hang up, I realize this means I'll need to go to the city this weekend. Callie and I are bridesmaids, and we're supposed to wear similar dresses in complimentary shades of green. This was Cammie's idea and rather sweet, since she thinks this means we'll be able to wear the dresses more than once. I've never had a bridesmaid's dress that was good for anything besides taking up space, but still I need to do some shopping—and soon. Callie has been very specific about the details. Three-quarter-length sleeves, tea-length skirt, not too frilly, no sequins or beadwork, but not too plain either. I'm tempted to just let her pick it out, but then I'd have to send her my measurements, and I'm not ready for that.

So on Saturday morning I head to Seattle to find a suitable bridesmaid's dress. I decide to make this as quick and painless as possible. In and out—just like the burger joint. I go downtown and start with Nordstrom and actually find one that I think will do. But that seems almost too easy. So I shop around a bit more, finally ending up in Pacific Place, my favorite downtown mall. After about an hour, I decide that I blew it by not getting that first dress right off the bat. Why am I making this so hard? I head for the exit, planning to hurry back to Nordstrom, when I hear someone call my name.

I turn to see my old flame, Eric, trailing me. He's waving at me as if he's trying to flag down a cab. I pause and wait for him to catch up. Not that I want to see him. I really don't. I am so done with this guy. But here we are, face to face, and for the life of me I cannot read his expression. Nor can I remember what I found attractive about this guy. He's nice looking enough, but nothing about him attracts me. Nothing magnetic or intriguing. Just handsome old Eric, looking slightly desperate.

"Cassie," he gasps, "I can't believe it's you. I was just thinking of you and trying to think of a way I could call you, and—"

"Look, I'm in a hurry," I say, glancing at my watch for effect. "Can you make this quick?"

He frowns. "Not exactly."

I actually start tapping my toe now—my caramel-colored Franco Sartos. I'm glad that I took time to put on a cute outfit today. No schlepping around from this girl anymore.

"You look great, by the way."

"Thanks." I look him straight in the eye. "How's Jessica?"

"Actually, that's what I wanted to tell you. Do you have time for a cup of coffee?"

"Coffee?" I let out an exasperated sigh. "Yeah, I guess so. But really, I'm in a hurry. I need to be back in Black Bear by six thirty."

His brows lift. "A date?"

Now the truth is, I promised to go to the high-school Christmas concert with Ross. We're doing a ski package giveaway, and it's kind of a promotional thing. But Eric doesn't need to know this. "Yes," I tell him, "and I can't be late."

So we go to a coffee kiosk, and I order a latte, making sure to pay for my own drink. I do not want to owe this guy anything. Then we sit down. For some reason I'm fuming, so I try to breathe deeply and chill. Eric has no power over me. He cannot hurt me again. Even so, I have this overwhelming and juvenile desire to hurt him. So I breathe a silent prayer, asking God to make me merciful. That'll take a real miracle.

"It really is good to see you," he says as he sits across from me. "You're looking fantastic too. I like what you've done with your hair." He smiles happily, as if he's just won the prize pumpkin.

"Thanks," I say. "It was time for a change." I tell him a bit about my job and how much I love it. "I had no idea that moving back home would be so good."

He sighs and shakes his head. "I wish you hadn't left, Cass."

Okay, be merciful, I remind myself. Be gracious. Kind words. "I think it was for the best, Eric."

He reaches across the small, marble-topped table now and takes my hand in his. I want to pull mine away, but I'm too stunned. "Cassie, I want you back. I want us back. I want everything the way it used to—"

I draw my hand back. "No," I say calmly, "that's not going to happen, Eric."

"But I thought you loved me."

I consider this. "I thought I did too."

"But you didn't?"

"I don't know. To be honest, I think I was in a rut. I was willing to settle."

He scowls now, sitting up straighter. "You think being with me was settling?"

"I didn't mean it like that," I say quickly. "I think I was just settling for everything in general. I wasn't happy with my job, but I stayed. I didn't like my apartment, but I had no plans to leave. Looking back, I can see that you and I weren't really right for each other either. But it was convenient."

"So that's it?" he asks, dismay all over his face.

"I think so," I admit. Then I smile. "I really wish you the best, Eric. You're a good guy, and some girl will be lucky to get you." Just not me! I'm so happy with this realization, but I hope I'm not grinning. I stand and place a hand on his shoulder in what I hope is a kind gesture. "And you should be thankful that you're not stuck with me, Eric. Really, it would've been such a mistake. It's a blessing that we found out before it was too late." Then I smile again, pick up my coffee, and tell him good-bye and good luck. As I walk away, I really do feel as if I've dodged a bullet.

Still, it's hard to erase his stunned expression from my mind's eye as I continue out the door and onto the street, making my way back to Nordstrom. I'm not sure if just his pride was wounded or if I actually hurt him. To my surprise I found I really didn't want to. But he was obviously shocked. Maybe he thought that all he had to do was snap his fingers and I'd come running back. That might've worked back in October. But not now. Not with this girl.

Eighteen

I make it back to Nordstrom and purchase the sage green silk dress that I think might actually meet with Callie's approval, although she'd probably approve even more if I bought it in a smaller size. The size ten did fit rather well except that it was a bit snug through the bust, and there's not much I can do about these big girls. I don't want to risk another seam-splitting situation on New Year's Eve when I still have Halloween to live down. Consequently I settle on the twelve, which is roomy and makes me feel thinner.

Anyway, I think Cammie will like it, and the color should look nice with Callie's dress, which is a slightly darker green. Pleased with my find, I shop around a bit more and find a couple more clothing items I cannot live without, as well as shoes for the wedding—a pair of Stuart Weitzman black pumps that are probably too expensive, even on sale, but are so stunning and sexy I can't resist them. Plus they're a classic style I could wear for years to come. And they make me look taller and thinner.

Jazzed about these purchases, I even do some Christmas

shopping. Then, poorer but happier, I'm back in my old Subaru and ready to go home.

I drive through town and feel this strange draw to First Avenue. Suddenly I'm driving past the Terrazzo de Giordano. I know I'm not going in, but I strain my eyes, wishing I could spy Will heading into work, maybe using a back door. This is ridiculous. I feel a bit like a stalker. Will probably doesn't even remember who I am. Finally, feeling seriously ashamed of myself, I head for the freeway. I can't get him off my mind. It's like I have this need to connect with him. But I'm not sure how. Maybe I'll send him a Christmas card.

I make it home just in time to change my clothes before Ross arrives. As he drives us to the high school, he asks about my day. I tell him about bumping into Eric and how great it felt to decline his offer to resume our romance.

"Poor Eric," says Ross as he pulls into the high-school parking lot.

"Poor Eric?" I repeat with a bit of indignation. "He cheated on me."

Ross nods and turns off his car. "Poor Eric for not realizing what he had before it was too late. You know, he was the loser in that breakup, not you."

"Oh…well, thanks."

As we're walking up to the school, in an uncharacteristic move, Ross puts his arm around my shoulders and gives me a little squeeze. "Sometimes I don't think you realize what a great woman you are, Cassie."

Okay, this pretty much blows my mind. Is Ross changing the rules here? Just as quickly as he put his arm around me, he put it back down by his side again. Maybe I just imagined the whole thing. Or else it was just a fatherly—make that *big-brotherly*—gesture. Nothing to get worked up about.

As we sit there listening to Christmas music, though, I can't help but compare Ross to Eric. Maybe it's his age or maturity, but Ross wins the comparison hands down. No contest. Still, even as I'm stacking up these two guys against each other, I can't help but think of Will again. Will looks pretty out of place in the lineup with these guys. Ross and Eric are both professionals—they look and dress and act the part—whereas Will is a bit of a bounder or a free spirit or maybe just less than self-motivated.

Why can't I get this guy out of my mind?

Less than two weeks before Christmas, I send out a few Christmas cards. I've never been much into this practice. Beyond those to my sisters and a couple of college friends and my parents (although I didn't send one to my dad last year), I usually send out just a handful. Consequently, I don't do the box thing. I just pick out some cards from the local Hallmark store, and out they go. This year I send a special card to my old address in the city. On it I write, "I hope you're doing well. I've found a good job and am enjoying the quiet life in Black Bear. Good luck and God bless. Love, Cassie." It's not much, and in a way it sounds like an ending, which is not what I meant. So I add a P.S. "If you're ever in the neighborhood, be sure to stop by." And I jot down my cell-phone number. In case he lost it. Then I stuff it into the envelope, and feeling a little nervous, I seal it, stamp it, and drop it along with the others into the mailbox at Black Bear Butte that afternoon.

The lodge is busier than ever during Christmas break, and part of my publicity campaign is to have our own Black Bear mascot on hand to greet kids and give out candy canes. This involved locating a really good black-bear costume from a great online costume company, then hiring a high-school kid named Brandon, who's also a good snowboarder, to play the role of Black Bear. To make our bear a little more friendly and approachable, he also wears a red and white Santa hat and a striped muffler. Black Bear can be spotted in and about the lodge or even riding up the easy lift chair and snowboarding down the bunny hill with comical style. He's been photographed by almost everyone and has even made it into several local newspapers. Plus, we feature him online now. Someone recently suggested we set up a Black Bear blog where he can post his thoughts on snowboarding and whatnot. Obviously, I'll have to play the part, since Brandon's not really much of a writer. But maybe after the Christmas rush settles down, I'll give it a try.

Less than a week before Christmas, however, Brandon gets the flu, and we have no Black Bear. I make the rounds, trying to find someone willing to step in and fill the gap, but all our employees are swamped with their own responsibilities and not too excited about wearing a bear suit all day long. Still, we have children who expect to see Black Bear today. The candy-cane basket is full and waiting. So it is that I decide to don the Black Bear costume myself. I'm a decent skier, and, hey, it might even be fun. Besides, with my marketing campaign fairly neatly tied up, there hasn't been too much on my plate recently. I let Marge know what my plan is and tell her I'll have my cell phone on me in case of any emergencies in the office. But I also ask her to keep my new identity under wraps, since I'm sure the other employees would love to give me a bad time about this. Then I close my office door and change into the ski clothes that I keep here at the lodge for those times I can make a run or two at the end of the day. And I get ready to put the bear outfit on top.

To say this costume smells like the boys' locker room in junior high might be an understatement. I actually give the fuzzy fabric a couple of expensive squirts of my Burberry Brit perfume before I climb in. Eventually I'm all zipped in and situated. I get the Santa hat and muffler in place, then retrieve the basket of candy canes and head out to meet my adoring little fans. Of course, they're not all adoring. I actually make a toddler cry when I bend down to give her a hug. And then there are the older kids who seem bent on harassing the bear.

I decide to escape a particularly obnoxious pair of boys by heading for the slope. Naturally, Black Bear gets special privileges at his own lodge, like not having to wait in lift lines and getting free food from the restaurant, so I zip past the lineup of beginner skiers, and with some help from Amy, the bunny-hill lift girl, I manage to get my furry hind end safely into the lift chair and take off. Feeling like a rock star, I wave to everyone as I ride up the short hill. Of course, getting off the lift chair is a little tricky, as is hold-ing ski poles with bear paws, and I nearly fall flat on my big snout as I plunge forward. But I manage to balance myself and slowly work my way back and forth down the hill, waving my poles to onlookers who cheer for me. This is actually pretty cool.

I do a variation of handing out candy canes and cruising the bunny hill for most of the day. It's a little past noon when I see Ross watching me with his hand over his mouth, as if he's suppressing laughter. Marge must've informed him of my whereabouts.

"How's it going, Black Bear?" he asks as he extends his hand to shake my paw.

"Just grrreat," I say in my deep Black Bear voice, which makes him throw back his head and laugh.

"So is this going to be a regular gig for you?" he asks quietly.

"You bet," I roar back at him, noticing that I'm being watched by some small sets of eyes. "I have no plans to hibernate *this* year. Not with great snow like this. I'm Black Bear, and this is *my* lodge!" Then I hold up one paw for a high-five, and he gives it to me.

"You go, Black Bear!"

A peppy Gloria Estefan song begins to play over the sound sys-tem, and I start doing a pretty uncoordinated but spirited bear dance to "Get on Your Feet." This naturally draws a little crowd, and soon I've got a bunch of kids dancing with me. I can't believe we pay Brandon to do this. This isn't work; this is a blast!

Time seems to fly, and before I know it, my shift as Black Bear is just about over. Unfortunately the obnoxious preteen boys are still giving me a bad time, so I decide to escape them with one last ride up the bunny hill. As I'm going up, I hear my cell phone ringing, so I fumble around until I find it and then answer.

"Cassie?" says a male voice.

"Yes?"

"This is Will."

Okay, now it's time to get off the lift, and yet I don't want to hang up. "Will," I say quickly, "hold on a sec, okay?" Then I manage to get off the chair with both poles and my cell phone all intact.

"Hey, Will," I say as I ski off to one side, "how's it going?"

"Really good."

"Cool." I wave at the little girls who are curiously watching Black Bear chatting on his cell phone. Why not?

"I got your Christmas card."

"You did?" Okay, not the smartest response, but what do you expect from a girl in a bear suit?

"I really appreciated—"

But his words are cut off, because in that same instant, I feel a big push from behind, and suddenly I'm barreling down the slope with both poles in one hand and my cell phone in the other, trying not to run down the beginner skiers who are weaving back and forth in front of me. Not wanting to lose my cell phone or wipe out the cute little preschooler in the pink ski outfit directly ahead, I first ski on one leg and then the other. I can hear people cheering for my brilliant stunt work. A little boy in bright orange takes a sharp turn, then falls down right in front of me, and it's all I can do not to plow straight through him. That's when I start to lose it. I feel myself careening too sharply to the left, and I know I won't be able to regain my balance this time.

I tumble first sideways, then in a somersault, and finally I land in a heap of fur and snow and am applauded by a happy crowd of onlookers who obviously think I did all this on purpose. Despite the throbbing pain in my left knee, I stand up and take a few bows, and the audience claps even louder. I'm thinking someone should pop in the "Get on Your Feet" song again. Although I doubt I can dance with this aching knee.

"Way to go, Black Bear," yells one of the obnoxious boys in a mean tone as his friend pumps his fist in the air. Guilty as presumed.

I growl at them, holding my paws high like I plan to catch and devour them whole, which might not be a bad idea. Then I realize I still have my cell phone in hand, but it looks like I've lost the connection. So I pocket it. Waving to my adoring fans, I start to make my exit, trying not to limp as I go. But then something makes me stop.

There amid the happy onlookers is a familiar face. To my total surprise, I realize it belongs to none other than Will Sorensen. He's not dressed for skiing but looks pretty cool in his jeans and faded denim jacket with a tweedy scarf wrapped around his neck.

"Will!" I say, sounding slightly hoarse. I think that bear voice has worn out my vocal cords.

"Huh?" he stares at me with a seriously puzzled expression,

which reminds me that I'm still in bear drag, and of course this makes me feel totally embarrassed. Why did I say anything? I could've dashed inside and changed. But instead I stupidly revealed my identity. I am so pathetic.

"Cassie?" he says in a lowered voice.

"Name's Black Bear," I growl at him for the sake of my fans. "You'll find Cassie in the building." Then I wave him toward the lodge. "Come on, I'll show you the way."

"Sure," he says, still looking puzzled.

"Mind if I take your arm?" I growl. "Twisted my knee coming down that hill."

"No problem," he says as he offers me his elbow.

I might look like a tough old bear on the outside, but I feel just a smidgen of a meltdown on the inside.

"You come up here to ski?" I growl at him as we go inside the lodge.

"Maybe…but mostly I came to see my friend Cassie." He turns and gives me another curious look.

"Her office is up those stairs," I say, wondering if my knee is going to handle it. "But let's take the elevator."

So, using Will as my crutch, I limp toward the elevator, and as soon as the doors close, I confess. "It's me in here, Will."

Of course, this cracks him up. He's still laughing as he escorts me to my office. But before we're all the way in, I hear Ross calling my name.

"Cassie?" he says, coming up behind me. "You okay?"

"She fell down," explains Will. "She might've hurt her knee."

So they both help me into my office and get me seated on one of the leather club chairs across from my desk. Then I remove the bear head and let out a loud groan as I rub my knee.

Will laughs again. "I can't believe that was you, Cassie. Is that your job here? You play the bear?"

Ross chuckles. "She was just filling in for the regular bear."

"Oh."

"I'm sorry," says Ross. "Let me introduce myself." So introductions are made, and I tell Ross what a great chef Will is and that he works at Terrazzo de Giordano.

"That's a great restaurant," says Ross. "I've eaten there a couple of times."

"Will took over my apartment when I moved to Black Bear," I continue, as if this all needs explaining, which I realize it doesn't, but I keep going anyway. "I haven't seen him since October."

"Now what about that knee?" asks Ross. "Do you think it's serious?"

"I think it seriously hurts," I say.

"How about if you get out of that costume?" says Ross. "I'll get Marge to send one of the medics up with some ice."

"Let me help you," offers Will as Ross leaves my office. He gently helps me unzip and peel myself out of the smelly bear skin, until it hangs around my ankles like a dead thing.

"Whew," I say as I sit back down and fan myself with my hands. "That's an improvement."

"How about those ski boots?" asks Will as he stoops down and releases the tension.

"Thanks," I tell him.

He gently eases them off, then removes the deflated bear, laying it across my desk almost reverently. And I lean back and let out a sigh of relief. "I feel better already."

Ross quickly returns with the medic in tow, and after a quick examination, which reveals the embarrassing fact that my legs need a shave, he tells me I might've pulled some ligaments. "But nothing appears to be broken," he says as he snugly wraps my knee in an elastic brace. "You'll still want to make an appointment with your doctor and get an x-ray. In the meantime, stay off of it, and keep it wrapped and on ice." He hands me a sample package of Advil. "And this might help too."

Ross hands me the water bottle from my desk. "So you're going to be okay, Black Bear?"

"I think so, but I guess I'll have to retire now."

"Well, Marge said Brandon called this afternoon, and he's feeling better. He thinks it was just a twenty-four-hour bug. He should be back tomorrow."

"Good."

"You take care now, Cassie," says the medic as he picks up his case and heads for the door.

I thank him. Then he and Ross both leave, so that it's just Will and me in here. I feel awkward and self-conscious.

"So...," I say as I unzip my L.L.Bean polar fleece jacket to let some cool air in, "what brings you to Black Bear?"

Now Will looks uncomfortable, and I feel bad for putting him on the spot like this. "I mean, it's great to see you and everything," I say quickly. "I'm just so surprised."

"Well, as I mentioned on the phone, uh, before we were disconnected." He chuckles as if he's recalling the whole unfortunate scene of the tumbling, bumbling bear tearing it up on the bunny hill. "I got your Christmas card, and I thought, hey, I've got a couple of days off, why don't I head on up here to see you." He grins. "So I did."

"Cool."

"I almost called you a few weeks ago," he says. "Mr. Snyder said you'd been by. But I figured you were just checking to make sure I hadn't made a mess of your place."

"Oh no," I say, "that wasn't it at all. I happened to be in town for some meetings and thought I'd pop in and say hi. How's the job?"

"It's been good. And they really seem to like me. But I'm starting to dream bigger now. I think I might start a place of my own... someday."

"Good for you."

"And you like your job? You finally found what you wanted to be when you grew up?"

"Sort of. I mean it's a fantastic job. And I love almost everything about it…"

"But not everything?" He studies me closely.

"I'm not sure."

He laughs. "Look at us. We've come such a long way in such a short time. And yet we're still not totally happy with it."

"We're just a couple of whiners, aren't we?" I tease.

"Guess we should just grow up and count our blessings."

I glance at my watch now. "Looks like my workday is finished."

"Do you have any plans for dinner?"

"Not really." If Will wasn't here, I wouldn't be surprised if Ross asked me to get a bite. I glance toward Ross's office and see that his lights are off. I doubt he's gone home this early, but he's definitely checked out of his office.

"Want to join me?"

I smile at Will. "I'd love to."

"I borrowed a car to come up here. I've thought about getting one, but it's so easy to ride my bike to work, and parking is such a pain in the city."

"I've got my car up here too," I say. "It's just an old beater, but it gets me back and forth okay."

"Do you think you can drive with that knee?"

I rub my left knee. "Yeah. It's the right leg that I need."

"Want me to help you down to your car?"

"That's a good idea." Then I point to the closet. "I've got some Uggs in there. Would you mind getting them?" I realize he might see anything in that closet, since that's where I keep spare clothes and other possibly embarrassing necessities. But under the circumstances, I don't even care.

I slip on the Uggs, remove the ice pack, and carefully stand. Testing my weight on my knee, I'm surprised that it's not too bad. "I think I'll be okay. But there's also a black Kate Spade bag in that closet. Do you mind getting it for me?"

He looks in the closet, finally holding up the bag. "This it?"

"Yep. Thanks." I attempt to hobble toward my desk.

"Remember the medic said to stay off it," he reminds me as he loops the strap of my bag over his shoulder, then puts his other arm around my waist. "You can lean on me."

"Nice look with the bag," I point out. "You're a real metrosexual male."

He laughs. "I hope that's a compliment." Then he helps me pack my laptop, and we're ready to get out of here. I feel like a clumsy participant in a three-legged race as we slowly make our way out to the elevator, then awkwardly proceed to the parking lot.

"I'm glad it's not icy today," I say as we head for my car. Will helps me in and puts my briefcase and other things in the back.

"Where shall we meet?"

I look down at my ski clothes. "I could go home and change," I say, suddenly feeling tired and hungry. "Or we could just go to the brewery—you know, keep it casual."

"I vote for the brewery."

I grin. "Me too."

So I give him brief directions. Black Bear isn't exactly a metropolis. Then I take off, driving carefully but quickly down the mountain. I hope I can get to the brewery just a few minutes ahead of him. This might give me time to do some damage control. I realize I probably look a fright after wearing that sweaty bear costume all day. And I'm sure I don't smell too great either. I just hope I remembered to put my Burberry Brit back in my bag.

Nineteen

I'm somewhat back to a presentable normal by the time Will arrives at the brewery—hair in place, mascara smudges removed, and fresh lip gloss applied. Fortunately, my perfume was in my bag, and I smell a bit better. I come out of the bathroom, still limping, and nearly run smack into Will.

"Good timing," he says as he hooks his hand beneath my arm. "Let me help you."

"Thanks," I tell him. "It's actually feeling a lot better."

"Hopefully it's nothing serious."

"Cassie!" calls out Gary Frye. He's waving from a table where several of my old friends, including Bridget and Penny, are seated.

"Come and join us," calls Bridget. She's eying Will and probably wondering what I'm doing with this guy when Ross and I have something going on. I haven't told her—or anyone for that matter—about Will. I mean, what is there to tell?

"These are some old high-school friends." I explain about Friday-night happy hour. "I'll just say a quick hello."

He nods. "Cool."

So I introduce Will as an old friend from the city, and he smiles and greets everyone politely.

"Keeping this guy a secret, are you?" teases Penny as she winks at Will. I'm thinking Penny's had a little too much to drink already, but I just smile at her.

"Will's not a secret," I say, "but we would like to catch up." I nod toward a table in the corner. "So if you'll excuse us."

They complain, but Will and I depart just the same. I don't want them to start grilling us about our relationship. Not that we have a relationship. But I want to know more about why Will came here today. Was it really because of my Christmas card? What did I say in it anyway?

"You really have a life," says Will as we sit down.

"Yeah, I guess so."

"And you've changed."

"Changed?"

He nods. "Your hair's different, and you look, well, great. But you've changed on the inside too."

I frown slightly. "Is that bad?"

He shakes his head. "No, that's good."

I smile. "Really?"

"Definitely. It's like you're more confident, more sure of yourself. Like you really know who you are now. You weren't like that before."

"Well, it hasn't been exactly easy. And it didn't happen overnight." I tell him a little about my mom and her shocking transformation and that she's been dating a guy my age. I go on and on, even telling him about my mall encounter with Eric and how glad I was to be over him. Will is a great listener.

"But enough about me," I say, feeling silly for being so self-absorbed. "How's it going with you? Have you seen Monica?" What I really want to know is whether he's got another girlfriend. But no way am I asking that.

"I've really been getting a lot of hours at work," he begins after the waiter brings our drinks and takes our orders. "In fact, this is the first time I've had a Friday off, but I sort of put my foot down and demanded it. I have to be back at work for tomorrow night, but I insisted on some time off during Christmas."

"Good for you."

"Yeah. And the manager was fairly decent about it. I guess I've proven myself, and they actually want to keep me around."

"Well, of course."

"I've already worked my way up to head chef," he says proudly.

"Congratulations!"

He nods and takes a sip of his Black Bear Porter. "Yeah, it's pretty cool." Then he looks at me. "I feel like I have you to thank for it, Cassie."

I wave my hand. "No. You're a great cook, Will. I had nothing—"

"You encouraged me. When I was totally bummed and ready to give up, you reached out to me." He shakes his head. "It still amazes me, because you were hurting pretty bad yourself."

I nod. "Yeah. But what you might not realize is that you helped me a lot too. That one night when I was so depressed—it seems unbelievable now—but I was actually considering taking some kind of pills or something." I sort of laugh. "But I didn't have much in the medicine cabinet, and I didn't think an overdose of laxatives would exactly do the trick."

He makes a face. "Yuck."

"Yeah, whatta way to go."

"I'm glad you didn't."

"Me too. Anyway, you were a real godsend to me, Will. I mean that. And I guess I've wanted to thank you too. I suppose that's why I sent the Christmas card."

Now there's a long silence. We both sip our beers, and I wonder if that's it. Nothing more to say.

"Oh, you asked about Monica…" He stops.

Suddenly I think, *Oh, no, they're back together*. I so don't want to hear this. I mean, sure, if they're back together, fine. I just don't want to know.

"Well, I got to thinking about what she did, using your credit card like that. And I decided to see if I could track her down through some of her old friends. I tried and tried, but all I came up with was dead ends. A couple of people think she's in Los Angeles, trying to get discovered and make it big."

"That sounds like Monica."

"Anyway, I've still got some people looking for her, and if I hear anything, I'll let you know. She needs to pay you back, Cassie."

I nod. "You're right. But I've pretty much kissed that money good-bye. And in a way, I'm glad."

"Huh?"

"Well, it was kind of a last straw for me. It forced me to move back home. And even though it was a little rough for a while, I'm happier here." I consider my next line, not sure that I want to toss it out, but then I figure it's simply the truth. "Not only that…it kind of connected me to you. I mean, crazy as it sounds, if Monica hadn't pulled a fast one on us, well, we never would've gotten to know each other. I'd still be thinking of you as that good-for-nothing loser who was sponging off poor Monica."

His brows lift. "That's what you thought?"

"Sorry." I shake my head. "Didn't mean to say that."

But he just laughs. "No, it's okay. Your character assessment wasn't far from the truth."

"Except I know now that Monica was the one who sponged off you. And me too. So anyway, for that reason, I don't really care about it anymore. There's a verse in the Bible that says all things work together for good if you love the Lord—or something to that effect. And I feel like maybe that's happening with me."

"Speaking of the Bible, and you're probably not going to believe this, but after you said you'd be praying for me, well, it got me thinking about my mom. She's pretty religious. I hadn't spoken to my parents since they got mad at me for dropping out of culinary school, which was after I dropped out of college. They pretty much cut me off when I hooked up with Monica. They thought it was sinful for us to be living together." He shakes his head. "But I honestly think it would've been a worse sin to marry her. She might've been good looking, but she was a mistake from the get-go."

"Kind of like Eric for me."

"Yeah. Anyway, after hearing some things you said, I decided maybe it was time to give up my little rebellion against my parents, and I gave my mom a call. We had a nice long talk. Then she sent me my old Bible, and I've actually been reading it."

"Seriously?"

He nods. "I know it probably seems pretty weird. Will Sorensen reading the Bible."

"I think it's pretty cool."

His expression turns sad. "The downside of getting in touch with my parents is that I found out my dad is dying."

"I'm sorry."

"Me too." He sighs. "But at least I've been able to talk to him, to mend bridges. I even offered to move back home and help out, but my parents are so glad that I have a good job and am getting back on my feet that they said to stick with it. But I promised to come home for a few days at Christmas."

"Will, I'm so happy for you," I say. "Your life is really on track."

"Thanks to you."

"Maybe God used me," I admit, "the same way he used you. But you've been making some great choices too. You'd better take some of the credit."

The waiter sets our food on the table. "So I just felt like I needed to come and say thanks," Will says. "It seemed like I owed you that much."

"You don't owe me a thing."

He starts to chuckle as he picks up a french fry.

"Something funny about your food?" I ask. "I'm sure it's nothing like what you're used to at Terrazzo de Giordano."

"No, that's not it." He grins. "I was just replaying that scene of Black Bear cartwheeling down the mountain.

"I did not cartwheel," I point out.

He laughs. "Well, whatever it was, I hope someone got it on film."

I laugh. "You know, that would be great to have on our Web site. Maybe I can talk Brandon, our regular bear, into reenacting it for me tomorrow."

"How's your knee?"

"Not too bad. I think it'll be fine if I give it some rest."

"You should probably still get it checked."

"Yeah. I'll make an appointment, maybe on Monday."

Will points another fry toward the entry. "Hey, isn't that Ross, the dude from the ski lodge?"

I look up and am surprised to see Ross coming into the brewery. Then I feel bad to see that he's by himself, because I know he doesn't like to eat alone. I wave to him, and he comes over to our table to say hello.

"How's the knee?" he asks with concern.

"I was just telling Will that I think it's going to be okay. Want to join us?"

He looks a little uncomfortable as he glances from me to Will, then shakes his head. "No, that's okay." He holds up a newspaper. "I thought I'd catch up on the latest."

"If you're sure."

"I'm sure." He smiles at Will. "You kids have fun." Then he goes to the other side of the room and slides into a booth.

"So what does Ross do?" asks Will.

"Ross owns Black Bear Butte," I tell him. "Well, he and his family own it. But he pretty much runs the place, and that makes him my boss."

Will nods. "I think he likes you."

"What do you mean?" I study Will.

He smiles. "I mean I think your boss thinks you're hot, Cassie."

I laugh nervously. "What on earth makes you think that?"

"I could tell by the way he looked at you just now and by the way he spoke to you. Trust me. I might be a guy, but I pick up on these things." His eyes twinkle. "It's my artistic and sensitive nature."

"Well, that's just—just—silly."

"Is Ross single?"

"Well, yes. But that doesn't mean anything. Probably what you picked up on is the fact that Ross and I are good friends. We often get a bite to eat together, and we do things together sometimes but just as friends. Co-workers, you know. Ross even made sure that I clearly understood that right from the beginning."

"Maybe he's the one who doesn't understand."

"Oh, Will." I wave my hand in dismissal. "Really, we're just friends." Then I change the subject by telling him about my mom going out with Ross. She thought there was something going on between the two of them, I explain, but Ross made it clear that he wasn't ready for anything serious yet. "I think it's sweet that his wife's memory means that much to him. I can't even imagine being loved like that."

Will nods thoughtfully. "Oh, it could happen, Cassie."

I feel myself blush and wonder if I read more into that sentence than was there. Once again I change the subject by telling him about the new French restaurant in town. Of course, I don't mention that it was Ross who took me there or that his friends are the owners.

"Cool," he says. "I love French cuisine. I'll have to try it out sometime."

"Well, you'll have to come back to Black Bear then."

He nods. "I might just do that."

"Are you driving back to the city tonight?"

"Actually, I got a room at the Ski Inn. Is it any good?"

"Well, it's the cheapest lodging in town, and college kids like to party there. Hopefully you'll get some sleep." Then I wink at him. "Unless you decide to party too."

"I think I've left my partying days behind."

"Speaking of college kids, it looks like winter-break invasion is in full swing." I nod to a rowdy bunch who have taken over the bar. Still garbed in outdoor wear, they probably just came down from the mountain too. "This is the time of year when the locals tend to lay low."

"Would that be you too?"

I shrug. "They don't intimidate me. I'd be more worried if they weren't here. My job is to lure as many customers as possible." I rub my sore knee. "I'd probably want to hang out and have some fun myself, but this knee is starting to feel like it could use some more ice."

Will picks up the check. "Then we should make sure you get safely home."

Knowing this isn't really a date, I open my purse to pay for my half, but Will stops me, saying it's his treat, and I don't argue. Actually all I can think is that I need to get home. My knee is throbbing now, and the elastic bandage feels like it's turned into a tourniquet. My toes are actually getting numb.

"Sorry to be such a party pooper," I tell Will as he helps me to my car. "But this knee is really starting to hurt. I guess maybe I won't wait until Monday to get checked after all."

"You should probably get some crutches," he suggests.

"Where do you get crutches, I wonder."

"You know, at a pharmacy. Haven't you ever been on crutches before?"

"Actually, I've been spared."

"Well, I played soccer for years, which resulted in a few sprains. I know a thing or two about crutches. How about if I pick some up for you?"

"But where?" I ask. "Our only pharmacy is closed now."

"What's the closest town with a Wal-Mart or ShopKo?"

I tell him, and he promises to be back in about an hour. "With crutches."

So I tell him where I live and that I'll see him later. As I drive home, I try to distract myself from the pain by thinking about what a sweet guy he is. I mean, how many guys would drive for an hour to pick up crutches for a friend? On his only day off? On Friday night, to boot!

I hobble into the house and am not surprised to see that Mom's not home. This probably means she's with Todd, and that still aggravates me. I thought Mom would've outgrown this phase by now. But it's like she's only getting worse. Like she really thinks she's in her thirties. I just don't get it.

Twenty

Searching for some kind of painkiller, I go through my mom's downstairs medicine cabinet and find an old prescription of Tylenol 3. It must be left over from when I came home to have my wisdom teeth out a few years ago. Even if it's past the expiration date, I decide to take two. Then I fill a Ziploc bag with ice, wrap it in a dishtowel, and make my way to the sunroom sofa. I unwrap the constricting bandage and situate the ice, then lean back and wait for the pain to go away.

"Cassie?" says my mom from somewhere above me.

I open my eyes, then blink, thinking maybe I'm dreaming as I see Mom holding what seem to be a pair of aluminum crutches and a bouquet of pink roses. "Huh?"

"What's going on?"

Still groggy, I try to remember. "Oh yeah," I say, pointing to my swollen knee. "I took a tumble on the bunny slope."

"On the bunny slope?" She looks skeptical.

"It's a long story."

"Well, I found these on the porch. I'm guessing they must be for you."

"Will," I say, suddenly remembering his mercy trip. "I must've been asleep. What time is it anyway?"

"It's after midnight," she says.

"Whoa," I sit up now. "I took two of your Tylenol 3 pills."

She laughs. "Good grief, that was from Cammie's wisdom teeth. They must be old by now. Did they even work?"

"Apparently."

"Well, maybe you should sleep down here tonight. Can I get you anything?"

I take advantage of my crippled state, allowing my mom to bring me some water and blankets and pillows. Finally she sets the pink roses, nicely arranged in a vase, on the coffee table before me.

"Thanks, Mom."

She also sets the bottle of pain medication on the table next to my water. "It says you can take two every four to six hours. And, judging by the size of the swelling, you might need to."

I thank her again and now feel bad for having been so down on her tonight, at least in my mind. "Did you have a nice evening with Todd?" I ask, hoping that I sound sincere and not patronizing.

She looks surprised. "As a matter of fact, I did."

I sigh. "Good."

"And who is this Will fellow? I don't believe I've met him."

"He's a friend from the city. He just happened to show up when I hurt my knee. He made a run to Ferris, I'm guessing to Wal-Mart, to pick up these crutches."

"That was nice." She points to the roses. "Those are nice too."

"He's a nice guy."

She frowns slightly. "So what's going on with you and Ross these days?"

"Me and Ross?" I shrug. "As I keep telling everyone, we're friends and co-workers, and that's about it."

"I wouldn't be so sure, Cassie. Folks in town seem to assume that you guys are an item."

Now I'm not sure how to react. The tone of her voice sounds slightly disapproving, like she's judging me, and I have no idea why. And it makes me mad. "So do the folks in town assume that you and Todd are an item too?"

She lets out an exasperated sigh. "Well, I just thought you should know, Cassie. I wasn't trying to pick a fight with you."

"I'm not fighting," I say defensively.

"It's late," she says. "Good night."

I take two more pain pills and wonder about the little exchange between Mom and me just now. Does she feel like we're in some sort of competition? Or is she just being a nosy mother? Or maybe she's still interested in Ross. If that's the case, why is she still going out with Todd? Is it possible she's trying to appear younger, for Ross's benefit, by stringing Todd along in their crazy dating game? And, if that's the case, which seems nuts, doesn't she realize that it only makes her look cheap and slutty?

"She's in the sunroom," I hear my mother saying as I wake up again.

Who is she talking to? And what time is it? I fumble for my

watch, squinting to read the dial. It's almost nine, but I'm still groggy from those last pain pills I took a couple of hours ago.

"Hey, Cassie," says Will as he comes into the sunroom with a large brown bag, which looks like it might contain groceries.

I sit up and pull the blanket around me, wondering if I have dried saliva on my chin or maybe eye buggers or bed head or raccoon eyes from smudged mascara. "Will?" I say as if I don't quite remember him. "What are you doing here?"

He grins. "Making you breakfast…if you don't mind."

"Breakfast?" I shake my head as if I'm trying to grasp the concept of food eaten in the morning.

"Yeah. I figured you wouldn't be up and about yet. I thought I could fix you some breakfast." He nods over his shoulder. "And your mom too, if that's okay."

"It's okay by me," calls my mom in a slightly flirty voice. "I adore a man who cooks."

He nods. "Cool. I'll just make myself at home then."

"Yeah, sure," I say as I swing my legs over the edge of the couch and fumble for the crutches.

"Let me help you adjust those," he says, coming to my side. "Stand up straight now." Then he actually puts his hands under my armpits, and I cannot imagine how nasty I must smell since I haven't showered since my tumbling-bear incident. Judging by the dead-animal taste in my mouth, my breath might be fatal. I try not to breathe as he adjusts the height of the crutches, then snaps them into place.

"How's that?"

I nod, worried that I might pass out from lack of oxygen. "Perfect," I say. Then I try to make my way out of the sunroom. "Look, I can walk," I call over my shoulder. "Now let's see if I can take a shower."

"Be careful on those stairs," calls Mom. Of course she's all dressed, looking cute and perky in her jeans and hoodie. I can only imagine what Will must be thinking—like *This is the mom? Whoa.*

"I better help you," says Will, still behind me.

"I'm okay," I assure him, thinking I do not want him to see or smell me like this.

"Let's just make sure you get upstairs okay," he says, his hand gently resting in the small of my back.

It does prove tricky. Will explains how to place the crutches and how to lift my weight, and I do nearly lose my balance a couple of times. "See," he says when we reach the top. "It takes a little practice. Make sure you yell when you're ready to come back down. Breakfast will be ready in about an hour. Does that work for you?"

"Sounds perfect," I tell him as I hobble toward my bedroom. Normally it wouldn't take me an hour to shower and dress, but working with my new handicap, I think it just might today. Plus, I figure I need to put some care into my appearance today. It's humiliating enough to have been seen by Will in my current condition, not to mention yesterday's bear routine. I'd like him to see me looking better today.

It does take most of an hour for the transformation, but when

I'm done, I think it was worth it. And when I call down the stairs for Will's assistance, I think he might even appreciate the improvement in my personal hygiene.

"Looking good," he says as he scampers up the stairs to help me. He gives me some pointers, then goes backward down the stairs ahead of me. I imagine myself tumbling forward, flattening him, and possibly killing us both. But somehow I manage to get all the way down without a hitch.

"Way to go," he says as we walk toward the kitchen. "You're already a pro at this."

"Smells good down here," I say.

"You should see what this guy has put together," says Mom. "Blintzes and crepes and fresh fruit, and let me tell you, I'm impressed."

"But it's not your usual high-fiber granola and soy milk," I remind her in a teasing tone. "However will you manage?"

"Sometimes you have to make sacrifices."

"Wow," I say when I see the table all set and looking like a spread for a culinary magazine. "This looks awesome." I glance at Mom. "Yeah, *some* sacrifice."

"Will even talked me into pulling out my old coffee maker," says Mom as we sit down.

"*Real* coffee?" I say hopefully.

"Here you go," says Will as he places a steaming cup in front of me. "Cream?"

"*Real* cream?" I gaze up at Will and wonder if I'm falling in love with this guy, or is it simply my stomach doing the thinking?

He laughs. "You sound as if you've been seriously deprived."

"Oh, I have," I assure him. "Mom has a strict regimen here. Things like cream and coffee and basically anything that tastes even slightly good are totally prohibited."

"Not today," says Will as he passes the cheese blintzes to me.

"Will tells me he's a professional chef," says Mom as we eat. "I told him I'd love to hire him to help with Cammie's wedding brunch."

"And I told her I'd love to come, but I seriously doubt I can get New Year's Eve off at the restaurant."

"Didn't you already hire the caterers?" I ask with a melt-in-your-mouth morsel of crepe still in my mouth.

"Yes, but they won't do anything as good as this."

"Obviously," I say, winking at Will.

"I don't usually get to fix brunch," he explains. "So it's fun for a change."

"You usually cook Italian then?" asks Mom.

"I do for now."

"Do you have other plans?" she asks.

"Well, I won't stay at Terrazzo forever, that's for sure."

"What would you like to do?" I ask, holding a bite of crepe in midair.

He seems to consider this. "Well, my dream used to be to have my own restaurant someday. Although I see that can be pretty demanding. At least it is at Terrazzo. The owner keeps complaining that he never gets a vacation. So maybe I'd do something different."

"What would it be?"

"I'm not sure. I'd want it to be something with a wide base of appeal. Not necessarily anything like haute cuisine since that can be a bit trendy, as in here today and gone tomorrow. I love making desserts, but I'm not sure that's enough to make a business out of."

"Well, there's always room for a good restaurant in Black Bear," says Mom. "You should consider setting it up here."

"I wish…" Then he shakes his head. "It'll probably be a few years before I save up enough for the kind of place I'd like to start." He chuckles. "As if I even know what that would be."

"Don't wait too long," says Mom as she helps herself to another blintz. "Our little town might look sleepy, but we're growing fast."

Will laughs. "Well, that little grocery store of yours looked pretty sleepy to me. It was a challenge to find the ingredients I needed this morning."

"I'll bet." I nod. "I keep telling the manager that the store needs to expand."

"Everyone's been telling them that for years," says Mom.

We talk more about our small town's future and what kinds of businesses we'd like to see here. But my knee is starting to throb again, and it seems that Mom is pretty much dominating the conversation, which I'm beginning to resent. Can't she see how ridiculous she looks, leaning over the table in her too-tight T-shirt that exposes way too much skin as she gives Will those big blue eyes?

"Excuse me," I say, suddenly standing and reaching for my crutches. "My knee is hurting. I think I'll go find some Advil."

"What are you going to do about that knee?" asks Will.

"We don't have any emergency medical facilities here in Black Bear," says my mom, "although we're trying to get something."

"How about in Ferris?" he asks. "That's a fairly large town."

"They have a hospital," I say, thinking I probably don't need to go there.

"Why don't I drive you over?" he suggests.

"Oh, I don't think it's necessary," I protest. "It's probably just a sprain."

"The medic said you might have torn some ligaments," he persists. "Wouldn't you rather take care of it now instead of putting it off until Monday?"

"But it might feel better on Monday," I say, sounding like a five-year-old.

Will doesn't accept my rationale. So, after cleaning up the brunch things, he insists on driving me to Ferris, where he patiently waits for me to get checked and x-rayed. I feel rather silly when the doctor proclaims my knee to be "most likely a bad sprain." Like I didn't know that. Still, she writes a new prescription for pain meds, which might be worthwhile, and tells me that my home treatment was just what the doctor would've ordered. "If it doesn't improve or gets worse, you might consider arthroscopic surgery." Then she gives me the business card of a sports physician and wraps my knee in a more substantial bandage. "This will support the joint without cutting off your blood supply," she explains.

I clomp back out to the waiting area and tell Will my less-than-exciting prognosis, apologizing for what was probably a waste of his time, but he insists it was worth it and seems genuinely glad it's not serious. By the time we're back home, he explains that he needs to return to the city now. "I'm working tonight. If I leave now, I should get there just in time."

"Thanks for everything," I tell him.

He smiles. "Just consider it my little payback to you for helping me last October."

I shake my head. "I think I must owe you big time now."

He hugs me. "Let's not keep score, okay? And take care of that knee. No more Black Bear stunt maneuvers down the mountain."

"That's for sure."

I stand by the front window, watching him back out and drive away. For some unexplainable reason, it feels like a small part of my soul is going with him, and I'm actually tearing up. I'm probably just worn out from my knee injury. Still, I wonder if I'll ever see him again. Is this the end of an odd little relationship? All accounts settled? Not that we're keeping score.

"He's a nice guy," says Mom from behind me.

"Yeah, he is," I admit, blinking back tears as I continue to gaze out the window. It looks like more snow is on the way. A good thing for the slopes. I take a deep breath as I turn around to face my mom. I briefly consider telling her more about how Will and I met and the whole Monica factor and how weird it was, but I just can't. Maybe it's the baby-pink rhinestone T-shirt, or maybe it's those snug, low-rise jeans, but this woman just doesn't look like a mother to me. Instead of someone to trust and confide in, she's practically the competition. And then I remember her flirty conversation with Will that upset me earlier. My mom, the cougar.

Okay, it probably doesn't help matters that I'm feeling sluggish and clumsy and heavy, struggling on these stupid crutches. It's like I'm the old woman here, and my mom is this spry, energetic young thing. So wrong.

"I think I'll take a nap," I say as I hobble toward the stairs.

I'm sure my distressed feelings regarding Will are a combination of several factors—including that I'm hormonal right now. Seriously, why would I be interested in a guy who's working as a cook, doesn't even own a car, not to mention real estate, and is probably still up to his eyeballs in debt? Add the fact that he's a couple of years younger than I am (I've always had a thing about needing a guy who's older than I am), and it's just totally ridiculous.

I reach my bed at last and dump myself onto it. I shouldn't trouble myself with any of this since I'm sure Will has absolutely no interest in me. He's just being a nice guy and showing his appreciation. End of story.

Twenty-One

"T hat friend of yours is a real hottie," says Bridget as we get coffee after church the next day. "He actually looks a little like Matthew McConaughey. I can understand why you've been keeping him in hiding."

"He hasn't been in hiding."

She chuckles. "Well, I wouldn't blame you if you did. Now tell me all about him. And is it serious? And how does Ross Goldberg fit into all this? And what is it with you Cantrell women? First your mom, and now you—it's like you guys are keeping all the good men to yourselves."

Okay, this makes me laugh. I begin by telling her about Will and how I helped him out in the city and how he wanted to show his appreciation. "And it was nice having him around after my knee injury."

"And that's all there is to it?"

"Pretty much so." I take a slow sip of my latte.

"Does that mean you are serious about Ross then?"

"Why are you so interested in my love life?" I ask. "Or rather lack of it?"

"Inquiring minds want to know."

So I give her my old we're-just-friends spiel again. But she's not buying it. I change the subject to her and her art. "How's the mural coming?"

"Oh, I finished it. Now I just need to figure out what to do with it."

I consider this. "Hey, maybe you should let me take a look at it. There's this big blank wall at the west entrance to the lodge. I think it could handle some art. I mean, if it worked. And if Ross liked it."

"Seriously?"

"Sure. Can I have a peek?"

She's already standing. "What're we waiting for?"

Soon I'm hobbling up the walk to Bridget's house, which turns out to be this incredibly cool bungalow. "This is charming," I tell her as she unlocks the door.

"Thanks. I like it."

I look around the interior of her house as we go in. "Really, Bridget, I so love this place—everything you've done. It's really cozy and homey."

"Except for that," she points to the huge painting that monopolizes her living room and dining area.

"Wow," I say as I step closer to look at an impressionistic take of the local mountains. "It's great."

"Do you think it could work at the lodge?"

I nod. "Definitely."

Now Bridget is practically jumping up and down as she claps her hands.

"But it's not up to me," I remind her.

She laughs. "Well, if anyone can talk Ross Goldberg into it, I'm guessing it would be you."

I give her a warning look. "Don't be so sure."

"But you will talk to him?"

"Hey," I say suddenly, "I have an even better idea. How would you feel about loaning it to us? We could go ahead and hang it during the holidays, and if Ross likes it, you can offer to sell it."

She nods. "At least it would get it out of my hair."

"And it'd give you some publicity—and Blue Pond too. Hey, maybe we can do some kind of cross promotion with the gallery and—"

"You really do have a marketing mind, don't you?"

I grin. "It's my job."

"Can you figure out a way to get it up there?" I ask. "And how to hang it?"

"Yep. I'll be on it first thing in the morning. Will that work?"

"Perfect."

Then she hugs me. "You're such a good friend, Cassidy. I'm so glad you moved back to Black Bear. Even if you do hog all the good men."

I roll my eyes.

"See you in the morning then?" I say as I hobble toward the door.

"You bet."

My crutches, combined with the goodwill of Christmas spirit, garner me some sympathy on Monday. And I use this to my benefit when I tell Ross what I've done with Bridget's art.

"Really?"

I can't read his expression. Is he vexed or simply curious? "She's getting it into place as we speak," I admit, leaning on my crutches. "I hope you don't mind."

"You really think it'll look okay up there?"

"I do. And it's better than that big bare wall." Then I tell him about my plan to do some cross promoting with Blue Pond. "I've been trying to come up with a way to connect with that gallery."

He slowly nods. "I like your thinking."

"I hope you like the painting too," I say. "And if you don't, it'll be gone after the holidays anyway."

By the afternoon, Ross not only likes the painting but is ready to make Bridget an offer. Everyone seems to think it looks perfect, almost as if it were a commissioned piece, and I feel like the belle of the ball. Well, other than these crutches, which are starting to wear some serious calluses on my armpits. The good news is that my knee is feeling a tiny bit better. My plan is to swim every day after work as a form of therapy for my knee. Ross has even suggested that I leave early to do this.

"It's a work-related injury," he says. "Do whatever you need to take care of it."

"You worried that I might sue?" I tease.

He smiles. "Not too worried. But maybe I can buy you off with some dinner tonight? You think you'll feel like eating after your workout?"

"I feel like eating right now." I laugh, then remember how it made me sad to see him eating alone on Friday night at the brewery. Who knows what he did for meals during the rest of the weekend? "But I'll feel even more like eating after I finish my laps."

"Great. Want to meet at the Den?" He kind of frowns. "We don't have too many options, do we?"

"Not really. But the Den is fine."

As I walk to my car, I call Bridget on my cell phone with the good news about her painting.

"No way!" she squeals. "He's going to make an offer?"

"Yes. So you should be thinking of what it's worth."

"You're the best, Cassidy. I owe you."

I feel happy as I drive toward town. Even with my banged-up knee, my life is in a much better place than it was just a few months ago. And yet...I can't quite put my finger on it, but it still feels like something is missing. Or maybe I'm just restless.

I have a good swim, and Ross and I have a nice dinner. He politely asks me a little about Will. How did we meet? What does he do? And I tell Ross about Will's interest in starting his own restaurant. "Maybe even in a town like Black Bear."

Ross nods with a slight frown. "I've seen so many new restaurants come and go in this town. It's not easy. I even worry about Alex and Elise and Petit Ours Noir. Business is okay now—the ski season is strong. But if things slow down, well, it can be hard on small businesses."

"Yes, I imagined that was the case."

"Speaking of Petit Ours Noir," he says, "they're having a special Christmas Eve dinner Thursday night, just family and friends, and I wondered if you'd like to join me. I realize your family will probably all be here by then, for the wedding and everything, but—"

"I'd love to come," I say.

He seems relieved. "Great."

This reminds me of something else. I'd been toying with the idea of asking Ross to be my date for Cammie's wedding. It seemed a little presumptuous at first, but now I'm thinking it might be okay. "Speaking of the wedding and my family," I begin, "do you think you'd be interested in playing the role of my date for the reception?" I give him a weak smile. "Callie has this dance planned for New Year's Eve. It's not going to be terribly spectacular—it's just at the community center—but she has reminded me several times that I should bring a dancing partner. Any interest?"

"Of course." He smiles. "I'm actually a fairly good dancer, although I'm probably a bit rusty."

"Well, I'm not the greatest, but I do know my way around the dance floor. Hopefully, I won't be doing the two-step on crutches."

"I'm sure we could figure out a way to make it work."

I realize this means that he should probably be invited to the wedding too. I make a mental note to mention this to Callie, although I wouldn't be surprised if she's already done it. For all I know, she's planning my wedding to Ross right along with Cammie's.

The lodge is busier than ever during the days preceding Christmas. But on Christmas Eve, it slows down a little.

"That's normal," says Ross when I express some concern. "People have things to do, getting ready for the holiday. The day after Christmas it'll be standing room only around this place."

Both of my sisters and Callie's hubby and boys have been staying at Mom's house for several days now, and it's been a bit of a madhouse. I find myself relieved to inform them that I have a dinner engagement for Christmas Eve. "It's a special dinner at Petit Ours Noir," I explain.

"I wish we'd known about it," says Callie, sounding slightly jealous. She's sitting on my bed now, pouting. "Maybe we could've booked it too. I've heard that French restaurant is pretty nice."

"Ross only invited me this week," I say as I slip my small diamond-stud earrings into place. "And it's a special dinner, just the owner's family and friends."

"Well, aren't you the lucky one?" says Callie as she leans back on the headboard and puts her feet up on my bed.

"Come on," Cammie urges from where she's leaning against my doorframe, "give Cass a break. I remember times you had a date on Christmas Eve, Callie." Then she turns to me. "By the way, you look great, Cassie. That black dress is phenomenal on you. Very sexy."

"Yeah, and those shoes aren't bad either," says Callie. "You sure they won't wreck your knee again?"

"No, it's feeling great," I assure her. "I've been off the crutches for two days, and it's just fine."

"Those shoes really are awesome," says Cammie as she looks at them more closely.

"You like them?" I strike a pose for her. "Stuart Weitzman. I was going to wear them for the wedding too."

"That reminds me," snaps Callie, still in a snit. "Besides the photo you e-mailed, I haven't actually seen your bridesmaid dress."

"I can show you now," I say as I go back into my closet and remove the garment bag. "Not that there's much we can do if you don't like it." I unzip the bag and hold out the sage green dress. "It's not fancy."

"It's pretty," says Cammie. "And that shade of green will be great with your dress, won't it, Callie?"

Callie examines it more closely. "This was the best you could do?"

I shrug, then hold the dress up to me. "It's not like it's easy to get to the city and shop," I point out. Then I actually tell them about running into Eric that day. Cammie, of course, is all sympathy. But Callie is still being a grump. I wonder if this is about my going to the French restaurant or something else.

"This is a size twelve," proclaims Callie, as if it's some federal offense.

"So?" I narrow my eyes at my older sister.

"So, I thought you'd lost weight, Cass."

"I have."

"But a twelve?"

"Callie," says Cammie, "we're all made differently, okay? Don't do this."

"But a *twelve,* Cass," says Callie. "You should be at least a ten by now."

"Look," I say, feeling hot tears in the back of my eyes. This is an old battle and one that I really don't want to fight tonight. "The ten fit pretty good. But it was tight across here." I point to the girls. "Get it? I didn't want to bust out at the seams during the wedding. Or show too much cleavage. Some people in this family might think it's okay to go prancing around in cute little T-shirts that are way too small and revealing, but that's not for me, okay?"

"Everything all right in here?" asks Mom, peeking her head into my room. Of course, she has on one of those very T-shirts right now. And I'm sure she's been listening.

"Just fine," I say sharply. "Callie is giving me fashion advice— like how I should wear a size ten instead of a twelve."

Cammie stands up and puts an arm around me. "I think you look fantastic, Cassie. Terribly sexy." She glances at our older sister, who's still glowering on the bed, and smiles at her. "I think Callie's just feeling a little jealous."

"I am not jealous," snaps Callie, getting up and pushing her way out of my bedroom.

Fortunately, I hear Andrew calling from downstairs, announcing that my man is here. So I grab my long coat, and Cammie tells me to have fun. "We'll be fine," she assures me as I head for the stairs. Then she winks. "You know how holidays can be."

I sigh as I carefully go down the stairs, taking it easy on my knee with these high heels. I do remember how holidays could get stressful. Often our parents would get into a fight. Or one of us girls—usually me—would be unhappy for various reasons. Yes, I do know how holidays can be, and that makes me even happier to be going out tonight. In fact, I feel a bit like Cinderella as I leave my mom and sisters behind. I'm so used to being the one who's left watching the others coming and going. It's strange to think of Callie being jealous of me tonight. Although it makes me feel just a little bit good, I feel bad for her too. I wonder if something bigger is wrong. Not that she'd ever admit it.

"You seem quiet tonight," says Ross when we're practically at the restaurant.

"Sorry," I say quickly. Then I give him a brief explanation of the dynamics at my house. Of course, I don't mention the size-twelve jab. It still hurts too much.

"Well, put those things behind you," he says as he escorts me up to Petit Ours Noir. "Tonight is for good food, good friends, good wine, and fun."

"Sounds delightful."

And it is. I can't imagine an evening more nearly perfect. But I still feel that something is missing. Maybe I'm just feeling guilty for abandoning my family. Or hurting my mom with the skanky-T-shirt comment. Still, for Ross's sake, I keep on my party face. I laugh and joke and delight in the food. But I'm truly thankful when the evening ends. I blame my knee for seeming tired as Ross drives me home. And he says he understands. Then, as if this were a real date, he walks me to the door.

"I never mentioned it earlier," he says as we stop at the top of the steps, "but you looked truly beautiful tonight, Cassidy. Really stunning. I know everyone thought I was with the most gorgeous woman in the room."

I could just about fall over. But I'm sure that would hurt my knee, which is actually a little sore now. "Well, I...uh...thanks, Ross," I finally manage to mutter.

And now, to my utter shock, he is leaning in—like he's about to kiss me. And I do not know what to do. I mean, sure, I've kissed guys before. Well, at least two or three. And I certainly got plenty of experience with Eric. But I'm totally unprepared for this. So I brace myself, tilt my head slightly up, close my eyes, and wait.

Ross plunks a sweet little kiss on my forehead. "Thanks for a delightful evening, Cassidy."

I smile, relieved that he didn't kiss me on the lips, yet somewhat disappointed too. Mostly I feel confused. "Thank you," I say quietly. "It was an amazing evening."

Twenty-Two

Still feeling stunned, I go inside the house to discover my mom and two sisters quietly sitting in the living room, almost as if they're waiting for me. I'm sure my cheeks are flushed, but I could easily blame that on the freezing temperatures.

"So?" says Callie with raised brows. "How'd it go? Did he propose?"

"Propose?" I gasp as I remove my coat, slip off my shoes, and collapse into my dad's old easy chair.

"We decided that was the only reason Ross would ask you out on Christmas Eve," says Mom. "To pop the question."

"Did he?" says Cammie.

"No," I say quickly, "of course not. Like I keep telling you guys, we're just friends." Okay, even as I say this, I'm not so sure. It does seem that something's changing.

"Hey," says Callie, "I was peeking out the window. I saw him walk you to the house. I saw his hand on your back, the look on his face…the kiss."

"A kiss on the forehead," I point out.

"So you say," says Callie, like she's a prosecuting attorney. "You looked like more than friends to me."

I sort of nod. "Well, maybe it's changing. But the truth is, I was surprised tonight. I mean, I really never dreamed Ross Goldberg would be seriously interested in someone like me."

"What do you mean someone like you?" protests Cammie. "You're a sweetheart, Cassie. Everyone loves you. Why wouldn't Ross fall in love with you too?"

I have to smile at my baby sister, sitting there in her pink-pig pajamas with her blond hair in two long braids, about to become a bride in a week, a doctor in a few months. "Same back at you, cutie pie."

"Okay, we've been talking...," says Cammie.

"Yeah, once Andrew and the boys went to bed," adds Callie.

"And we've decided that a truce is in order," continues Cammie. She looks at Callie now. "So?"

"So, I'm sorry about what I said in your room, Cassie." Callie looks at me with those big blues. "It was really rotten. And Cammie was right. I was jealous of you."

I blink. "Seriously? You were jealous of me?"

Callie nods with tears brimming in her eyes. "Yes. I was thinking of how you have your freedom. You're dating a cool guy. You're wearing cool shoes. It's like I wanted your life."

"No way," I say. "What about your life? You're married to a great guy. Have two gorgeous sons—"

"Sons who run me ragged," she spurts. "Sons who never stop moving from the minute they pop out of bed in the morning until they finally collapse at night. And then I want to collapse too. Andrew and I don't even have sex anymore—not without scheduling it. And he's so busy with work, and I'm so tired, and—and—I'm pregnant again!" Then she bursts into tears, burying her face in her hands.

Mom scoots closer to her, pats her back, and says, "It'll be okay, sweetie."

"Congratulations," says Cammie.

Callie looks up with watery eyes. "I don't want to have another baby."

"You're just worn out," I tell her. "You've probably worked way too hard on this wedding, and you're chasing the twins all the time. You need a break, Callie."

She nods with a chin that's still quivering. "Yes. Yes, I do."

"And I'm sorry too," I say to her. "I didn't realize things were hard for you. I mean, I'm usually jealous of you. You seem to have it all, Callie. You're so together."

"It's just an act."

"Well, you're good at it." Then I look at Mom. "Okay, if it's time for apologies, I guess I owe you one too."

She waves her hand at me. "It's okay. I think I had that coming."

"But the truth is, I've been jealous of you, Mom."

She laughs. "Well, that's just crazy."

"But it's true. From the moment I came home, I've been jealous. And, to be honest, sort of mad too. I wanted you to be the old you, and I know that's not fair."

"I haven't been much of a mom, have I?"

I shrug. "Maybe it was time for me to grow up."

"Well, if confessions are in order," she says, "I've been jealous of all of you."

"What?" says Callie.

Mom points at her oldest daughter. "Jealous of you for being such a babe." She shakes her head. "The sad thing is that I used to look like you."

"You still do," says Callie. "Have you looked in the mirror lately?"

"Okay, maybe an older version of you." Then she points at Cammie. "And, little one, I've been jealous of you."

Cammie looks shocked. "Why?"

"Because you've been so dedicated to your education. Goodness gracious, my girl, you're about to become a doctor. Not only that, but you're a good Christian who plans to live her life for others." Mom shakes her head. "I guess I'm as proud as I am jealous."

"Thanks." Cammie grins.

"And you." Mom points at me now. "I've been terribly jealous of you lately."

"Oh, come on," I say, thinking this is going too far.

"It's true. You have managed to hook the most eligible bachelor in town."

"I haven't hooked—"

"Oh yes you have, Cassie. I'm sure you have."

"But you told me you weren't interested."

"Of course I told you that. But only because he'd already told me that he wasn't interested in me. I was just a friend to him, someone to ward off the loneliness. Then my daughter comes in and steals the show."

Okay, this makes me laugh. "You mean I stole the show by doing things like splitting open the seat of my pants at the Halloween party—"

"What?" demands Callie.

So I tell them the story. I also tell them about some of my other embarrassing moments. Soon we are all laughing so hard that we're crying. Better yet, we're all friends again—and family.

"You know," says Callie as she wipes her eyes, "Andrew was just saying how the Cantrell women must have really great genes."

"Yes, Mom's jeans are Juicy," I tease.

"What?" Cammie looks slightly shocked.

"It's a designer brand," explains Callie. "Juicy Couture. And she looks great in them, by the way. But I'm talking about genetic genes. Andrew was saying that we must have good genes, and it got me thinking about Nana Merritt."

"I can barely remember her," says Cammie.

"That's because you were only three when she died," says Mom.

"How old was Nana?" I ask.

"Fifty-five," says Mom sadly.

"Fifty-five?" I echo.

Mom nods. "Yes. And I suppose that has something to do with my attempt to regain my youth. That and being dumped by your father for a younger, trendier version."

"Nana died from breast cancer, didn't she?" says Callie suddenly.

"Yes. And I had a little scare myself about a year ago."

"You never told us," I say.

"Because it turned out to be benign. But it was my wake-up call. I decided that I was going to take control. And if I only had a year left to live, I was going to have fun doing it."

"But you're okay, aren't you, Mom?" Cammie looks really concerned.

"Yes, I'm fine. And I'm going in for regular checkups."

"Good."

"Uh, speaking of Dad…," Callie says slowly.

"Were we speaking of him?" asks Mom in a blasé tone.

"Well, you sort of mentioned him," says Callie. She glances at Cammie. "Why don't you handle this?"

Cammie clears her throat. "I know that you guys are all still furious at Dad. And, of course, I am too. But I've also forgiven him. And even though Callie warned me not to, I've invited him to my wedding."

The silence is so thick you would need a chainsaw to cut it. I stare at Mom and can tell that she's not okay with this. But she doesn't say a word.

"I was really mad at Cammie at first," says Callie. "Then I realized it's her wedding, and if she wants her dad here, well, what can I say?"

"Can I explain?" says Cammie, looking directly at Mom now. Mom just nods.

"I called Dad and told him that I was still angry and hurt by what he'd done to you. I told him that I'd really struggled with forgiving him, but that I finally realized I had to forgive him. Then we talked for a long time. And while I don't agree with everything he said, and I don't condone what he did, I sort of understand how it happened. And I could tell that he's sorry."

"He's sorry?" Mom looks shocked.

"Yes. He's sorry and embarrassed, and he knows he's a big jerk."

Mom actually smiles now. "He said that?"

"Yes."

"Well, that's something."

"We talked a couple of times before I realized that I wanted him at my wedding," continues Cammie. "I got to remembering all the good things about Dad. How he used to take us camping and fishing and skiing. How he was my soccer coach. Remember how he got Cassie into Little League when girls weren't especially welcome?"

I nod as I remember this.

"And despite all that's happened, I just really wanted him to walk me down the aisle," she finishes. "And I hope that's okay with everyone."

Suddenly we're all crying again. Not tears of laughter either.

But we hug and wipe our eyes and finally decide that it's okay if Dad walks Cammie down the aisle.

"I suppose that means he's bringing Michelle," says Mom.

"I don't know for sure…"

Now Mom gets a funny look on her face and actually starts to giggle. "You poor girls…" She laughs even harder. "Your father is dating a girl who's young enough to be his daughter…and I'm… I'm dating a boy you went to high school with. Oh my word!"

"Yeah, our parents are pretty embarrassing," says Callie, laughing right along with her.

"We'll be the talk of the town," I say. "People will be saying, what's become of those cradle-robbing Cantrells?"

"I hope Ross isn't too concerned about keeping up appearances," gasps Callie between giggles. "If he is, he's marrying into the wrong family."

"We're not getting married," I sternly remind her.

"Well, just in case." She winks at me.

We joke some more about how our family has gone from respectable to scandalous. And finally we're all so worn out that we call it a night and go to bed.

Twenty-Three

*C*hristmas comes and goes, and I think my sisters and mom and I are closer than we've been in years. Oh, it's not peachy-keen perfect. But all things considered, it's pretty good. Mom's wardrobe calms down a bit too. I have to give Callie credit for this, because they went shopping together, and Callie was probably a good, if expensive, influence.

As the end of the year draws near, we work together on the last-minute tasks for Cammie's wedding. I have to give Callie credit for this too; she's managed to put together a nice event that hasn't broken the bank.

"If I ever get married," I tell her as we're getting dressed for the big day, "I'd love to have you help me with the planning."

She zips up my dress. "If you marry Ross Goldberg, you can count on it."

"Oh?" I turn and look at her. "But if I should marry someone else?"

"You could still count on it." She grins and pats her tummy. "Well, unless I'm giving birth to triplets or something."

"Have you seen Dad yet?" I whisper.

She nods solemnly. "He brought Michelle."

Now I'm not a person who normally swears, but this pushes me over the edge. Still, I say it under my breath. "Where are they now?" I hiss.

"Dad's with Clay and the groomsmen. I don't know about Michelle."

"Has Mom seen Dad yet?"

"I don't think so."

I take in a deep breath. I have absolutely no desire to see my dad. I cannot imagine how Mom must feel. I so wish he had chosen not to come. But then I look over and see sweet Cammie. Mom's helping her with her veil. For Cammie's sake, I can get over this. For Cammie's sake, we all can.

"You look so beautiful," I say as I go over and watch Mom fluffing the veil.

"The sweetest bride ever," says Callie as she fusses with one of Cammie's stray blond curls.

I glance at Mom and can tell she's extremely nervous. I know this has more to do with Dad than the wedding, and I ache for her. "Mom," I begin slowly, "you look beautiful too. You've got to be the hottest mother of the bride I've ever seen."

She laughs and looks self-conscious. "But not too young?"

"You look perfect," says Callie as she smoothes Mom's hair.

"Stunning," says Cammie.

Mom stands straighter and smiles. "Then we must be just

about the best-looking wedding party ever to grace the aisle of this church."

This makes me laugh. "Well, from what I've heard, this church hasn't seen too many weddings. At least not lately."

"That's because everyone who goes here is over seventy," Callie points out.

"But it's a beautiful church," says Cammie. "And even though we didn't come here that often as kids, I have good memories of being here."

"I always liked it too," admits Mom. "I've even toyed with the idea of coming back."

"You should," I tell her. "They could use some young folks."

She grins. "Go figure."

We primp a little more, but we can tell by the music coming from the sanctuary that the time is drawing near. Then someone taps on the door, and it's time for Mom to be escorted to her seat.

"Chin up," says Callie.

"Knock 'em dead," I tell her, and she smiles at me knowingly.

Soon we're all taking our turns slowly walking down the aisle. Cammie insisted on not rehearsing this event. She said she thought wedding rehearsals were silly, but Callie and I think she wanted to spare Mom from any extra time with Dad. Since we're a pretty small wedding party and it's a fairly simple wedding, all goes smoothly. Finally Callie and I are in place and looking back down the aisle. I'm surprised to see Cammie, who looks adorable, being escorted by a man who looks a lot older than the father I remember. His hair is almost totally gray, and while it's rather distinguished looking, it also ages him. He looks tired, sort of worn out and wrinkled, and I wonder if his lifestyle has taken a toll on him. To my surprise, I actually feel sorry for him. It was his choice to have an affair and to leave Mom, but look what it got him. He's alienated from his family. He probably won't get much time with his grandchildren. He was barely invited to this wedding. Then there are holidays and family reunions and all sorts of things that he will probably miss out on. It's actually really sad. *Was it worth it, Dad?*

I look at Mom, standing bravely with her eyes locked on Cammie as Dad escorts his youngest daughter down the aisle. I think Mom's going to be okay. She's going to survive this. She has her girls to surround her, to laugh with her and cry with her and hold her up if it gets too hard and heavy.

Cammie looks incredibly sweet and pretty today. I'm so happy for her. And now I focus entirely on Cammie and Clay. I cry as they say their vows, because somehow I know that they mean these words from the bottom of their hearts. I believe they will do everything in their power to keep the promises made today.

I realize I want that too.

I notice Ross sitting about midway down on the bride's side. He looks debonair and handsome in his dark suit. He smiles pleasantly, I think at me, and I realize that our relationship could be taking a turn. Why am I not sure I want that? I look back at Cammie and Clay as they exchange rings and finally kiss.

Ross drives me to the reception dinner. He is the perfect date. Polite and considerate. A great conversationalist. Well read and well traveled. Interested and interesting. Handsome. And yet...he's not quite right for me. I know this instinctively. Something inside tells me he is not a good fit. A good friend, definitely. But we are not a match made in heaven.

Callie could never understand this. She thinks he's the perfect catch. Even my mother agrees. But I know he's not the one for me. The only way I can explain this is to remember those silly Valentino boots I bought last fall. They looked so good with their impressive name in their fancy box. Even the tissue paper was divine. And yet those boots were beyond my budget, outside my comfort zone. Not only did the price tag make me feel guilty, but when I wore them, they pinched my toes and caused blisters on my feet. I've only worn them a couple of times since then, and both times I couldn't wait to kick them off and slip into my Uggs. Yes, I suppose I am an Ugg sort of girl.

Even so, I enjoy my time with Ross. We dance a lot, and although my fancy pumps eventually become so uncomfortable that I have to dance in my bare feet, we still have fun. I suppose I preoccupy myself with Ross to escape having to face my dad. Although I'm working on forgiving him, trying to follow Cammie's brave example, I'm still struggling a bit.

But there is no escape. Dad corners Ross and me at a side table where we're taking a break and enjoying some champagne. "Hello, Cassidy," he says, then nods to Ross. "How are you doing, Ross?"

Ross reaches out and shakes Dad's hand. "Life's good, Craig," he says. "Can't complain." I don't know why this little exchange surprises me. Obviously they would've known each other through business and whatnot when Dad lived here. After all, Black Bear is a small town. And yet it feels weird to me, sort of *Twilight Zone*ish, as they sit there shooting the breeze like a couple of old buddies.

"You're looking well, Cassie," my dad says to me. "I hear you're working at the ski lodge."

I nod. "Yeah. Ross is my boss."

He chuckles. "Hey, that rhymes."

"Where's Michelle?" I ask, perhaps a bit too pointedly.

"She's visiting with an old friend."

"Oh yeah," I say. "I almost forgot she was from here too."

"I think I'll freshen our drinks," says Ross. I'm sure he's uncomfortable with where this is heading. Actually, I appreciate the privacy. Once again, he's the perfect date.

My dad takes an empty chair. "I know this is hard for you and everyone," he says slowly. "But I don't want to lose you girls. I've made some mistakes, some things I'm really sorry about and can't undo, but I hope you'll find it in your heart to forgive me, Cass."

This is shocking, quite possibly the last thing I expected. I don't think I can remember my dad ever admitting to a mistake—

not to me anyway. It wasn't his style. His humility knocks me off my high horse, and I'm not sure how to react.

"It's okay, Dad," I say quickly, without really thinking. I just want to get this over with. To move on. "I'm already working on forgiving you, but it might take me longer than Cammie. She was always a lot more angelic than I was."

Dad grins. "You and me both, Cassie."

"Well, I hope can learn from your mistakes too, Dad."

He nods with a slight frown. "I hope someone can."

We talk a bit more, but it's awkward and uncomfortable, and I'm so relieved when Ross returns and jumps in with some small talk. Then my dad excuses himself, and I take a deep breath.

"You okay?"

I nod. "Yeah, thanks for helping."

"Your dad's not really a bad guy, Cassie. He's made some mistakes, but his heart is good."

"I know." Now I feel like I'm on the verge of tears. "It's just hard, you know."

"If it makes you feel any better, I sort of know how he feels."

I look at Ross. "What do you mean?"

"It's not something I like to talk about, and I'm certainly not proud of it, but I did something like that to Gwen. Back before she got sick. It was stupid and selfish, and I still feel guilty about it."

I don't know what to say to this. Ross is forty-six years old. It's possible that he wasn't the perfect spouse. And yet I had imagined that he was.

"Do you think less of me now?"

I shake my head. "No, I actually respect you even more for telling me."

"No one really knows about it. I trust that you'll respect that."

"Of course. You can trust me."

We dance to a couple more songs, and I try to figure out what his confession means. Is he trying to get closer to me—or push me away? I'm not sure that it matters. I decide I will receive it at face value. I will receive it as the friend I continue to tell him and everyone else that I am.

The newlyweds slip away before midnight, but the rest of us stick around to see the New Year in. And when midnight strikes, I'm not that surprised that Ross kisses me. This time on the lips. Just because I'm curious, I kiss him back.

There are no fireworks. Despite the party poppers exploding and bells ringing and horns blowing, all is quiet inside me. I know without a doubt that Ross is not the one.

"You seem sad," he says as he drives me home.

"I guess I'm sort of tired and confused," I admit.

"Was I wrong to kiss you?" he asks as he pulls in front of Mom's house.

"No, not really." I turn and face him now, telling myself that it's time to act like a grownup. No games. No stringing this out for the sake of egos—not his or mine. Even if it puts my job in jeopardy, I need to be honest and clear. "I think I needed you to kiss me tonight," I say slowly. "I think it helped to settle what I sort of already knew."

"That we should only be friends?"

I nod, hopeful. "Yes. Is that what you felt too?"

"I wasn't sure, but it crossed my mind tonight. I have felt an attraction to you, Cassidy. I have for some time now." He actually smiles. "It gave me hope. I thought maybe I was ready to get back into the dating game, that maybe I could get serious about a woman again."

"And you can," I tell him. "It just won't be me."

He nods. "I can respect that."

"Do I still have a job?"

He laughs now. "Of course. I'm not about to let my best marketing woman go."

Suddenly I remember something Bridget said last week. "I probably shouldn't even say this, Ross…"

"Yes?"

"Well, I happen to know someone who thinks you're quite a guy."

"Not your mom?"

I laugh. "No. Although I think she and Todd might be cooling it."

"Who then?"

"Bridget Ferrington."

He looks surprised. "Are you serious?"

"Totally. She's made it clear to me that she'd like to get to know you better. She thinks you're pretty cool. Probably even cooler after you bought her mural."

"Really?"

Okay, I can see the wheels turning in his head now. So much so that I almost feel jealous. But not quite.

"You should give her a call."

"Really? Bridget is interested in an old dude like me?"

"Hey, Bridget is the same age as me," I remind him.

"I know." He nods. "But you're mature for your age, Cassie."

"I hope that's a compliment."

"It is."

"Well, why don't you call Bridget then? Tell her you guys have my stamp of approval—not that you need it."

"Thanks, Cassie. I'll give that some serious consideration."

"See you on Monday."

"And Happy New Year!"

"Yeah, that's right. Happy New Year to you too."

Twenty-Four

By the middle of January, Bridget and Ross have become a fairly serious item in this town. Of course, everyone assumes this is because Ross dumped me for her. Although it hurts my pride more than I care to admit, I'm so relieved to be out of the uncertainty of the relationship that I don't really mind. Sometimes, just to throw the gossipers off, we all three have dinner together and really yuk it up.

"I'll bet they think I'm dating both of you," Ross said the other night.

"I'm really not into that kind of thing," I tell him.

"Me neither," says Bridget, turning her nose up.

As this chilly January wears on, loneliness sets in, and I almost resent having given up Ross. Okay, I realize that's incredibly immature, not to mention selfish, but it's the sad and embarrassing truth. It was nice having someone to go to dinner with, someone who treated me special. And, although Mom and Todd are history, she's now dating Mike Reynolds, a respectable widower who owns the newspaper.

Business at the lodge remains consistent, and the snow is still better than average, but even so I keep getting this feeling that my usefulness at Black Bear Butte is wearing thin. There are only so many things you can do to a marketing campaign once it's solidly launched. Especially when the season is halfway through. I even mention this concern to Ross, but he doesn't agree with me. He assures me there's still much to be done. But I worry that he might be keeping me on as a charity case.

Then one afternoon in early February, shortly after I get home and kick off my shoes and put up my feet, Will calls. I can feel my heart flutter just to hear his voice. But I'm worried that he sounds a little sad or maybe very serious.

"My dad passed away last week," he eventually tells me. "The funeral was today, and I guess I'm a little blue."

"I'm so sorry."

"We knew it was coming. He got lots worse during the holidays. I actually moved back home shortly after Christmas, just to help out. He went downhill quickly, and it was pretty overwhelming for my mom. My parents were fairly old when they finally had me, and I'm an only child."

"I didn't know that."

"Yeah. My mom's a lot older than your mom. She's in her seventies and pretty worn out from everything."

"It's great that you can be there for her—and were there for your dad before he passed on."

"Yeah, I'm glad I came. It gave my dad and me a chance to talk. At least at first, when he was well enough. But the past couple of weeks have been pretty quiet. He was mostly knocked out by the pain medication. He wanted to have his final days at home."

"But he went peacefully?"

"Yeah, he really did."

"So did you quit your job at Terrazzo de Giordano?"

"Oh, they told me it was mine if I came back. But I gave up the apartment in the city." He sighs. "Our apartment."

This actually makes me laugh. "Well, it's not like we really *shared* it, Will."

"We sort of shared it."

"Okay." I try not to imagine what it would be like to share an apartment with Will—I mean, after a wedding.

"So, how are you doing?"

I sigh and wonder what the honest answer to this would be. "I don't know," I finally admit.

"What's wrong, Cassie?"

"I'm not sure. I guess I feel a little restless or something."

"Are you still dating Ross?"

"How did you know about that?" I ask. "I mean, I wasn't really dating him, not as in seriously."

"Your mom mentioned it. And I could sort of tell. Remember how I mentioned that I thought he was into you."

"Oh, yeah. Well, no, I broke it off. We were together at my sister's wedding on New Year's Eve, and I could just tell it was all wrong for me. So I told him."

"Really?"

"Yeah, and now he's actually dating a good friend of mine. They are totally great together."

"And you're okay with that?"

"Do you mean is that why I'm feeling a little out of sorts?"

"I guess."

"No, not at all. I think I'm a little lonely. But it's more than that, Will. I mean, I do like my job, and I like this town and everything. But I feel as if there's something more for me. I just can't put my finger on it."

"I know what you mean."

We talk some more about the kinds of lives we wish we were living. And it's amazing how we really want some of the same things. We both want satisfying jobs that engage us creatively. But we don't want our jobs to be the central focus of our lives. Will is worried that owning a restaurant, although it sounds exciting, could be too demanding. Plus, we both want to get more involved in recreational activities, and we both like the outdoors and want to do some traveling. After about an hour, I start to worry. This conversation almost seems to be going too far, getting too deep. Not that we're talking about anything sexual—it's nothing like that. But it's more like my heart is getting way too involved, like my soul keeps trying to connect to this man. And I find that a little scary. I worry that I'm just desperate. Or, even worse, that I'm imagining he's saying things that he really is not.

"Well, I should probably go," he says. "I promised my mom I'd make dinner tonight. A lot of her friends have been bringing casseroles and those sorts of things lately, and she and I are both craving a nice steak and green salad."

"Sounds yummy," I say as I consider my own lackluster prospect of canned soup again.

"You take care, okay?"

"Yeah, you too."

After I hang up, I start to cry. I tell myself it's just PMS as I wipe my tears on a dishtowel. Or a little pity party. I heat my soup, read the newspaper with Felix in my lap, watch the Food Network, and call it a night.

The next evening after I get home from work, Will calls again. This time we talk even longer, and when we hang up, I don't cry. Then he calls the next night. And the next and the next. I can't imagine what his phone bill is going to be, but I have a feeling his mother won't care. She seems so happy to have him staying with her. And based on some things he's barely mentioned, I have a suspicion that his family has money. I don't know why I find this so surprising. I guess it's because I still have that first loser-dude image of Will indelibly stamped on my mind. It's highly prejudicial, and it was really a wrong impression. But the idea of his parents being well-off doesn't quite fit. Still, as he tells me more about his dad, who was an aeronautic engineer for NASA before he retired, and his mother, who started an interior design shop in the sixties and just retired from it about ten years ago, I realize there's a lot I don't know about this guy.

"I used to think I was born about two decades too late," he tells me one night a couple of weeks after his dad's funeral. "I mean, not only were my parents in their forties when I came along, but I had the spirit of a flower child." He laughs. "Back in middle school when everyone else was dressing like yuppies, I wanted to be a hippie."

"Did you smoke grass?"

"Of course."

"A real rebel boy."

"You bet."

"But you're not now?"

"Well, I'm drug free." He chuckles. "But I'm still a bit of a rebel, I think, and a free spirit. I don't see myself ever falling into the money-is-everything trap. At least I hope not."

"How's your mom getting along?" I ask.

"Better. She's actually talking about getting a condo in Florida with one of her girlfriends. She always wanted to be a snowbird, but my dad liked the winters."

"She should do that," I say. "Florida actually sounds delightful to me right now." Then I tell him about our record-breaking lows this week and how it affected business on the slopes. "It was so dead out there that I tried skiing yesterday and nearly froze my nose off."

"Well, don't do that," he says. "You have a cute nose."

"Thanks." I smile. "But we're hoping it'll warm up a little before the Presidents' Day weekend, since that's usually pretty busy."

"Do you work tomorrow?" he asks unexpectedly.

"Yeah, sure," I tell him. "Why?"

"I just wondered since it's sort of a holiday."

Then I remember what I'd been trying to forget. "Valentine's Day?" I laugh. "Well, Ross might close the lodge for Thanksgiving and Christmas, but Valentine's Day does not fall into that category. In fact, next year he plans to have the lodge open for all holidays. He's thinking that some people don't have families or things to do, and the slope is a great getaway for them."

"Yeah, I've even been thinking about getting out the old board and waxing it."

"I didn't know you were a boarder," I say.

He laughs. "I'm a rebel, remember. You don't think I'd be a skier, do you?"

"You should bring your board up here," I tell him. "Maybe I'll race you down."

"Last time I saw you skiing was a little scary, Cassie."

"Hey, I'm much better when I'm not wearing a bear suit."

"Well, I might just take you up on that little challenge," he says.

The temperature is slightly warmer the next day, but I still layer on the clothes, and as usual it takes about five freezing minutes before my Subaru's heater kicks on. As I drive up to the lodge, I wonder how long I'll be able to do this. I mean, other than the ice and snow, the drive is beautiful, and the lodge is a great place to work, but I cannot imagine myself doing this for years to come. And I wonder what will keep me busy once the ski season ends in the spring. Still, I try not to think about these things as I scurry across the freshly plowed parking lot and into the warmth of the lodge.

"Hey, you," says Bridget as I reach the top of the stairs. She's wearing her coat and appears to be going down.

"What are you doing here?" I ask, although it seems she's here almost as much as I am.

She puts her fingers to her lips and nods back toward Ross's office. "A Valentine's surprise."

I nod. "Oh."

"Yeah, I'm trying to make a neat getaway. Did you see him down there?"

"No. But he's probably out plowing."

She laughs. "It's so funny how he likes running that thing. Like a little boy with his big toys."

"What did you get him for Valentine's Day?"

"Go take a peek in his office. Then call me and tell me what you think."

So she goes one way, and I go the other, and before I even take off my coat and things, I slip into Ross's office and look at his desk. But it looks the same as usual. Then I glance around the spacious and uncluttered office, and I see it. Bridget has hung a beautiful painting of the lodge with the mountain behind it. Done in her amazing impressionistic style, it's absolutely perfect. I hear Ross talking to Marge, so I hurry out and into my own office, where I start peeling off coat and vest and scarf and gloves, then sit down to check e-mails.

"Did you see it?" asks Ross as he comes into my office with a beaming smile.

I grin at him. "Isn't it awesome?"

"It is."

"And it gives me an idea."

"Uh-huh?" He nods. "It gives me an idea too." Of course, I can tell by his dreamy expression that our minds are on two completely different tracks.

"Earth to Ross," I say. "My idea is, how about if we use that piece for next year's promotion campaign? Wouldn't it look great on the brochures and Web site and everything?"

"That's a fantastic idea, Cassidy."

"I'm sure Bridget will like it too."

So as soon as he's gone, I call Bridget and tell her my idea as well as Ross's reaction.

"Oh, I'm getting another call," she says quickly.

"Oh my," I say dramatically, "I wonder who that could be..."

"Later."

Then I hang up and wonder what those two will be doing tonight, although I'm sure it will be very romantic. Probably a quiet table at Petit Ours Noir. I also wonder, judging by the look in Ross's eyes, if there could be a ring involved. Or maybe that's moving too fast. Still, it's obvious they're crazy about each other. Selfishly, I hope that's the case. I recently told Bridget that if they should get married, she has to promise to rent her little house to me.

Shortly before noon a delivery girl comes in with a big vase of red roses and sets them on Marge's desk. I try not to feel envious as I walk by. Marge is at lunch now, but I'm sure she'll be pleased to see that her husband, a guy I never would've guessed was romantic, actually sent her roses.

My plan for the lunch hour is to take a few quick runs, unless it's too cold, and then grab a bowl of chili in the cafeteria. Sure, it's about the same thing I do every day, but the skiing is good exercise, and the chili is better than the canned soup I'll probably have at home. I ride the lift by myself, remembering what Will said about popping up here, and I think how nice it would be if he'd do that today. But by the time I've done three runs, I give up on his making an appearance and go to the cafeteria for my chili.

I can't help but notice how many couples are here today, and I wonder if they've come for a romantic little getaway. Of course, this gives me an idea for next year. Why not have a romantic ski-package promotion? We could partner with one of the better motels in town and offer a discount and maybe even put together a gift basket from the local shops. Excited about my new idea, I finish my chili, then hurry to my office to make some notes.

"These are for you," says Marge as she brings the vase of red roses into my office and plants them on my desk.

"Really?" I blink. "I thought they were for you."

She laughs. "Harv hasn't sent me roses in ages. His idea of Valentine's romance is to bring me a heart-shaped pepperoni pizza to eat in front of a good basketball game."

"Oh." I'm glad she doesn't stick around to see who sent these.

But Marge is like that. She knows how to mind her own business as well as stay on top of things. A real gift. I slip the small card out of the envelope and slowly read, "These roses remind me of you. Stay warm. Your rebel boy." A thrill of happiness rushes through me. Of course, these are from Will. But *red* roses? Does he realize the significance? Or was it just a coincidence? And if he sent *red* roses intentionally, what does that mean to me? Am I ready to take this step?

"Wow," says Ross as he peeks into my office. "Who sent those?"

I feel my cheeks flush. "A friend," I say.

"Uh-huh?" He steps into my office now. "A friend?" He studies me. "Would it be a friend from the city? A nice-looking young man who's in need of a haircut?"

"I like his hair."

Ross laughs. "So it is Will."

I nod.

"Wait till Bridget hears this."

"What do you mean?"

"She's certain that you and Will are meant to be."

"Oh she is?" Okay, I'm trying to think of a way to change the subject since I'm not totally sure how I feel about that possibility yet. Then I remember my romantic getaway package idea, and I shoot it at Ross. "What do you think?"

"I think it's brilliant."

"I'm going to start working on it now. I mean, it's not like it has to be exclusively for Valentine's Day."

"Of course not." He nods to my roses. "I need to call Bridget."

"Big mouth." I make a face at him, and he laughs.

In the middle of the afternoon, when our UPS usually arrives, Marge brings in something else for me. "You're popular today," she says as she sets a neatly wrapped brown box on my desk. I can tell by the handwritten address that this is not business related, but I start opening it before she's out the door. To my surprise and delight, it's a box of homemade chocolates! The handwritten note on top says, "Made with love for you." Of course, I know who made them. I eat several before I realize that I must share these before I devour the entire box, which will mean I'll have to spend the entire evening at the fitness center, and I can't think of anything more pathetic than working out alone on Valentine's Day evening.

"These are marvelous," says Marge after I make her take another one.

"What's this?" says Ross, coming out of his office.

"My valentine also knows how to make chocolates," I brag as I hold the box out to him.

"No kidding? Will made these?"

"Try one."

He takes one of the dark-chocolate cashew turtles, and as he slowly chews, a euphoric smile creeps onto his face. "These are amazing."

I nod. "Yep, I know."

"May I?" He's looking at the box.

"Of course. There's no way I can eat all of these."

"Oh, man," he says as he savors another. "These are decadent."

"Exactly," says Marge. "That's just what I was thinking."

"Will should open a chocolate shop," says Ross.

I feel my eyes widen. "You're absolutely right."

"I'd be a customer," says Marge.

"I'd be a backer," says Ross. "I'd even carry them here."

A chocolate shop. Of course! I'm excited. I wonder if this could be the business that Will is looking for. I remember his concern that a restaurant business can take over your life. A chocolatier wouldn't have to give up his life. I'm tempted to call him right now, but I don't want to be hasty. Instead, I decide to wait for our nightly phone call. I'll just introduce the idea to him casually. But before I do that, I decide I should also pray. Will and I have both been saying that we want our lives to be directed by God. He's come a long way in the past few months. I don't want to encourage him to make a move in the wrong direction.

ill goes absolutely nuts over my idea. "That is so incredibly perfect, Cassie!" he says with unbridled excitement. "If it could really work. I love making chocolates and confections and desserts. I had a blast putting that box together for you. I even made one for my mom, and she was totally impressed."

"It wouldn't be as demanding as running a restaurant," I point out. "You wouldn't need to be open in the evenings. And you could take vacations if you wanted." I tell him some more of my ideas, about how he could sell to restaurants and maybe even market his chocolates online.

"I need you to be my marketing manager," he says quietly.

"That would be so fun."

"Really?"

"Yeah." Then I tell him about my childhood memory of running the lemonade stand and how Bridget told me that might hold the clues to my happiest career choice. "Maybe you'd want to develop a franchise in Black Bear," I say shyly. "I mean, after you get established. Maybe I could run it for you."

"What if wanted my home base to be in Black Bear?"

"Seriously?"

"Why not?"

"What about your mom?"

He tells me that she and her friend have already booked their flight to Florida. "They're going to look around for a while, and she plans to put her house on the market by summer. She says it's too big for her to keep up. I wouldn't be surprised if she became a year-round Florida resident. If not, she could easily buy a second home wherever she likes. Maybe even wherever I finally decide to set up my business."

"You'd really consider settling here in Black Bear?"

"Of course. I fell in love with the town…" There's a long pause now. "Of course, it might've had something to do with falling in love with someone who lives in the town."

I swallow hard, almost afraid to believe what I am hearing. "Me?"

He laughs. "Of course you!"

"Really?"

"Really, Cassie. I've been wanting to tell you for ages. But so much was going on. My life has been crazy, and I don't have a real job now. Then my dad…and, well, I just figured I had no right to even consider that you might take me seriously." Another long pause. "I mean, if you even do…"

"Of course I do."

"You do?"

I laugh. "Okay, I guess I'm a little stunned. I mean, it's so crazy."

"Crazy good?"

"Yeah, crazy good."

We talk for another hour, and by the time we hang up, I know I'm in over my head. But I've never felt happier. I've never felt more excited about the future. I've never felt like I loved anyone more than I love Will. I think I fell for him the night he fixed me dinner at the old apartment. I just didn't know it—or couldn't admit it. But now I want the whole world to know.

By the end of the week, we have a plan. Will wants to stick around until his mom and her friend head down to Florida. She is showing him the things she wants put into storage for later use in her condo. Then she wants him to have an estate sale to get rid of everything else. "But that's not all," he says in a happy voice.

"What?"

"Apparently my dad had an insurance policy that Mom nearly forgot about. It was through NASA and has matured rather nicely over the years. Anyway, she feels that Dad would want me to have it to launch my new business."

"No way!"

"Yep. She said that she doesn't need it and that she's well taken care of even if she lives to be 150. So there you have it. I'm good to go."

"Will, that's great."

"I was hoping you could look around Black Bear for me… maybe get some ideas for a good location and that sort of thing. Do you have time for that?"

"Oh, man, I would make time for that, Will. You are definitely talking to the right woman!"

He laughs. "That's what I figured." He tells me he'll be shopping online for the equipment he'll need. "I figure it'll take me until mid-March to really be ready for a move. In the meantime, I'd like to come over to visit this weekend."

"Cool."

"And if you're not busy…"

"Hopefully I'll be busy with you!"

"Well, it's a date then."

And is it ever a date! A date that lasts the entire weekend, starting with Friday night happy hour at the brewery, then skiing at Black Bear Butte on Saturday, followed by an amazing dinner at Petit Ours Noir that night, which Will totally loves. He picks me up for church on Sunday morning, and Bridget invites us to join her and Ross for lunch at her house afterward. As it turns out, it's a celebration lunch: they did get engaged last night!

By Sunday afternoon, Will and I are standing in front of my mom's house, and I don't want to let him go. "It went by so fast," I tell him.

"I'll come again next weekend," he promises as he kisses me good-bye. It's not our first kiss, and I know it won't be our last. But, honestly, I think I could kiss this man forever.

Finally I pull myself away and tell him to drive safely. "Say hello to your mom for me."

"That's right," he says suddenly. "She wants to meet you. I told her that before she trips on down to Florida, I should bring her over. Would you mind?"

"I'd love to meet her."

By spring break I have met Will's mom, a completely delightful woman who recently bought a wonderful condo in Key Largo and wants Will and me to come visit as soon as she and her friend are settled. I also found the perfect spot for Will's business. It used to be a shoe shop and is on Main Street and has a tiny apartment upstairs. The architecture is absolutely charming, and Will fell in love with it and immediately put down a deposit. My mom, our Realtor, says it should close in April, and Will plans to be finished packing up his family home by then.

In the meantime I tried to give Ross my notice, but he talked me into becoming a freelance marketing consultant for him and others, which actually sounds rather nice to me. He feels that my marketing expertise and creativity might be useful to several businesses in town, including Alex's French restaurant, which is still struggling. But, I assured him, my main priority is going to be Will and his business. I'm already putting together a marketing plan that's going to totally rock.

Just a couple of weeks ago, and not long after getting engaged, Bridget and Ross shocked everyone by eloping to Las Vegas. At first I was slightly alarmed by this unexpected move, but they seemed totally happy when they got back. Ross actually walks around the lodge whistling and even goes home early sometimes, so I think it must've been a good decision. Plus Ross has been coming to church with her.

The happy consequence of their hasty marriage is that Bridget honored her promise to rent her little bungalow to me with an option to buy. On April first I actually move into this darling cottage.

The weather is perfect, and I am happier than I've ever been as I unpack boxes and spread what few furnishings I have around this adorable house. Last week Will talked me into keeping some furniture he's decided to save from his family home. He would put them in his apartment over the shop except that it's about the size of a postage stamp, and he plans to keep it minimalist. "It'll save renting a storage unit," he told me. "That is, if you don't mind."

"Just no old lady things," I warned him.

He nodded and grinned. "You mean you don't want the old pink Victorian lamps with tassels? Not the rose-colored sofa with its ruffled pillows?"

I frowned at him and wondered what I was getting into.

But when he backs the moving van into my narrow driveway this afternoon and starts unloading, I know I've hit the jackpot. "These belonged to your family?" I ask, astounded as he unloads another amazing mission-style piece. This one is a narrow table that looks stunning in the small entryway. I can't wait to put a lamp and vase of flowers on it, maybe a mirror above it.

"My mom was really into the craftsman style for a while, but she wants something less heavy and dark for Florida," he says. "But I've always liked Gustav Stickley, as well as Frank Lloyd Wright."

"I *love* Frank Lloyd Wright," I exclaim. "And those pieces are totally perfect in here."

"So you're not wishing for those Victorian lamps and the rose sofa?"

"You *were* pulling my leg."

"A little." He pauses after setting a leather-covered craftsman recliner by the small fireplace, then pulls me into his arms. "So you like my furniture, huh?"

"I *love* your furniture!" Then I frown slightly. "But what happens when you get your own place? Do I lose all this?"

He laughs. "Not if you agree to marry me."

I blink, then stare at him in unbelief. Did he really just say what I think he said, or am I hallucinating?

"So to keep the furniture," I repeat, "I have to marry you?" I use a teasing tone—just in case I really am confused or delusional. After all, I remind myself, this *is* April first.

Will fakes a hurt expression. "You mean you'd marry me just to keep my furniture?"

"It's awfully nice furniture," I say, kissing him gently on the lips. "But even if you gave it all away, Will, I'd still marry you."

"So can I take that as a yes?"

I nod. "Unless this is some ill-planned April Fools' joke. It better not be."

He seals the deal with a slow, passionate kiss. "This is no joke, Cassie. I might've been fooled a few times in my life, but this is the real deal. I love you. You are the only one for me. I'm absolutely positive about that."

"Me too," I say quietly, suddenly remembering my goofy analogy of the toe-pinching Valentinos that were a big mistake and how they compared with my snuggly, comfy Uggs that I could wear forever. I'll probably never tell Will about my crazy little metaphor. But it works for me—this guy is a perfect fit!

"I love you!" I tell him, wrapping my arms more tightly around his neck. "You're the only one for me!"

About the Author

MELODY CARLSON is the award-winning author of over one hundred books for adults, children, and teens. She is the mother of two grown sons and lives near the Cascade Mountains in central Oregon with her husband and a chocolate Lab retriever. She is a full-time writer and an avid gardener, biker, skier, and hiker.